Pr

JOHN D. MACDONALD

"The Dickens of mid-century America—popular, prolific and... conscience-ridden about his environment... a thoroughly American author."

The Boston Globe

"It will be for his crisply written, smoothly plotted mysteries that MacDonald will be remembered."

USA Today

"In McGee mysteries and other novels as well, MacDonald's voice was one of a social historian."

Los Angeles Times

"MacDonald had the marvelous ability to create attention-getting characters who doubled as social critics. In MacDonald novels, it is the rule rather than the exception to find, in the midst of violence and mayhem, a sentence, a paragraph, or several pages of rumination on love, morality, religion, architecture, politics, business, the general state of the world or of Florida."

Sarasota Herald-Tribune

Fawcett Books
by John D. MacDonald

All These Condemned
April Evil
Area of Suspicion
Barrier Island
The Beach Girls
Border Town Girl
The Brass Cupcake
A Bullet for Cinderella
Cancel All Our Vows
Clemmie
Condominium
Contrary Pleasure
The Crossroads
Cry Hard, Cry Fast
The Damned
Dead Low Tide
Deadly Welcome
Death Trap
The Deceivers
The Drowner
The Empty Trap
The End of the Night
End of the Tiger and Other Stories
The Executioners
A Flash of Green
A Friendship: The Letters of Dan Rowan and John D. MacDonald, 1967–1974
The Girl, the Gold Watch and Everything
The Good Old Stuff
Judge Me Not
A Key to the Suite
The Last One Left
A Man of Affairs
More Good Old Stuff
Murder for the Bride
Murder in the Wind
The Neon Jungle
Nothing Can Go Wrong
One Monday We Killed Them All
One More Sunday
On the Run
The Only Girl in the Game
Please Write For Details
The Price of Murder
Seven
Slam the Big Door
Soft Touch
Where is Janice Gantry?
You Live Once

TRAVIS McGEE SERIES

Bright Orange for the Shroud
Cinnamon Skin
Darker Than Amber
A Deadly Shade of Gold
The Deep Blue Good-By
The Dreadful Lemon Sky
Dress Her in Indigo
The Empty Copper Sea
Free Fall in Crimson
The Girl in the Plain Brown Wrapper
The Green Ripper
The Lonely Silver Rain
The Long Lavender Look
Nightmare in Pink
The Official Travis McGee Quizbook
One Fearful Yellow Eye
Pale Gray for Guilt
A Purple Place for Dying
The Quick Red Fox
The Scarlet Ruse
A Tan and Sandy Silence
The Turquoise Lament

THE GIRL THE GOLD WATCH & EVERYTHING

John D. MacDonald

FAWCETT GOLD MEDAL • NEW YORK

A Fawcett Gold Medal Book
Published by Ballantine Books

Published in the United States by Ballantine Books, a division of Random House, Inc., New York, and simultaneously in Canada by Random House of Canada Limited, Toronto.

ISBN 0-449-12769-9

Manufactured in the United States of America

First Fawcett Gold Medal Edition: January 1963
First Ballantine Books Edition: November 1982
Twenty-first Printing: November 1988

THE GIRL
THE GOLD WATCH
&
EVERYTHING

Dear Fred,

You didn't tell me it was going to be easy. But you didn't tell me it was going to be like this. Find Kirby Winter. Bring him back. Spare no expense. And you assigned me a good man to help out. At least Huddleston **used** *to be a good man. Today you wouldn't know him. He stares into space and he sighs, and all I can get out of him is sometimes an aimless giggle.*

We found Kirby Winter, boss. We found him twice. And if you want him found a third time, you better send somebody else. But it will be a waste of money.

In fact, Fred, I think you better tell the client to give up. If this Kirby Winter **did** *hold out a couple of million bucks from his Uncle Omar's estate, nobody is going to get it away from him.*

I know what you're thinking. You're thinking Kirby Winter bought me off, and Huddleston too. I wish to God he had. I'd sleep better.

All I can do is tell you just what happened. The tip-off was absolutely correct. We found him right here in a big suite in the Del Prado, and he'd been right here in Mexico City registered under his own name for two weeks. He's not trying to hide, at least not very much, Fred. Kirby Winter and party. The party is a party of one, exactly the same broad that was with him in Sao Paulo three months ago, that gorgeous hillbilly broad that looks sweet as angels; but don't let that fool you a minute.

What I can't understand, Fred, is how both you and the client got the feeling this Kirby Winter is sort of innocent and helpless. Maybe that's his past history, but he got over it. This is a very self-confident guy, believe me. And as far as style and dash are concerned, Onassis should have it so rich. He and his hillbilly broad, they have a very fine time. If he's scared of having somebody show up and take some of that money away from him, he doesn't show it a bit.

Well, once we had them located, we figured out how to get them back into the States. I had to do most of the arrangements myself because ever since all those funny things happened in Sao Paulo, Huddleston has been a little unsure of himself.

I set up a private plane, big enough for the four of us and the pilot, with enough range to get us over the border. As you suggested, it seemed best to bring the girl along too. Then the problem was get them from the hotel to the airport. I decided we'd make it fast and simple. Bust in, hold a gun on them, give them each a big enough shot to keep them very, very quiet and humble and eager to please. In that condition we could walk them down to a car and be off. And I'd let you know where to arrange to have us met.

I bought a passkey. They went out about nine last night, and Huddleston and I decided we'd wait and welcome them when they got back. So we let ourselves in and settled down to wait. We both had guns. I had the hypo all ready. I had a man ready to pull up out in front as soon as I gave the word. And the pilot was standing by.

They came in about midnight, laughing and talking. As soon as they were far enough into the room, we stepped out and covered them. I ask you, Fred, how could anything go wrong? I am not a careless guy.

But it went wrong, Fred. All you can do is try to believe what I'm going to tell you. They jumped a little and stared at us, and then they started acting as if it was the biggest joke in the world. It reminded me so much of Sao Paulo, I felt very nervous. And Huddleston's color wasn't very good. I told them that if they co-operated, nobody was going to get hurt. This Kirby Winter—and he is sort of a mild-looking guy—stared at me and shook his head sort of sadly and said that after Sao Paulo, they thought we'd give up, so that meant they hadn't made their point clear enough, so they'd make it a lot clearer this time. Huddleston told him to shut up. I went toward them with the hypo, figuring to take care of him first. Fred, I was being **very** *careful.*

Suddenly the hypo was gone. I stopped and looked at my empty hand. Kirby Winter and that tow-headed hillbilly girl were smiling at me. I looked at Huddleston. Fred, I swear, in the twinkling of an eye he had taken off every stitch and he was wearing a big blue sash tied with a bow around his waist, and printed on his chest in lipstick it said "Surprise!"

Remembering Sao Paulo, I decided that if things started to go wrong, I'd even them up by shooting Kirby Winter in the leg. As you know, I am fast and accurate, and I probably would have hit him just where I wanted to, except that when I tried to fire, I had a perfume atomizer in my hand instead of a gun.

Just as I stared at Kirby Winter, in that very same instant, Fred, without any warning at all, I was in the elevator and the door was closing. There was an elevator operator and three middle-aged tourist ladies and Huddleston in there with me. The door closed and we started down and the ladies started screaming and fainting. It was a mess in that elevator, Fred. Just like Huddleston, the only thing I had on was a sash, only mine was pink. And on my chest it was printed "Adios, amigo!" And we were both shaved absolutely bald and soaked in perfume, Fred. And that hysterical elevator operator ran us right down to the main lobby and opened the door. And Huddleston was so shook up, he tried to run.

Anyway, the wheels are turning, and if everything goes well, and if you send the money I wired for, they may let us out of here by tomorrow. Our lawyer says there aren't any major charges, but there sure are a lot of small ones. And he checked and found out that Kirby Winter and party checked out about noon today.

Personally, I don't think Huddleston is going to be of much use to anybody from now on. And I can't vouch for myself. If you think we were bought off, you'll have to admit it was a pretty strange way of covering up.

As I said, if your client wants Kirby Winter found again, you can send somebody else. I have been trying to examine what happened to us with a completely open mind. The easiest answer is to say that it is hypnosis. But Fred, I think it is just plain old-fashioned magic like we used to read about when we were kids. Why not? If there's magic in the world still going on, the ones who can do it won't let it get into the papers, will they?

And that uncle of Winter's, that Omar Krepps. Wasn't he supposed to be a very mysterious guy? A wizard, sort of? Maybe before he died he taught Kirby Winter how to use the spells or rub the lamp or whatever the hell he does.

And look at Sao Paulo. Winter and that nifty little broad of his took six of the biggest casinos for about seventy grand apiece while they were there. And if that isn't magic, Fred, tell me what it is? An invention they're using?

Honest to God, Fred, the way I feel right now, if that little hillbilly girl should suddenly appear right in this cell and turn into a purple kangaroo, it wouldn't shock me a bit. You take so much and you come to the end of being shocked. You know what I mean?

Maybe the client believes and maybe you believe that this Kirby Winter used to be sort of a goof. But, believe me, something changed him. And unless you find out what it was and how it happened, there's no use sending anybody else after him. The way they looked at us, Fred, honest, it was like they were a pair of Martians. Or the way you and I would laugh at a puppy that growls at you. Fondly, you know. And superior.

I hope the money is on the way, because if it isn't, we might be in here a long, long time. No matter when we get out, I'm thinking I might go into some other line of work. I've sort of lost my confidence.

Very truly yours,
Sam Giotti

Chapter One

Slowly, with a dedicated effort, Kirby tipped the universe back into focus. He heard the after-image of his voice going on and on, a tiresome encyclical of complaint, a pean to the scuffed spirit. The woman across the table from him was in silhouette against the window—a window big as a tennis court on edge—and through the window was an ocean, rosy with dusk or dawn. It made a peach gleam on her bare tanned shoulders and backlighted a creamy weight of blondness.

Atlantic, he thought. Once he had established the ocean, he found the time relationship simplified. Looking from Florida, it had to be dawn.

"You are Charla," he said carefully.

"Of course, dear Kirby," she said, amused, slightly guttural, almost laughing. "Your good new friend, Charla."

The man sat at Kirby's left, a solid, polished man, tailored, clipped, manicured. He made a soft sound of amusement. "A Spanish verb," he said. "Charlar. To chat. To make meaningless talk. An irony because her great talent is not in talking, but in listening."

"My great talent, Joseph?" she said with mock astonishment.

"Your most unusual one, my dear. But we have both enjoyed listening to Kirby."

Kirby nailed it all to a wall inside his head, like small signs. Charla, Joseph, Atlantic, dawn. He sought other clues. It could be Saturday morning. The burial service had been on Friday at eleven. The conference with the lawyers had been at two in the afternoon. And he had begun drinking at three.

He turned his head with care and looked at the empty

lounge. A barman in white jacket stood under prism lights paled by the dawn, arms folded, chin on his chest.

"Do they keep these places open all night?" Kirby asked.

"Hardly ever," Joseph said. "But they respond nicely to any small gift of money. A gesture of friendship. At the official closing time, Kirby, you still had much to say."

It was brighter in the lounge. They looked at him fondly. They were mature, handsome people. They were the finest two people he had ever met. They had slight accents, an international flavor, and they looked at him with warmth and with love.

Suddenly he had a horrid suspicion. "Are you—are you some kind of journalists—or anything like that?"

They both laughed aloud. "Oh no, my sweet," Charla said.

He felt ashamed of himself. "Uncle Omar is—was—death on any kind of publicity. We always had to be so careful. He paid a firm in New York thirty thousand dollars a year to keep him out of the papers. But people were always prying. They'd get some tiny little rumor about Omar Krepps and make a great big story out of it, and Uncle Omar would be absolutely furious."

Charla put her hand over his, a warm pressure. "But dear Kirby, it does not matter now, does it?"

"I guess not."

"My brother and I are not journalists, of course, but you could speak to journalists, you know. You could let the world know what a vile thing he did to you, what a horrid way he repaid your years of selfless devotion."

She was so understanding, Kirby wanted to weep. But he felt an uncomfortable twinge of honesty. "Not so selfless. I mean, you have an uncle worth fifty-million dollars, there's an ulterior motive."

"But you told us how you had quit many times," Joseph said. The warmth of Charla's hand was removed. Kirby missed it.

"But I always went back," Kirby admitted. "He'd tell me I was his favorite nephew. He'd tell me he needed me. For what? All he ever did was keep me on the run. No chance to have a life of my own. Crazy errands all over the world. Eleven years of it, ever since I got out of college. Even there, he told me the courses to take. That old man ran my whole life."

"You told us, my dear," Charla said, her voice breaking. "All those years of devotion."

"And then," Joseph said sternly, "not a penny."

The brightness of the dawn was beginning to hurt Kirby's eyes. He yawned. When he opened his eyes, Joseph and Charla were standing. Joseph went over to the barman. Charla touched his shoulder. "Come, dear. You're exhausted."

He went with her without question, out through glass doors, across a vast and unfamiliar lobby. When they were a dozen feet from the elevators he stopped. She looked up at him in question. Her face was so flawless, the eyes huge, gray-green, the parted lips moist, the honeyed skin darker than her hair, that for the moment he forgot what he was going to say.

"Darling?" she said.

"I'm not staying here, am I?"

"Joseph thought it would be better."

"Where is he?"

"We said good night to him, Kirby dear."

"Did we?"

"Come, dear."

The elevator climbed through a fragrant silken silence. He drifted down a long corridor. She took a key from a jeweled purse and let them into the suite. She closed the blinds against the dawn sunlight and took him to a bedroom. The bed was turned down. New pyjamas and an assortment of new toilet articles were laid out for him.

"Joseph thinks of everything," she said. "Once he owned some hotels, but when they began to bore him, he sold them, Kirby, dear, you must have a hot shower. Then you will sleep."

When he came back to the bedroom in the new pyjamas, she was waiting for him. She had changed to a robe of some soft fabric in a shade of gold. She had brushed her hair. She stood up and seemed very small to him without her high heels. The fitted robe sheathed and revealed a figure to fog the lenses of the little men who took pictures for the center-folds of the more forthright magazines. It curved and cushioned into all the right dimensions and then, implausibly, curved just a little bit more. Though he felt, with thunderous pulse, as though someone were thumping him lightly on the top of the head with a padded stick, and though he felt appallingly winsome, like a boy groom, he also felt a solemn sense of responsibility. Here was a totally first-class woman, mature, fragrant, expensive, sophisticated, silken and immaculate. And one could not sidle up to her, dragging one foot and saying shucks. Heartening himself with a thousand memories of Cary Grant, he tried to saunter up to the woman, wearing a smile that was tender, knowing and suitably ravenous.

But he sauntered his bare toes into the cruel narrow leg of a small table. With a whine of anguish he lunged, off balance, at the woman—clutching at her with more the idea of breaking his fall than with any sense of improper purpose. The flailing leap alarmed her and she darted to one side emitting a small hiss of dismay. One frantic hand caught the strong golden fabric at the throat of her fitted robe. For one full half-turn, the durable fabric sustained them in the beginning of a skater's whirl, but then there was a ripping sound, and as he tumbled into a far corner he caught a glimpse of her as she plummeted out of the robe, spinning, struck the edge of the bed, bounced once and disappeared over the far edge with a soft padded thud.

He sat up, pushed the ruined robe aside, clasped his toes in both hands and made small comforting sounds.

Her tousled head appeared slowly, warily, looking at him from beyond the bed, her eyes wide. "Darling!" she said. "You are so impulsive!"

He stared at her with his face of pain. "Kindly shut up. This has been happening ever since I can remember, and I can do without the funny jokes."

"You always do this!"

"I always do something. Usually I merely run away. In the summer of 1958 I went with a beautiful woman to her suite on the seventh floor of the Continental Hilton in Mexico City. Three minutes after I closed the door, an earthquake began. Plaster fell. The hotel cracked open. We had to feel our way down the stairs in the dark. The lobby was full of broken glass. So please shut up, Charla."

"Throw me my robe, dear."

He balled it up and threw it to her. He got up and hobbled to the bed and sat down. She came around the foot of the bed and sat beside him. The robe, belted in a new way, covered her.

"Poor Kirby," she said.

"Sure."

She patted his arm. She chuckled. "I've never been undressed quite that fast before."

"Very hilarious," he said.

She touched his chin, turned his head so that he looked down into her eyes. For the moment she looked very sad. "You do tempt me, dear. Because you are so very sweet and nice. Too many charades these days. And too many men who are not like you in any respect."

"If they were all like me, the survival of the race would be in doubt."

She pulled him closer. He kissed her, abashedly at first and then with mounting enthusiasm. When he toppled her back, she wiggled free and shook her head and made a face at him. "No, dear. Joseph and I are very fond of you. And you have had a ghastly time. And Joseph told me to care for you. Now hop into bed like a sweet lamb, and take off the top of the pretty pyjamas and lay face down and I shall make you feel very, very good."

"But—"

"Darling, don't be a bore, please. I don't want to change our friendship so soon, do you?"

"If you're asking me—"

"Hush. Some day, soon maybe, you will become my lover. Who can tell? Is it not more fun to guess? Be a good boy."

He stretched out as instructed. She came back after turning out all the lights but one. She poured something cool and aromatic onto his back and began to knead the muscles of his back and shoulders and the nape of his neck with clever fingers.

"My word, you have lovely muscles, dear," she said.

"Dynamic tension."

"What?"

"Exercises anyone can do."

"Oh. Now just let everything fall away. Slide down into

the darkness, sweet Kirby. Abandon yourself to pure sensation."

"Um."

"Rest, my dear. Rest."

Her soothing hands stroked the tension out of him. He was so completely exhausted he could have fallen into sleep like falling ten thousand feet into a midnight swamp. But her touch, her gentle teasing voice, the awareness of her fragrant and erotic presence kept him suspended, floating on the surface of sleep. She hummed and the tune seemed familiar, as though he had heard it in a foreign movie.

He reached back through time to the previous Wednesday, at midnight. Fifty-seven hours ago? That was when the word had reached him at his hotel in Montevideo. The old man was dead. Omar Krepps. Uncle Omar. It was shocking to think that even death itself had the power to reach out and take that strange, invulnerable little man.

As he thought of the return trip he sank deeper in the pool of sleep and his images became confused, changed by Charla. The breast-nosed jet took off down a pale silken runway of tenderest flesh while the nude and shadowy hostesses gathered close around him, humming to him. In the midst of this half-sleep he was vaguely aware of Charla turning him, helping him into the pyjama top. Her mouth came down upon his, sweet, deft and heavy, and as he tried to lift leaden arms to hold her close, she was gone. He thought he heard her say, "I'm so sorry, dear." He wondered what she felt sorry about. The other light went off. The latch clicked. He fell off the edge of the world.

Chapter Two

Kirby was hauled up out of sleep by a rangy young girl he had never seen before. She shook him awake. All the lights in the room were on. He braced himself up on his elbows. She was pacing around the bed so rapidly it was difficult to keep her in focus. She was yelling at him, and the words made no sense. She had a wildly cropped mop of palomino hair, fierce green eyes bulging with fury, a lean face dark with rage. She wore a coral shirt, striped stretch pants, and waved a straw purse the size of a snare drum.

It took him long dull seconds to realize she was yelling in a language he did not understand.

When she paused for breath, he said faintly, "No comprendo, Señorita."

She switched immediately into a torrent of fluent Spanish. He spoke it reasonably well, but not that well. He caught just enough to realize it was idiomatic, graphic and probably would have sent a Mexico City cab driver running for shelter, his hands clapped over his ears.

"Mas despacio, por favor," he pleaded when she paused for the next breath.

She looked at him narrowly. "Will English do?"

"Do what?"

"Where is my goddam aunt, and what the hell right does she think she has pulling one of her cute tricks and getting me thrown the hell off the first decent television script I've seen in a year? She can't call me down here like I'm some kind of a slave. Where's that spooky Joseph, buddy? Don't you *dare* try to cover for either one of them, buster. I've handled her sniveling little secretarial types before. I want the facts, and I want them right now!"

She put a small nose with abruptly flared nostrils five

inches from his and glared directly into his eyes. "Well?" she said.

"Facts?"

"Facts, fellow."

She had an almost imperceptible accent, but there was an illusive familiarity about it.

"I think you're in the wrong room."

"I *know* I'm in the wrong room. The other rooms in the suite are empty. That's why I'm in this room. Don't stall."

"The suite?"

She stamped her foot. "The suite! Yes, the suite! My God, start tracking, fellow. Hook up with reality. This big lush suite in the Hotel Elise, eighth floor, Miami Beach, ten o'clock on this gaudy Saturday night in April, in this suite registered in the name of Charla Maria Markopoulo O'Rourke, buster, my unsainted aunt, this suite it cost me a twenty-buck bribe to get into after steaming all the way from the Coast on a jet."

"Charla!" he said. And knew where he was, and why the girl's accent, though less than Charla's, had seemed familiar. Up until that moment he had thought himself in Montevideo. "Uncle Omar is dead," he said.

"Don't waste those sick codes on me, buster. I unjoined Charla's wolf pack ages ago. Little Filiatra changed her name and her outlook and her habits because she got sick up to here of all the cute, dirty, sick little tricks. I'm Betsy Alden now, by choice, and I'm a citizen and a good actress, and she gets me reinstated fast or I'm going to belt her loose from her cunning little brain."

"If you'd back away a little, I could think better."

She went to the foot of the bed and glowered at him. "Where is she?"

"Look. You seem to have the idea I work for her."

"Please don't try to be cute, friend."

"Honest to God, my name is Kirby Winter. I had a terrible day yesterday. I got drunk. I never met Charla until late yesterday some time. I didn't even know the rest of her name. I don't know who you are. I don't know where she is. I don't have the slightest idea of what you're talking about."

The girl stared at him, biting her lip. He saw the suspicion and the anger slowly fade away. And then she looked at him with cold, mocking contempt.

"So terribly, terribly sorry, Mr. Winter. I guess I just wasn't thinking. I should have guessed you wouldn't be on the team. You don't look bright enough. You do look more the fun and games type. Muscled and clean and earnest. But not even knowing her right name? My word! Charla must be getting really hasty and desperate. Isn't she a little elderly for you?"

Contempt was more distressing than her inexplicable anger.

"But I was only—"

"Check the bureau before you leave, Mr. Winter. She tips very generously, I've been told."

The girl whirled and left the room, slamming the door behind her. The slam re-echoed through all the brassy corridors of his hangover, and made his stomach lurch. Suddenly he was covered with icy sweat. He lay back and closed his eyes, wrestling the furry Angel Nausea. He wished the damned girl, in spite of her moral judgments, had had the grace to turn the lights off. He wondered if one could perish of thirst while being wracked with nausea. In a little while—in just a little while—he would get up and turn off the lights . . . .

There was daylight beyond the closed blinds. The room lights were off. He got up and found his way to the bathroom. He looked at his self-winding watch. It had stopped. He felt weak, rested, thirsty and ravenous. He looked into the mirror and saw his own mild and fatuous smile, blurred by a gingery stubble of beard. He wondered if he had merely dreamed the angry girl. And Montevideo. And the funeral. He was certain he hadn't dreamed Charla. He was totally certain of that. He remembered his inheritance and immediately felt chagrined and depressed. But he felt too good to stay depressed.

After the long shower, a shave with the new razor, and a minty scrubbing with an unfamiliar toothpaste, he knotted a big towel around his waist and went back to the bedroom. Someone had opened the blinds. Golden sunlight poured in. There was a huge glass of iced orange juice on the bedside table, and a note written in violet ink in a bold yet feminine hand on heavy blue-gray stationery embossed with the initials C. M. M. O'R. It looked like some odd abbreviation of Commodore, and he knew that the angry girl had not been something dreamt. Charla Maria Markosomething O'Rourke.

"Kirby, dear. I heard the shower and took steps. You must have been at the very end of your rope, poor thing. Little men are hurrying to you with a sort of care package. Your clothes have been bundled off, pockets empty, look on the dressing stand. Packages in the chair. I bought them by guess alone last evening before the lower level shops closed. When the animal has been clothed and fed, you'll find me on the sun balcony. I need not ask you if you slept well. Good morning, darling. Your Charla."

He looked out his windows. They faced east. The sun was more than halfway up the sky. The door to the main part of the suite was ajar. He picked up the phone and asked what time it was. "Twelve minutes after ten on a beautiful Sunday morning in Florida," the girl said pertly.

Twenty-seven hours in the sack, he estimated. He went to the chair where the packages were stacked. White nylon tricot boxer shorts, waist thirty-two. Correct. Rope sandals, marked L. Comfortable. Gray dacron slacks, cuffed. Perfect at the waist. Possibly one-half inch shorter in the inseam than he usually wore them. Close enough. One short-sleeved sports shirt with a button-down collar. Fine for size and styling. But the colors—narrow vertical stripes in gray, pale blue, coral and light yellow, each narrow stripe divided from the next one by a narrow black line, and the fabric was a lightweight silk. As he was buttoning the shirt there was a knock at the corridor door. Two uniformed waiters, deft, smiling, courteous, came in with a large clinking cart and quickly set up his vast breakfast, hot in the tureens, on the snowy linen. They had a Sunday paper for him. He tried to hide the fact he was salivating like a wolf. Everything has been taken care of, sir. Thank you, sir. If you need anything else, sir. He wanted them to go before he grabbed the eggs barehanded.

"Shall I open the champagne now, sir?"

"The what!"

"The champagne, sir."

"Oh. Of course. The champagne. Just leave it the way it is."

Not until he had nothing left but a second cup of coffee was he able to even pretend to look at the newspaper. And then he could not keep his mind on it. Too many other mysteries were unsolved. He turned and lifted the champagne out of the crushed ice. It was not a split. It was a full and elegant bottle. He was wrapping it in a fresh napkin when he noticed the two champagne glasses on the nearby tray-table.

How big a hint does a man need, he thought. He took the bottle and the glasses, and, feeling incomparably elegant, went off in search of Charla O'Rourke. He found one empty bedroom without a sun balcony. He found a second and much larger bedroom with open French doors facing the east. He walked, smiling, squinting, trying to think of some suave opening statement, into the hot bright glare. Charla was stretched out on her back on a wide long sun-cot of aluminum and white plastic webbing, her arms over her head. Sun had reddened the gold of her body. She was agleam with oil and perspiration. He stood and boggled at her, all suave statements forgotten. He tightened his grip on the champagne bottle just in time. She seemed to be asleep. At least she was breathing deeply and slowly. She wore three items—a ridiculous wisp of white G string, white plastic cups on her eyes, and a blue towel worn as a turban. He stood in an awed, oafish silence, aware of the sound of the ocean surf far below, of a drone of traffic on Collins Avenue, of faint music from somewhere. Not plump at all, he thought. Where did I get that impression? Firm as an acrobat, but just with more curves than there's room for. More than anybody should have.

She plucked the plastic cups from her eyes and sat up. She smiled at him. "Poor dear, you must have been exhausted!"

"Gahr," he said in a wispy voice.

"And you brought the champagne. How dear of you! Is something the matter? Oh, of course. The puritan syndrome." She reached for a short white terry jacket and put it on without haste. He found himself wishing she would button it and wishing she wouldn't. She didn't. "We spend so much time at Cannes, I forget your odd taboos. Now you may stop boggling at me, dear boy. Do you think I've had enough?"

"Gahr?"

She pressed a firm thumb into the honey-pink round top of her thigh. They both watched the white mark fade slowly. They watched it intently. "Quite enough, I would say," she said. "Some people find a dark tan quite attractive, but it does change the texture of the skin, you know. It becomes quite rough, comparatively." She rose lithely and walked by him and into the relative gloom of the big bedroom, saying, "Come on in, dear." He followed her, carrying the bottle and the glasses, his mind absolutely blank.

He did not see her stop abruptly when she was three steps inside the room. He did not see her stop and turn. His eyes had not compensated. He walked into her, and in the instantaneous impression of heat and oil and perfume of that impact, he dropped the bottle onto his foot. He saw her floundering backward, grabbed at her with the hand which had held the bottle, misjudged his distance, struck her rather solidly on a terried shoulder and knocked her over a footstool. She lit solidly and said something in a language he did not understand. Somehow he was glad he did not understand it.

She crawled over and retrieved the unbroken bottle and stood up. "If you'll stop hopping up and down on one foot, Mr. Winter, you can pour me a glass of champagne."

"I'm sorry."

"Thank God you didn't get playful until we got off that balcony, Kirby."

"Charla, I just—"

"I know, dear." She worked the wire loose, deftly popped the cork. The champagne, after the thump, foamed abundantly as she filled the two glasses. She put down the bottle, took one glass from him, looked speculatively at him as she sipped. "Instead of perfume, dear, bring me liniment, instead of jewels, bandages. Now fill my glass again and be patient while I tub this oil away. Could I trust you to scrub my back?"

"Gahr."

"No, we had best not risk that. Here's to caution, Kirby dear. Champagne is dripping off your chin. Wait for me in the next room, please."

He carried the bottle and his glass into the large sitting room of the suite, walking on knees as reliable as wet yarn. He sat down with care, emptied his glass and filled it again. He felt as if he had a permanent double exposure on the sensitive retinas. No matter where he looked, he saw Charla supine, foreshortened, in deathless Kodachrome, in an incomparable clarity of focus, a vividness of the great, round, firm, self-sustaining weight of breasts, with their buttery tan, the skin without grain or sag or flaw, the nipples a darker hue, large but not gross, aimed, slightly divergent, at the tropic-blue morning sky.

When he shook his head violently, the pervasive image blurred. When he shook his head again, the image slipped back and down into the cluttered warehouse of memory. It lay atop the rest of the debris, instantaneously available.

He heard the end of the metallic thunder of the water roaring into her tub, and as he fancied her stepping into it, he groaned aloud. O thank you, Uncle Omar. Thank you for instilling a helpless youth with such grave suspicions of women and all their works, that here and now, in my maturity, in my thirty-second year, I cannot confront a lovely and half-naked lady without getting cramps in my toes and saying gahr.

But he had the dim suspicion that such were the obvious riches of Charla that even a far more worldly man might have experienced a visceral tremor or two.

Considering the wretched paucity of his experience and the extent of his carefully concealed shyness, he marveled that when he had come upon her there, he had not merely given a mad cackle of laughter and vaulted the cement railing a hundred feet above the gaudy roofs of the beach cabanas.

He knew well the forlorn pattern of his increasingly compulsive search for sexual self-confidence. In this world that Hugh Heffner had made, he alone seemed forever bunnyless. And it was becoming less a matter of hunger than of pride.

He knew that women found him reasonably attractive. And he had laboriously developed that brand of semi-insinuating small talk which gave women the impression he was as accustomed to the casual diversion as the next fellow. But there was the damnable shyness to contend with. Where do you start? How to start? In situations where unattached women were abundant, he had developed into a fine art the knack of making each of them believe he was intimately concerned with one of the others.

Once in a great while he would finally overcome the shyness, turn into the final pattern for the attack on target, and then have the situation blow up in his face. He knew he was not a clownish man. It depressed him to look back on too many slapstick situations. One would think it possible for a man of dignity to approach a woman like Charla without suddenly, inadvertently, peeling her like a grape and hurling her over a bed. His face grew hot as he remembered.

It was, he suspected, because he tightened up in the clutch. With the bases loaded, two out, and a three-nothing count on the clean-up hitter, the rookie comes in, steps on the rubber, glares sternly at the batter—and drops the ball.

Sometimes nature intervened. As in the case of the earthquake. A man could begin to believe he was hexed.

Sometimes, as with Andrea last year in Rome, it seemed pure accident. He had rescued her from a yelping throng which had confused her with Elizabeth Taylor. The talk had been amusing. They were staying in the same hotel, on the same floor. She was alone, trying to recover her morale after a bad marriage and a messy divorce. It was understood, without words, that he would walk a dozen feet down the corridor and tap at her door and she would let him in.

The prospect terrified him. He had presented too glib and sophisticated a front. She would expect a suave continental competence, a complete and masterful experience. And it was rather much to expect of a fellow whose most recent—in fact, whose only affair—had taken place twelve years earlier in the back seat of a 1947 Hudson in Johnstown, Pennsylvania, in a public park during a rainstorm with a noisy, pockmarked girl named Hazel Broochuk, and had lasted for about twelve incomparably clumsy minutes.

Though these were hardly the experience factors one would bring to an assignation with a woman who could be mistaken for Liz, he steeled himself to carry out the impersonation to the best of his ability. After a scalding bath, he donned his wool robe and marched up and down his room, fists clenched, jaw set. To the sound of trumpets, he turned toward his door, marched out into the corridor and firmly yanked the door shut. He yanked the door shut on a substantial hunk of the hem of the robe. The door locked itself. The keys were inside, on the bureau. Maybe in the world there were men of sufficient aplomb to go tap on the door sans robe. It certainly would reduce any areas of confusion as to the purpose of the small-hours' visit. But Kirby Winter was not one of them.

And the worst time of all, perhaps, was when, emboldened by brandy, hand in hand with a sweet laughing little darling of a girl, they had run like the wind from the big house in

Nassau down toward the beach cabana in the moonlight. And halfway there the wire clothesline had caught him just under the chin.

But for each opportunity denied him by the fates, there had been twice that number he had run away from, in sweaty terror. He sneered at himself and sipped the champagne. You are a clown and a coward, Kirby Winter—a lousy, neurotic, mixed-up coward, and yet you go around making women believe you're a gay dog. Gahr, indeed.

Charla came into the room. She planted herself in the corner of the couch near him before he could begin to stand up. She was barefoot. She wore short pink shorts and a candy-striped halter and a pink ribbon in her hair. He realized that if he focused beyond her instead of right at her, she looked about fifteen. Startlingly precocious perhaps, but no more than fifteen. Only the direct gaze detected the webbed flesh under her eyes, the lines bracketing the mouth, the slight sag of tissue under her chin.

"Again, dear," she said, holding her empty glass toward him. He filled it and his own and put the bottle back on the ice. "That shirt is really handsome."

"Thank you. It's very nice. The other things are nice too. But I really can't accept—"

She made a face at him. "So grim and stuffy all of a sudden? Are you cross when you wake up? I am. That's why I left you alone, Kirby dear."

"No. Not cross, I guess. It's just—"

"Pressing wasn't enough for your suit. It'll be back this afternoon. With your tie and socks and so on, dear. Really, I threw your shirt away. I hope it didn't have some sort of sentimental value. It was actually shabby. Please tell me you *do* feel better. I mean, when one makes a special effort to—"

"I feel a lot better, Charla."

She pulled her knees onto the couch and sat crosswise, wrinkling her eyes at him as she sipped her drink. She was long-waisted, he saw. The weight of hips and breasts made her waist look smaller than it was. Her glossy legs were short and rather heavy, but seemed exactly suitable for her.

"Mad with me?" she asked.

"Should I be?"

"Oh, because I teased you a little. Do you remember?"

"Yes."

"Such a cruel thing a woman can do, isn't it?"

"I guess so."

"I may tease some more, you know."

He shifted uneasily. "I guess you might."

"But some time I might not be teasing at all." She stared at him, her eyes wide and innocent. "Poor little man. How will you be able to tell when the time comes when I don't tease?"

He cast about for a change of subject. "That girl."

"Oh, yes. She disturbed you. My niece. Now she calls herself Betsy Alden. I was very cross with her, Kirby. I still am."

"She made quite a fuss."

Charla shrugged. "I seem to have done some horrible, damaging thing to her career. I didn't realize. I wanted her to come here to see me. After all, I am her only aunt. She wouldn't come. She had some silly idea of her play-acting being more important. So—I remembered an old friend and called him up. He called a good friend of his. Suddenly they didn't need her. Is this so terrible?"

"Only if she can't find another job."

"She says she'll have trouble. She cursed me. She was very noisy and vulgar. Once upon a time she was a very sweet child. It's hard to believe."

"Did she leave?"

"Oh, no! She has to stay here. Because she will now have to beg me to undo the terrible damage she thinks I've done. After she becomes sweet enough to me, then I shall phone my friend again, and then she will be in demand again for those idiotic television things. It's what she seems to want, poor child."

"At first she thought I worked for you. And then she got another idea about me, and that wasn't right either."

Charla's smile was curiously unpleasant. "She mentioned that. I admit it is not accurate. But it could have been, so easily, don't you think?"

"I guess so."

"You seem so solemn today, Kirby. Even, forgive me, a little bit stuffy. You talked so much on Friday night, and were so charming and hurt."

"I must have been a nuisance. I want to thank you for—giving me a chance to sleep it off. And I really must be going."

"Oh, not until Joseph comes and we tell you our idea."

"Idea?"

"Come, dear. We know you have no specific plans. You told us that."

"Did I? I'll have to find something—"

"Maybe you've found it, Kirby. You have certain attributes Joseph and I could use, you know. You make a good impression, dear. You look very decent and earnest and reliable and trustworthy. Many people look like that, but it is a false front. You are what you seem to be, dear."

"I beg your pardon?"

"And you have such a great capacity for loyalty. I'm certain your Uncle Omar was pleased with you, and made wonderful use of you. He trained you. And really good people are so hard to find these days. And you're at home in so many countries. We have little problems you could help us with."

"What sort of problems?"

She shrugged. "Here's one at random. We have one nice little ship. The *Princess Markopoulo,* Panamanian registry. We think the captain and the agent are conspiring against us. The profits are so tiny. You could go aboard as my special representative and find out what is wrong. There are always problems. And we don't want to give up the way we live and handle them ourselves. It would be too dull. You would be busy. It would be amusing. And we would pay you well. Between assignments you could be with us. We would pay you twice what your Uncle Omar paid you."

"Do you know what he paid me?"

"You told us, dear. And you've saved a veritable fortune! Eight thousand dollars. Dear Kirby, that would last me perhaps one month. And you will have to find work."

"I must have done a lot of talking."

"You told us your inheritance from your dear dead uncle. A pocket watch and a letter."

"And I don't even get the letter until a year from now," he said, and divided the small amount of champagne left.

She hitched closer to him, touched her glass against his, looked into his eyes. "So why not have the amusing life? It is good fortune for all of us we met the other night. We are very good friends, no? Here is what we shall do, Kirby

Winter. You settle what must be settled here. By then the *Glorianna* will be here. And we shall have a cruise."

"The *Glorianna?*"

"My dear toy yacht, dearest. Holland built. Lovely staterooms and a crew of five. We always have charming guests aboard. Much fun, much wine, maybe a little love. My crew is bringing her down from Bermuda now. The best food in the world, my dear. We insist on that. Spend a month as our guest and then we shall decide your future. Why do you look so troubled?"

He shrugged. "Superstitious, maybe. Things like this just don't fall into my lap, Charla."

She put her empty glass aside and moved closer to him. She took his hand and lifted it to her lips. It made him feel curiously girlish and awkward. She looked at him with a sweet gravity. "You do make me like you—too much, perhaps. We should have met another time. When there were no jobs to offer, when you were not troubled and disappointed. When we could both be honest."

"What do you mean?"

"I meant nothing. A woman's chatter." There was a knock at the door and she asked him to let in Joseph. With great enthusiasm Charla told Joseph that Kirby had agreed to come cruising on the *Glorianna* and then he would take the job they had decided to offer him. Kirby found himself shaking Joseph's hand and being effusively congratulated. Things seemed to be moving too fast. He tried to find the right opening to tell Joseph it was not that definite, and suddenly realized he was being instructed to move out of his own hotel and move here, to the Hotel Elise.

"But I—but I—"

Joseph put a fatherly hand on Kirby's shoulder. Charla was on Kirby's other side. She slid her arm around his waist, hugged herself close to him. In the arctic reaches of his mind, walls of ice toppled into the sea.

"Nonsense, my boy," Joseph said. "The hotel is not full. I happen to own a certain percentage of it. When you return with your luggage you will be all registered. Because I am busy on small matters, Charla is often lonesome. We would be grateful, both of us. You will be doing us a favor."

"Well, I guess I could—"

"Splendid!" they cried simultaneously, and Charla gave him

a heartier little hug, full of rounded dizzying pleasures. Her glowing face was upturned toward his, her eyes full of warm promise. Joseph had taken a gold cigarette case from his pocket. It slipped from his hand. Both men stooped simultaneously and cracked skulls. Kirby straightened up, off balance, half-blinded by the white burst of shock and pain. He swung his arm up to catch his balance and caught Charla smartly under the point of the chin with his elbow. Her teeth made a chopping sound and her eyes glazed and she wobbled momentarily.

She looked at him fearfully and made a curious gesture and spoke in a foreign language. It sounded like an incantation, and in the middle of it he thought he heard her say, "Omar Krepps".

"Shut up!" Joseph said to her in a deadly tone. He was holding a palm against his brow.

"I'm sorry," Kirby said miserably. "I just seem to—"

"It was an accident," Charla said. "Are you hurt, dear Kirby?"

"I—I'd better be on my way, I guess."

Chapter Three

As Kirby opened the rear door of the cab to get in, a girl eeled by him and took the cab.

"Hey!" he said indignantly.

Betsy Alden glowered at him. "Just shut up and get in, stupid!"

He hesitated, got in beside her and said, "But what are—"

"Driver! Go north on Collins, please. I'll tell you where."

"But I want to go—"

"Will you shut up!"

They rode a dozen blocks in silence. He looked at her rigid profile, thinking she would be quite a pretty girl if she wasn't always mad. The taxi was caught by a light. "Right here," she said and quickly handed the money to the driver and got out. When Kirby caught up with her, she was walking south, carefully examining the oncoming traffic.

"Will you kindly tell me—"

"In here, I guess," she said, caught at his arm and swung him along with her into a narrow walkway leading to the side entrance of one of the smaller beach hotels. Once in the lobby she looked around like a questing cat, then headed for a short flight of stairs to the mezzanine. He followed her up the stairs. She wore a green skirt and a white blouse. She had changed to a smaller purse. Her toffee hair was more orderly. Following her up the stairs he realized she was singularly expressive. Even in the flex of lean haunches under the swing of the skirt she seemed to project both stealth and indignation.

"Sit over there," she said, indicating a fake Victorian couch upholstered in shiny plastic under a fake Utrillo upon an imitation driftwood wall. He sat on the couch. She stood by the railing, looking down into the lobby for what seemed to be a long time, then shrugged and came slowly over and sat beside him.

"I'll tell you one thing and you remember it, Winter," she said. "No matter how careful you are, it might not be enough." She gave him a very direct green stare.

"Are you all right?"

"How are you reacting to my dear Aunt Charla? How's your pulse?"

"Miss Alden, I have the feeling we aren't communicating."

"When she wants to really set the hook, she can make any Gabor look like Apple Annie. There's fine steam coming off you, Winter."

"She's an unusual woman."

"And she takes no chances. She had to have me here on standby. Just in case you'd rather settle for something younger, taller and not quite so meaty. But I told her a long time ago I'm through playing her games. She can take care of her own pigeons without any help from me. I got off her merry-go-round when I was twenty years old. And I was a very old twenty. Charla would be all right—she might even be fun—if she weren't so damned greedy."

"What is that about a pigeon?"

"What else do you think you are? Do you think she's smitten by your charm?"

"She got smitten a few times."

"What?"

"Miss Alden. Just for laughs. What are we talking about?"

She frowned at him. A strand of the tan-gold hair fell across her forehead and she pushed it back. "I checked the newspapers. Omar Krepps was your uncle. That's what we're talking about."

"I don't understand."

"When I was fifteen years old she yanked me out of school in Switzerland and began lugging me around the world with her. She and Joseph are operators, Winter. Canadian gold, African oil, Indian opium, Brazilian girls—you name it, and they've bought it and sold it. They aren't the biggest and they aren't the shrewdest, but they keep getting richer, and it's never fast enough to suit them. They are in and out of cartel and syndicate operations with other chums of the same ilk, and their happiest little game is trying to cheat each other. I was only fifteen, but I soon learned that in their circles, the name Omar Krepps terrified them. Almost a superstitious terror. Too many times Krepps would suddenly appear, skim the cream off a deal and leave with the money. I believe they and some of their friends tried to have him killed, but it never worked."

"Kill Uncle Omar?"

"Shut up and listen. And believe. That fat little old man seemed able to be nine places at once. One time he skinned them good, intercepted cash on its way to a number account in Zurich somehow, and just took it, and they could do nothing about it because they'd in effect stolen it first—Joseph and Charla and some of their thieving pals. At that time Charla was wearing a ring that opened up. A poison ring, I guess, with an emerald. She opened it idly one day and there was a little wad of paper in it. She unfolded it. It said, 'Thanks, O. Krepps.' When she came out of her faint she had the wildest case of hysterics you ever saw, and she had to go into a hospital for a week. You see, the ring hadn't been off her finger since before the money was taken."

"I can't really believe Uncle Omar would—"

"Let me finish. Krepps died last Wednesday. They were in Bermuda. They flew here Thursday morning. You arrived at dawn on Friday, and by dawn on Saturday you're in bed in Charla's suite. How much accident is involved in that?"

"I thought I met them by accident."

"That pair doesn't cotton to the random stranger. There's always a reason for every move. What do they want from you?"

"They've invited me on a cruise."

"Tell me all of it, Winter. Every word you can remember."

He told her an edited version of it.

She scowled. "And your Uncle Omar left you practically nothing? I guess they must want to pick your brains and find out how he operated."

"But I didn't have anything to do with—making money. I don't know anything about the business end of it. He told me what courses to take in college. When I got out I went to work for him, doing the very same thing right from the beginning."

"Doing what?"

"Giving money away."

"What!"

"Just that," he said helplessly. "He had some sort of clipping service and translation service and I would go and make investigations and give the money away if in my opinion everything was on the level—and if it could be kept quiet."

"Much money?"

"I think it averages out somewhere around three million a year."

"To charities?"

"Sometimes. Sometimes to individuals trying to get something started, or small companies in trouble."

"Why did he want to give it away?"

"He never seemed very serious about anything. He never explained. He just said he did it to keep his luck good. He was a jolly little man. He didn't like to talk seriously. He liked to tell long jokes and do card tricks and show you how he could take his vest off without taking his coat off."

"Did you see much of him?"

"About once a year. He was always going off alone. It made people nervous. He had apartments and houses here and there, and it was hard to tell just where he'd be. But I never ran out of work, no matter how long he was out of touch. And he hated publicity of any kind."

"You are not lying to me," she said. It was more statement than question.

"No. While he was alive I wasn't supposed to tell anybody what I did for him. Now I guess it doesn't matter too much. The notoriety he got in the very beginning—I guess it made him secretive."

"What notoriety?"

"A long time ago. My parents were drowned in a boating accident when I was seven, and I went to live with Uncle Omar and Aunt Thelma. She was his older sister. She was good to me, but she certainly made Uncle Omar's life miserable. We lived in an old house in Pittsburgh. Uncle Omar taught high school chemistry and physics. He had a workshop in the basement where he tried to invent things. I guess it was the only place in the house where he was happy. Aunt Thelma was always crabbing about the money he spent on tools and equipment and supplies, and complaining about the electric bills. When I was eleven years old he quit right in the middle of a school term and went out to

Reno and won a hundred and twenty-six thousand dollars. It was in all the papers. They called him a mathematical genius. They hounded him. Every nut in the country made his life miserable. He put money in the bank for us and disappeared. He was gone almost a year. He reappeared in Reno and lost a hundred thousand dollars there, and then nobody was very interested in him any more. After that he took us down to Texas where he'd built a house on an island in the Gulf off Brownsville. He set up a trust fund for Aunt Thelma and sent her back to Pittsburgh. I stayed there with him for a little while before I went back. By then he had a lot of business interests all over the world. He supported me and paid for my education and gave me my job when I graduated. But—he didn't leave me anything, and I don't know anything about his business interests. In fact, I didn't know him very well. The papers say it's a fifty-million-dollar estate. He left me his watch and a letter to be handed to me one year from last Wednesday."

"And you told Charla that?"

"Yes."

"And told her what you've been doing for a living?"

"I guess I did."

"And you've gone all these years without even trying to make any guesses about your uncle?"

At the moment Betsy Alden irritated him. "I may act like an idiot, but I have average intelligence, Miss Alden. My uncle left that cellar all of a sudden. And how many high school teachers become international financiers?"

"So he found something that gave him an edge."

"An edge over other people, so he gave a lot of the money away. Maybe it was conscience. At least it made him feel better."

She nodded rather smugly. "And so Charla is terribly interested in that letter. Isn't it obvious?"

"But she can't—I can't get it for a year."

"Mr. Winter, any explanation of how one little man could terrorize Charla and her group, fleece them, and end up worth fifty-million dollars is worth a year of effort. And by the end of the year she can have you in such captivity, you'll turn the letter over to her without even opening it, and whinnying with delight at the chance to please her in some small way."

"You have a dandy opinion of me."

"I know Charla. I've seen her at work."

"Where do you come in? What do you want? Do you want the letter?"

"All I want, believe me, is some leverage. I don't care how or where I get it, but I want to be able to pressure Charla into fixing it so I can go back to work where I belong. She brought pressure down on me." She stabbed Kirby in the chest with her finger. "And if I can use you to get her off my back forever, I would be a very happy girl. And at the same time I might be doing you a favor, like keeping you from sinking into a swamp."

"Do you hate her that much?"

"Hate is complex. This is a simple emotion. Contempt. She's really quite easy to understand. Her only motivation is greed. Greed for money, power, pretty things, admiration, sensual pleasure. She likes to use power, Winter. So does Joseph, but she's captain of that team."

"He's your uncle?"

"Hardly. She calls him her brother, but he's more a sort of half brother-in-law. And not what you'd want to call a wholesome relationship. But they do seem so charming, don't they? It makes them a deadly team."

"I keep feeling that you are dramatizing this. I just can't believe they—"

"Wait a minute. I just thought of something. You are his only living blood relation. And it was in the papers, so Charla must know that. So in addition to whatever is in the will, won't you get his personal papers and records?"

"I guess so. I hadn't thought about it."

"Believe me, Charla will. And Charla has. Now don't you dare turn anything over to her."

"What do you think I am?"

"Don't be angry. We know there's something she wants, badly. So we have to find out just what it is she wants. Once we find out what it is, then you can decide whether you want to sell it to her, whatever it is. If you do, let me be your agent. I'll get you more than anybody else could."

"People keep moving too fast lately."

"I'm essentially rougher than you are, Kirby Winter. I'm a graduate student of the school of Charla. You move into the Elise. If you start dragging your feet now, they may change tactics." She scribbled an address and a phone number and handed him the piece of paper. "When you find out anything definite, get in touch with me here. It's a little apartment I've borrowed from a hokey friend. He's on one of his annual tours of duty in New York. He goes up there and does commercials so he can afford to live down here and write plays. He's sick with love for me. Look, Kirby. You don't have to like me and you don't have to trust me. What are you losing so far? And call me Betsy."

"Losing nothing, so far. Possibly my mind. Nothing important though."

"Play along and play it very cozy, and when you do find out what they're after, then you can decide whether or not to get in touch with me. Okay?"

"Okay, Betsy."

Her eyes changed. "When people don't push me around, I'm nicer than this, really."

"And I'm less confused, as a rule."

"I don't know anything about your tastes—or your opportunities, but the less you give away to Charla, the more you'll get of her." She looked slightly uncomfortable. "Just don't let it dazzle you, Kirby. Just keep remembering she's one of the world's great experts on—horizontal persuasion. Keep your head, and we can make her pay and pay and pay."

"If there's anything to sell."

"If she wasn't convinced there is, she wouldn't be here." She patted his arm and stood up quickly. "I'll be waiting to hear from you. Wait five minutes before you leave."

Chapter Four

There were nine messages in his box at the Hotel Birdline in downtown Miami. They all requested that he return the phone calls of Mr. D. LeRoy Wintermore, of Wintermore, Stabile, Schamway and Mertz, the law firm which handled Uncle Omar's personal matters—as opposed to the captive attorneys who handled the corporate affairs of Krepps Enterprises and all the other interlocking corporations.

Wintermore was a fragile snow-crested old man with, as Kirby had once heard his Uncle Omar say, a skeptical attitude toward all established institutions, including the law.

Kirby packed his two suitcases of personal gear before phoning Wintermore. It took him seven minutes. He phoned the number on the most recent slip and found he had reached D. LeRoy Wintermore at his home. It was Sunday, of course, but it did not feel like Sunday.

"Dear boy!" Wintermore said. "I was fretful about you. When you found what—uh—dispensation Omar had made, you seemed a shade surly."

"I wasn't exactly ecstatic. I don't think I'm greedy especially, but after all, there is supposed to be fifty-million kicking around some place."

"Possibly it was his intention to improve your character, Kirby."

"I have more than I can use now."

"At any rate, there seem to be a few minor difficulties to be ironed out. They want you at a high level conference at the Krepps offices tomorrow morning at ten."

"They?"

"Your uncle's elite corps of earnest executives. I shall be there too, by request, and if it appears that you need legal representation, I shall be ready to stand at your side. Fearlessly."

"What's up?"

"I have no idea, but they seem to have the impression there was some sort of collusion going on between you and Omar. Hidden assets. Something idiotic. They seem agitated. And something else has disturbed them. Since last Wednesday, every one of Omar's houses and apartments has been thoroughly ransacked."

"Really?"

"And they seem to want to connect it all up with whatever mysterious services you performed for Omar."

"Did he ever tell you what my work was?"

"Dear boy, I never asked."

"Mr. Wintermore, even though the only things mentioned in the will are the watch and the letter, won't I get all Uncle Omar's personal records and papers?"

"In the normal course of events, you would."

"But now I won't?"

"Omar had a rather serious warning of his heart condition three months ago. He came to my office and took personal material from our files and left us just the basic essential documents. I asked him what he was going to do with the papers he took. He said he was going to burn them. He smiled rather broadly and said he was going to burn everything. And then he took a silver dollar out of my left ear. He was extremely clever with his magic tricks. It is my understanding he did burn everything, except for one case of documents now in the main vault at Krepps Enterprises. A lovely man, dear boy. Lovely. But with a secrecy fetish. And the executive staff over there seem to find you infected by the same disease."

"I was following orders. I'll be there at ten, Mr. Wintermore."

He hung up and looked around the room and wondered if he would ever find reason to check into the Hotel Birdline again. It was centrally located, but sometimes the nights were made hideous by people hammering on the wrong doors and cawing in the hallways and striking one another with the damp sounds of expert impact until the sirens came. But it was cheap and reasonably clean and he could always get a room in or out of season, and the management stored, free of charge, that small store of personal possessions he did not take along with him on his world-wide errands of mercy, support and investment.

Now he carried his suitcases down to the desk, experiencing stomach pains which reminded him he'd forgotten lunch. Hoover Hess, the owner, was working the desk. He was a loose, asthmatic, scurfy man with the habitual expression of someone having his leg removed without anesthetic. His smile was a special agony. He had gone as high as a seventh mortgage and been down as low as a second. He averaged out at about four.

He smiled. "Hey, Kirb, this thing with your uncle. I'm sorry as hell. It happens like that sometimes. Bam! You're gone before you got time to fall down. How old was he?"

"Just turned seventy, Hoover."

"Well, I guess now you're set, hey?"

"Not exactly. I want to check out. I'll be over at the Elise on the Beach."

"Like I said, set. Taking a suite? Why not? Live it up, Kirb. Order up some broads. Order up some tailors. Drink that stuff from the good years."

"Well, I'll be sort of a guest over there, Hoover."

"Sure. Until the legal thing clears and they give you the bundle. I understand. And I'm sorry to lose a good customer. What I want you should do, Kirb, when you get the bundle, we'll sit down some place and let me show you the books on this thing. What I figure, consolidate the mortgages. It would be just the right kind investment for you."

"I really won't have anything to invest, Hoover."

"I know how it goes. You got to have an answer. Every clown in the world comes around with hot deals, but you know me a long time, right? You don't have to give Hoover Hess any brushoff. I know you good too, Kirb. You play it just right. Nice and smooth and quiet. No fuss from any broad you bring here, right?"

"But I didn't—"

Hoover Hess waved a pale freckled hand. "Sure. Be cute. That's the way you play it. The one I see those times, she was a lady. The glasses is always good, the flat heels, the outfit like a school teacher. Some guy hasn't been around, he gets fooled, right? But you been around, you watch her walk, and you know it's class stuff, chin up, swinging that little round can only one sweet little inch side to side walking through here to the crummy elevator."

Kirby suddenly realized Hess was talking about Miss Farnham, Wilma Farnham, the only other staff member of Uncle Omar's secret give-away program, the one-woman clipping service, keeper of the files, translator of foreign news items, totally devoted to Uncle Omar's hidden program. She had been on the job six years, working out of a small office in a building far from the main offices of Krepps Enterprises. His field reports went to that office. The money was arranged through that office. Uncle Omar had assigned rough priorities to the projects she dug up. Then the two of them, Kirby and Miss Farnham, had worked out the schedules. When he was in town they often had evening conferences over work in progress and future missions in his room at the Birdline. She always pushed hard for the health things, the bush hospitals, the village ambulance services, the child nutrition programs. She was consistently dubious about the struggling little entrepreneurs, and always made Kirby feel she thought him too gullible for the job. She had worshipped Uncle Omar. He felt guilty, realizing this was the first time since returning he had wondered what would become of her now. But there stood Hoover Hess, leering at him.

Feeling that he was betraying and degrading Miss Farnham, he gave Hess a broad, knowing, conspiratorial wink.

"Out of them glasses," Hess said, "and out of them old-lady clothes, with her hair mussed and a drink in her, I bet she's a pistol, Kirb."

"How much do I owe you this time?"

"You're past checkout, but I won't charge you for today. You come in dawn Friday. Make it three nights, plus two phone calls. Comes to eighteen eighty-four. No credit card?"

"I had to turn them in."

"So who needs cards with so much cash coming? You can just sign if you want."

"I'll pay cash, Hoover. Thanks."

When he had his change, he walked to the lobby booth. No point in trying the office to get Wilma Farnham. It was listed under O.K. Devices. O. K. for Omar Krepps. He looked up Miss Farnham's private number. After the phone rang eight times he gave up and took a cab back out to the

Beach and checked into the Hotel Elise. The desk clerks were extraordinarily cordial. Room 840 was ready for Mr. Winter. It was approximately six times the size of his room at the Birdline, with chaises, tables, gentle music, six shower controls, a sun deck, an ocean view, vases of cut flowers, bowls of fruit, his dry-cleaned suit hanging in the closet, the other laundry on a low chest of drawers. When he was alone, he went out onto the sun deck. He could not see the deck where he had walked out to be confronted by Charla supine, but he estimated it was perhaps forty feet to his right, screened by an architectural concession to privacy. He looked down. Little brown people were stretched out on the bright sun cots near the cabanas, looking like doll bodies awaiting the attentions of the costumer. He went back into the room and over to the biggest bowl of fruit. When he looked at it, it made him think of Charla. He selected a pear, and it turned out to be such a superior pear, he had to eat it over the bathroom sink, a deep oval of stainless steel set into a long countertop covered with cherry-colored tile. He looked at the rounded shape of the sink and thought of Charla. He bit into the pear and thought of Charla. He glared into his own mirrored eyes and thought of Charla. Finally he had to dry his sweaty face on a hand towel and go stand in front of the nearest air-conditioning vent.

He went down into the ornate maze of bars and shops and dining rooms in the bowels of the hotel and found a grill room that would serve him a steak sandwich and coffee. It was after four. He tried to sort things out logically. He wasn't very good at it. Miss Farnham had always seemed skeptical of his attempts at orderly analysis. Uncle Omar had never seemed to mind when he reached conclusions he could not justify through any exercise of logic.

Betsy Alden presented too many possibilities. He did not even want to think about her. Thinking about her was like having a dull headache. She could be a neurotic having hallucinations. She could be absolutely accurate. Or she could be at any point between those two extremes.

I am not, he thought, so remarkable, so enchanting, so superior, that Joseph and Charla lay all this on because they can't help themselves. All over the world, whenever they found out I might come up with funds, I've been hustled, but never so good, never so completely. So they do want something. And it isn't the way you hustle a potential employee. As far as I know, I haven't got anything they want. But they think I have it or will have it. There is something somebody wants. It did well by Uncle Omar. Well enough, so that all the outposts have been ransacked, but according to Mr. Wintermore, there would have been nothing in any one of them, not even at the island.

I told them I have nothing. I'm still being hustled. I was too drunk to lie, so they must think I have something I don't know I have, or will get something later that I don't know about. The letter. As good a guess as any. Or maybe, as Betsy suggested, the personal papers.

So what are the ethics? Go along with it? Tell Betsy when I get a clue? Do I owe her anything? Maybe. It depends on how accurate she was. A little free ride shouldn't corrode the soul.

But how much corrosion is implicit in Charla Maria Markopoulo O'Rourke? Suddenly he realized he could readily check it out, indirectly at least. If Charla and Joseph were as influential as they seemed to be, and as powerful as Betsy implied, the Miami papers would have something about them in the morgue.

"Darling!" Charla said, sliding into the booth to sit facing him, reaching across to take his hand in hers. "Wherever have you been?" She wore a blue and white cotton print cut alarmingly low, and a totally frivolous hat. He felt the heat of her hands through white gloves. She stared at him so earnestly, so glowingly, so heatedly, he almost turned around to see who she could be looking at directly behind him. It was a dark corner of the grill, a paneled booth, a lamp with an orange shade. The impact of her made her seem larger than life, a face seen by courtesy of Eastman color when you sit too close to the screen. The nose was snubbed, the cheeks broad, the gray-green eyes slightly Asiatic, the hair milky, heavy, the shade of old ivory, mouth broad, lips heavy and slightly parted and delicately moist, disclosing the small, white, even teeth.

"Just—uh—errands," he said.

She released his hands, pouted at him. "I've been forlorn. I've missed you terribly. I even wondered if you'd been waylaid by my poor little confused niece."

"Uh—no."

"That's good, dear. She may try to tell you some of her mad nonsense. I should warn you in advance, I guess. I feel disloyal telling you these things about her because, after all, she is the daughter of one of my half-sisters. I guess we should have realized we'd have a problem with her when she was expelled from that nice school in Switzerland. But she did seem so sweet, at fifteen. We did our best by her, Kirby, but she has—a very weak grasp on reality. Possibly we should have institutionalized her. But—family, you know—one keeps trying. Actually, that's why I had her come here this time. More bad reports. But it might not do any good. She seems totally rebellious."

"Bad reports?"

"We try to keep track of her, discreetly. Darling Kirby, I don't want to bore you with family problems. But she is really terribly—unstable. She acts out her own fantasies."

"Oh?"

"She has accused me and Joseph of truly horrible behavior, and I haven't known whether to laugh or cry. Unscrupulous men have taken advantage of the way she seems compelled to act out the dreams in her strange mind."

"I beg your pardon?"

"She seems very erratic this time. She may approach you, Kirby. And she may try to make you a key figure in one of her fantasies. And when she does, she will probably throw herself at you."

"Throw herself at me?"

"It will just be another little drama she is constantly writing for herself in her mind. If it should happen, I can't tell you what to do. You seem like a most decent person, Kirby. If you refuse to play the male lead opposite her paranoid heroine, she'll probably find someone who will. She's reasonably attractive. Maybe it would be best if you—humored her. You would be gentle, wouldn't you?"

"B-But—"

"Thank you so much, dear. Just indulge her. Say what she wants to hear. I'll be trying to find another opening for her. I have some good friends in the entertainment world. Don't you think it is better for her to be free than to be shut away somewhere?"

"I guess so."

"One doctor suggested that it is a sublimation of something she does not want to face. By accusing me of vicious, horrible, incredible things she seems to ease her own feelings of guilt. To her I am some sort of dream figure living amidst monstrous conspiracies. Joseph and I joke about it sometimes, but it is a heartbreaking kind of humor. We're really not complicated. Perhaps we like to live too well, but we can afford it—even though we are always being cheated somehow. And maybe you will be taking that worry off our minds, dear."

"I haven't really—"

"They gave you an impossible room and I made them change it. Tomorrow you and I are going shopping. I know exactly the sort of clothing you should be wearing. And that haircut is really tiresome if I may say so. It's as if you are trying to sneak through life without being noticed, Kirby. And you have *so* much possibility. When I'm through with you, you'll walk through the world as if you own it and women will turn to stare at you and their eyes will go wide and their little hands will get moist and they'll make sly little plots to meet you."

"I don't think I exactly want that kind of—"

"You'll *relish* it, believe me. Come on now, dear. Joseph will be waiting for us in the suite. We'll have some drinks there, and the limousine will pick us up at seven-thirty and take us to a perfectly fabulous restaurant."

By ten-thirty that evening, Kirby Winter found himself taking particular pains to enunciate clearly. And sometimes, if he closed one eye, he could keep Joseph in better focus.

"Nice of you to invite me on a cruise," he said. "But I don't want to feel—"

"Obligated?" Joseph cried. "Nonsense! It is our pleasure!"

Kirby carefully turned his head and said, "Where'd she go?"

"To freshen her make-up perhaps."

"I don't dance often, Joe. I didn't mean to come down on her foot like that."

"She forgave you."

"But I keep remembering that scream."

"She is just unusually sensitive to pain, Kirby. Her nerves are closer to the surface than most. But since she is equivalently sensitized to pleasure, I imagine it is a characteristic she would not willingly give up."

" 'Mazing woman," Kirby said solemnly. " 'Mazing."

"I was just thinking, my boy, if you should feel you might be leading a parasitic life on the *Glorianna,* if it would offend your instincts, there is one project you might take on. And a worthwhile one I would say."

"Like what?"

"You were close to Omar Krepps. A fantastic man, fantastic career. But the world knows little about him. He saw to that. I think it would be a rather nice gesture of devotion and respect, dear boy, if you busied yourself with a biography of him. Later we could get some professional to put it in proper shape for publication. Just think of all his quiet charities which will never be recorded unless you do it. And there might be a kind of poetic justice in it. It might make you a bit of money."

"Interesting," Kirby said.

"I imagine that for a project like that, you could gather up his personal papers, documents and records."

"And bring them aboard, huh?"

"You'd be working aboard, would you not?"

"The mystery of Omar Krepps."

"Might make rather a nice title, that."

"Sometimes you sound English."

"I did have some schooling in England."

"You know, I bet you'd like to help me sort out those cases of personal records."

"Is there that much!"

"Hell, yes."

"I'd be happy to help, of course, if you need me."

Kirby felt shrewd as a fox. "All in storage under my name at the Hotel Birdline. Cases of crud. Diaries."

"I had no idea you had all that. You didn't mention it the other night."

"Forgot it."

"When the *Glorianna* gets in, we can have it all brought aboard."

"Oh sure."

"Aren't you acting a little strange, Kirby?"

"Me? Strange?" As he grinned the room tilted and then came slowly back. He felt reckless. "Joseph, old buddy, we're all strange, each in our own little way. You, me, Charla and Betsy."

"Betsy?"

He grinned broadly and drained his Irish coffee. "She's maybe the weirdest one of all. She can tell what's going to happen before it even happens. She's a witch, maybe."

Joseph's big, bronzed, glossy face was suddenly like something on a coin. "Just what did she predict, Kirby?"

Suddenly, too late, the alarms rang. The fox became a rabbit and ran under a bush.

"Who predict what, Joseph?"

"Has Betsy been talking to you?"

"Excuse. I think maybe I might be going to be a little bit sick."

He went into the men's room, leaned close to the mirror, and made strange savage faces at himself until somebody else came in. . . .

"Naughty boy," the gentle, chiding, loving voice said, husky-sweet in the night. "Oh, yes indeed, a very naughty boy." Fingers stroked his forehead. He opened his eyes cautiously. He saw a dark edge of building overhead, and half a sky full of stars. A head, bending over him, blocked out some of the stars. The face was in dark shadow, but light came from somewhere behind her, silvering the outline of her head.

"Dear God," he whispered.

"Oh yes, darling boy, you drank much too much. And such a waste, really. Such a waste of all manner of good things."

He moved his head slightly. There was a smooth, rounded, pneumatic warmth under the nape of his neck. As he began to wonder just what it was, a stir of the warm night breeze ran along his body and he felt as if he was entirely naked. He moved one hand cautiously. He was naked. He sat up abruptly in spite of the pain which split his head in two. He got his head up into the light for a moment before Charla took him by the shoulders and yanked him back down so firmly his head bounced once off the resilience of her thigh then settled into its previous position. At least he had gathered some information. He was on a sun deck, on a sun cot, and from the micro-glimpse of the room beyond, he guessed it was his own. Charla sat at the end of the cot, his head on her lap. And at least there was a reassuring layer of fabric over the rubbery convexity of his fleshy pillow.

"Don't leap like that, dear one," she said.

"I was just—"

"So naughty," she crooned. "Getting so squiffed. Lying to me. You shouldn't lie to me. You did see Betsy."

"For a minute." He hesitated. "Where my clothes?"

"Right here on the floor, sweet. After we got you up here and you passed out out here on the deck, you felt so sweaty and hot and miserable, I took them off."

"Oh."

"I'm really very angry with you. You don't know who your real friends are, do you?"

"I don't feel very good."

"Of course you don't! And you haven't acted very well. Just rest now. You've spoiled it all for us, for tonight. Didn't you know you were spoiling things for your Charla?"

"I didn't know it was—"

"Did you think I'd be so vulgar as to make an appointment? I'm a woman, darling. Maybe there'll be another night. Maybe not. Who can say?"

"The liquor hit me."

The fingertips closed his eyelids, then moved gently across his lips. "Maybe you were exhausted, dear. Maybe poor, stringy, little Betsy used all your resources."

"No! We just sat in a hotel and talked."

"Her hotel?"

"No. Just a hotel. In the lobby."

"And you listened to that poor crazed mind and began to doubt us. Where is she staying, dear?"

"An apartment."

"Do you know the address?"

"She didn't tell me."

"Don't you think you've done enough lying for one night?"

"Really, she didn't tell me. She said she'd get in touch."

"She knows you've moved here?"

"Yes."

"And when she does get in touch with you, you'll let me know, won't you, lover. Immediately."

"Oh yes. I'll do that, Charla."

She sighed. He felt the perfumed warmth of her exhalation against his face. "You have put me off, you know. Just a little. I told you, I have to be a little more than half in love. I think I was. But not now."

"I'm sorry. Please forgive me."

She held his head, eased herself out from under him and lowered his head to the woven plastic of the sun cot. She stood beside the cot for a moment looking down at him. Because of the darkness of the night, he was just able to keep from making some violent, ludicrous concession to modesty.

"I'll try to forgive you, darling. But you really must be very good from now on. I must leave you now."

The remembered mouth came slowly down upon his, flexing, changing, with soft heated movements. His arms went around her without volition, holding her with an increasing strength until suddenly he made a great Hoo-Aah sound and leaped like a stung horse, galvanized by the sudden, shocking, forceful, momentary grasp. She pulled free and, from the doorway into the room, laughed in a gentle mocking way, and was gone.

He lay quivering under the stars, then went in and had an icy shower, and left a call for nine o'clock. It was a few minutes before three. He found a switch for the deck light and picked up his clothes. After he sorted them out and hung them up, he turned off the deck light and went out again into the April night to sit on the wide concrete wall at the end of the deck, sit naked on the abrasive texture, his back against the solidity of the hotel, knees flexed, forearms on his knees, hands slack, cigarette in the corner of his mouth. He could look to his left and straight down, down past architectural solutions, straight down through an obscured and dizzy vista to a tiled death below. He could look straight out at a night-dark sea and sense the slow pulse of the swells and the tides. He could look to his right and see the few highlights of the aseptic sun cot, a prop in a play now over. The wind was fresher, almost cool enough to be uncomfortable. His heart rapped a little too fast, and he had a dull headache. But these physical stigmata were minor compared with his emotional trauma. Charla, with a single vulgar tweak, had reduced him to clownishness, had turned consternation into farce, had shown, symbolically, her ability to destroy his pride, dignity and manhood at her option.

He thought sourly of all the should-have-done things. Another man, a real man, might well have burst from the couch with a roar of rage at such playful violation of privacy, grasped her, swung her onto the couch and ravished her there, under the stars, a fitting punishment for impertinence. (But maybe that was really what she was asking of him!)

He wondered what, long ago, had created this incapacity to deal with people like Charla. He looked out at the sea and wondered why he should be afraid of anything, of anyone. The sea went on, and the shore people changed, but there were stars so lasting that the sea itself was smaller than the life of one man in comparison. Compared to the sea, compared to the stars, of what moment was one snatch of the fishwife hand, one small humiliation, on one night, for one man?

He thought of her hands, small, strong, quite square-looking, beautifully kept, the nails long and curving, the pads of the palms prominent.

He groaned and snapped his cigarette toward the sea and went to bed.

Chapter Five

The executive conference room was sixteen stories above the street, with a huge window framing the bay, a segment of causeway and distant pastel confections of hotels out on the beach. The decor was lime and white, and the big round table and the captains' chairs were lusterless black.

There were eight men at the table. D. LeRoy Wintermore sat at Kirby's left. At his right was a square, pale, motionless fellow named Hilton Hibber, representing the trust department of the bank named executor in Omar Krepps' will. The other five men were Krepps Enterprises executives. They depressed Kirby. They always had. He could not tell them apart. They all had names like Grumby and Groombaw and Gorman. They all had snowy linen, gold accessories and an air of reverence. And they all had big fleshy faces weathered to a look of distinction, perfect governors on television dramas.

And he had always found their general attitude tiresome. They seemed to resent the frivolity of the decision to have the main offices in Miami. And somehow they had pigeonholed Omar Krepps as being a rather ludicrous eccentric, a little man who complicated their grave chores by hopping around picking up odd bits and pieces of businesses which they then had to fit into the measured structure of empire. And they had never tired of trying to tuck O.K. Devices into the fold. In far countries Kirby had always been getting little multicolored forms with small holes in them and blanks for him to fill out. Uncle Omar had told him to ignore them and he did. But they kept trying, and sometimes they would write him sad scolding letters.

The middle one called the meeting to order and said, "Let me recap the terms of Mr. Krepps' will, gentlemen. All the assets of the estate are to be turned over to the Omar Krepps Foundation. Krepps Enterprises will be slowly liquidated over a period of time as its holdings in other corporations are transferred. We five executives of K.E. become officers and directors of the Foundation, in addition to our continuing corporate duties. It has occurred to us, Mr. Winter, that it would be fitting that you should be connected with the Foundation in some active capacity. We are mindful of the fact that Mr. Krepps left you no money in his will. We shall need an executive secretary for the Foundation, and we are prepared to offer you a salary of twenty-five thousand dollars a year."

"I haven't asked for anything," Kirby said.

The five looked sternly at him. "You are unemployed, are you not?" the spokesman asked.

"At the moment."

"Gentlemen!" said D. LeRoy Wintermore suavely. "You are giving me and my client here the impression some deal is underway. But we cannot properly assess its merits until we know what you expect of him."

"Your client?" the spokesman asked. "Isn't that a conflict of interest?"

"No indeed," the old man said.

Hilton Hibber cleared his throat. "Perhaps I can shed some light. In going over the summary records for tax purposes, I find that over the past eleven years, some twenty-seven million dollars in cash and liquid assets have been drained from the asset structure of K.E. and turned over to O.K. Devices. Inasmuch as all taxes were paid on this money, Internal Revenue took no particular interest in it. But O.K. Devices was entirely owned by Omar Krepps. And now they wish to consider that twenty-seven million part of the estate. If they do, scraping up the tax money on that amount would gut the structure of K.E. and reduce the scope of the Foundation seriously. The current books of O.K. Devices were turned over to me. They were maintained by Miss Wilma Farnham, who, aside from Mr. Winter, was the only other employee of O.K. Devices. The books show a current asset value of four hundred dollars. There are no notes payable or receivable, no accounts payable or receivable." He hesitated and took out a white handkerchief and wiped his face, though the conference room was cool. "In fact, there are no records at all, aside from the depreciation account on office equipment."

"And we know why there are no records," the spokesman said in a strangled tone. "Miss Farnham claims she was following Mr. Krepps' instructions. She hired a truck and helpers, and on the day following the death of Mr. Krepps, she took all the files and records to a remote area and burned them. She stacked them, poured kerosene on them, and burned them, by God!"

"Most unfortunate," Mr. Wintermore murmured.

"Furthermore," Mr. Hibber said, "the Revenue people will assume this was done to conceal the location of the hidden assets. Obviously they will eventually subpoena both Miss Farnham and Mr. Winter in an attempt to extract information regarding these assets. So I suggest that—uh—cooperation at this point on the part of Mr. Winter might be beneficial to all."

Everyone looked at Kirby Winter. "Let me understand this," he said. "You're in a tax jam. You don't know what I've been doing for the past eleven years, and you are dying to know. If I explain what I've been doing and what happened to the twenty-seven million dollars, then I get a nice reward of an undemanding job for life."

The spokesman smiled. "Badly stated, of course. But if you should refuse the offer, you can't blame us for suspecting that some of this missing money might be—diverted to your private account."

"That statement is slanderous, sir," Wintermore said tartly.

The spokesman shrugged. "Perhaps. But we're all realists here. We have to protect ourselves."

Kirby leaned back in his chair and studied the intent faces. "You just want to know where all that money is, huh?"

He saw six eager nods, six pairs of glittering eyes.

He smiled at them. "It's gone."

"Gone!" It was a sound of anguish.

"Sure. I gave it all away."

Consternation turned immediately to indignation. The spokesman said, "This is hardly the time for frivolous responses, Winter. Mr. Krepps was eccentric. But not that eccentric." He leaned forward and struck the table with his fist. "Where is that money?"

"I gave it away," Kirby said. "You asked me. I told you. I gave it away."

"My client has given you his answer," Wintermore said.

"In view of Mr. Winter's attitude, I see little point in continuing this meeting," the spokesman said. "His attitude is not unlike Miss Farnham's attitude. Obviously they are agreed not to co-operate with us. May I ask your plans, Mr. Winter?"

"I might go on a cruise."

"With twenty-seven million dollars?" Hibber asked in a cold voice.

"I never carry more than fifty dollars in cash."

"Where do you keep the rest of it?"

"I gave it all away." He leaned to his right and whispered to the elderly attorney.

Wintermore straightened up and said, "As the only living relative, my client is entitled to whatever personal papers and documents Mr. Krepps left here."

All five executives looked uncomfortable. "He left a case of documents in the vault here," the spokesman explained. "When we were faced with—this problem, we examined them. It would seem to be—some sort of a joke. The case contains fifty or so pounds of texts and pamphlets on jokes and magic. Decks of marked cards. Handkerchief tricks. Interlocking rings. The old man was—rather strange you know. The case is back in the vault—any time you care to send for it."

On the taxi ride back to Wintermore's office, the old man was silent and thoughtful. When they were in his private office, he began to make a strange sound. Kirby looked at him with alarm. Wintermore's face was dark. Suddenly Kirby realized the old lawyer was laughing.

"Oh dear, oh dear," Wintermore said. "Forgive me. I have added up all the little clues in a long friendship. Oh dear. Yes indeed. There is no other answer. You did give the money away."

"That's what I told them."

"But you see, they can never believe it. It is a concept so monstrous, they rebel at it. Omar delighted in practical jokes. And this is the biggest practical joke in financial history. Wherever he is, he is laughing as helplessly as I am. Those p-poor earnest fellows! And I am sure Miss Farnham was following his instructions when she burned the records." Wintermore blew his nose and stood up and said, "I'll get your watch."

"Doesn't the will have to be probated or something first?"

"Not for keepsakes, Kirby."

Wintermore came back in a few moments with a fat, old-fashioned, gold pocket watch on a worn chain. The watch was running and on time. On the other end of the chain was a charm in the shape of a little gold telescope. Kirby looked at the watch and then he looked through the telescope, turning it toward the windows. The light illuminated a little interior scene done with photographic realism. Kirby gasped and stared and then looked questioningly at Wintermore.

"My dear fellow, your uncle did not care to live with a woman. But that does not mean he found them entirely useless. He was a man, even as you and I."

"I feel as if I never knew him at all."

"He was not an easy man to know."

"He always seemed—impatient with me, as if I was a disappointment."

Wintermore leaned back in his leather armchair. "He didn't say much about you, Kirby, but when he did I detected a certain amount of anxiety. It was as if he was terribly anxious that you should be ready. As if some great trial or task would eventually be given you. I wouldn't say he faulted you for diligence or imagination. But he seemed to be waiting, with decreasing patience, for you to stand on your own two feet."

"God knows I tried to quit often enough."

"Quit and go crawl into a hole was the way he put it, I believe. Once he wondered aloud in my presence if you were going to be a ninny all your life. Forgive me, but the quote is exact."

"I don't feel hurt. I've wondered the same thing."

"If Omar could have seen you this morning, he would have been heartened."

"Would he?"

"You were splendid, my boy. Skeptical, indignant, indifferent. I would have expected you to apologize to those five impressive gentlemen for any inconvenience you had caused them, make a full statement of what your duties have been, and gladly accept the position they offered."

"You know, I'm surprised I didn't. But people have been pushing me around ever since I got back here."

"You baffled them, Kirby. You gave them no leverage, no handle, no button to push. So naturally they think you were speaking with the independence of hidden millions."

"So Uncle would have been heartened. So what? It came a little late, didn't it?"

"It would seem so."

Kirby looked again through the telescope, sighed and put the watch in his pocket. "Let them squirm for a while. I'll take them off the hook when I'm ready. Or maybe I won't. I don't know."

"They won't just sit there wringing their hands, you know. Expect some sort of counterattack."

"When it comes, you can tell me what to do. You're my attorney."

"It would be interesting to know what Omar had in mind. I do wish we could open that letter he left for you. But I have had a long and ethical career, young man, because I have had the good judgment never to trust myself. We have a Mr. Vitts in this office, a man of truly psychotic dependability. I had him put that letter in his personal safety deposit box. Mr. Vitts delights in sacred trusts. Boiling him in oil would not give anyone access to that letter one day sooner."

"Before the year is up, I may have a better idea of what's in it."

"If you ever have a plausible guess please tell me. Omar was a strange fellow. He made no wrong moves. I've often wondered at the secret of his success, and the only answer that seems even halfway reasonable is that, long ago, he devised certain mathematical procedures which enabled him to predict future events. I keep wondering if those formulae are in that letter. It would account for his anxiety about you. The ability to predict would be a terrifying responsibility."

Kirby frowned and nodded. "It would account for those gambling winnings when I was a kid. And then he lost them back on purpose, so people would leave him alone."

"I intend to live through this year, too. Just to learn what is in the letter."

Kirby walked from Wintermore's office to a neighborhood drugstore for a sandwich and coffee. One little word kept rebounding from the cerebral walls. Ninny. It was a nineteenth-century word, yet he could not find a modern equivalent with the same shade of meaning. Probably it was a corruption of nincompoop. Ninny—that soft, smiling, self-effacing, apologetic fellow, the type who is terribly sorry when you happen to step on his foot, the kind you can borrow money from in the certainty he will never demand you repay it. And if he was a little brown dog, he'd wear his tail tucked slightly under, and wag it nervously, endlessly.

He wondered at his own degree of ninnyism. How severe was it? How incurable was it? Could a man walk through life in a constant readiness to duck? On the other hand, were not the opposite traits rather unpleasant? Arrogance, belligerence, domination. Yet the arrogant man seemed to have considerably less difficulty with one primary aspect of existence.

"Girls," he said aloud. A fat woman on the adjoining stool turned and gave him a long cold stare. Kirby felt himself flush and felt his mouth begin to stretch into a meek smile of apology. As he began to hunch over, he straightened his shoulders, lifted his chin and said, "Madame, I was talking to myself, not to you. If you feel you're in the presence of a dangerous nut, I suggest you move to another stool."

"Whaddaya? Some wise guy?"

"You glared at me, so I responded."

"All kinda nuts in Miami," she muttered and hunched herself over her tuna fish.

Kirby felt a small glow of pride. Perhaps not completely a ninny. But one had to start in small ways. One had to emerge, step by step, from ninnyism, acquiring confidence at each small victory.

Actually, at the conference, he hadn't given a true ninny reaction. Ninnyism would require making a detailed statement of what he had been doing for O. K. Devices, and making them believe it. He had told the truth, but as a gesture of revolt, had made it sound like an evasion. In all honesty he had to admit that it was the intransigence of Miss Wilma Farnham which had backstopped his moments of rebellion. Let the executives sweat.

When a chunky girl came to take his money he braced himself and said, "The coffee is lousy."

"Huh?"

"The coffee is lousy."

She gave him a melting smile. "Boy! It sure is."

He went to the phone booths and called Wilma Farnham at her apartment. She answered on the second ring, her voice cool and precise.

"Kirby Winter. I tried to get you yesterday," he said.

"Yes?"

"Well, I thought we ought to talk."

"You did?"

"What's the matter with you?"

"Nothing's the matter with me, Mr. Winter. The office has been closed. I've turned the books over to the attorneys. I'm seeking other employment. Mr. Krepps left me a generous bequest, but I shan't receive it for some months they tell me. The relationship is over, I would say. Good-by, Mr. Winter."

He called her back. "What could you possibly have to say to me, Mr. Winter?"

"Listen, Miss Farnham. Wilma. I heard you burned all the records."

"That is correct."

"So it looks as if the tax people might subpoena us—"

"Mr. Winter! I knew you would call me. I knew that the instant Mr. Krepps died you'd forget your word of honor to him. I intend to *keep* my word, Mr. Winter. I would rot in prison rather than break my word to that great man. But I knew you would immediately start currying favor with everybody by telling them everything you know. Believe me, there is no longer any documentation for anything you have told them or will tell them. And you cannot wheedle me into breaking my word, or frighten me into breaking my word. You are a miserable, sycophantic weakling, Mr. Winter, and I would say your uncle overestimated you all your life. Don't bother me again, please."

And once again the line was dead.

Twenty minutes later he was pressing the bell for her apartment. When she answered over the communicator and he told her who he was, there was a silence. The lock was not released. He pressed other bells at random. The door buzzed and he pushed it open and went into the tiny lobby. The elevator was in use. He went up two flights of stairs, found her apartment in the rear and beat upon the door with his fist.

"Go away!" she yelled.

He kept hammering. A door down the hall opened. A woman stared at him. He gave her a maniac grin and she ducked back into her apartment.

Finally the door swung open. Wilma Farnham tried to block the way, but he pushed roughly by her, turned and shut the door.

"How dare you!"

"Now *there's* a great line. It swings, Wilma."

"You're stinking drunk!"

"I'm stinking indignant. Now you sit down, shut up and listen." He took her by the shoulders, walked her backward into the couch and let go. She fell back with a gasp of shock and anger.

"Nothing you can say to me—"

"Shut up!" He stared at her. She wore a burly, shapeless, terry-cloth robe in a distinctly unpleasant shade of brown. Her brown hair fell to her shoulders. She was not wearing her glasses. Her small face was wrinkled with distaste, and she squinted at him myopically. "What the hell gives you the impression you've got this monopoly on loyalty and virtue and honor, Wilma? What makes you so damn quick to judge everybody else, on no evidence at all? What gives you the right to assume you know the slightest damned thing about me, or how I'd react to anything?"

"B-but you always just sort of drift with—"

"Shut up! You did as you were told. That's fine. My congratulations. But it doesn't make you unique. I did as I was told, too. I did not tell them one damn thing."

She stared at him. "You're trying to trick me somehow."

"For God's sake, call any of the brass. Ask them."

She looked at him dubiously. "Not a thing?"

"Nothing."

"But those lawyers told me you would tell everything. They said it was the only way you'd get a dime out of the estate."

"They made just as bad a guess as you did."

"Did you just say—nothing? Just refuse to talk?"

"I did better than that. I told them something they couldn't possibly accept—something they couldn't possible believe."

"What?"

"I told them I gave it all away."

Her eyes were suddenly too round for squinting. "But—that's—"

Suddenly she began to giggle. He would not have thought her capable of any sound so girlish. Then she began to guffaw. He laughed with her. Her hoots and shouts of laughter became wilder, and the tears were running down her small face, and suddenly he realized her laughter had turned into great sobs, great wrenching spasms of grief and pain.

He went to her, sat with her. She lunged gratefully into his arms, ramming her head into the side of his throat, snorting, snuffling, bellowing, her narrow body making little spasmed leapings with her sobs, and he could make out a few words here and there. "Sorry—so alone—ashamed—didn't mean—"

He held her and patted her and said, "There, there, there."

At last she began to quiet down. He became conscious of the fresh clean smell of her hair, and of the soft warmth of her against him, and of a hint of pleasant contour under the dreary robe. She gave a single great hiccup from time to time. Abruptly, she stiffened in his arms, thrust herself away and scrambled to the far end of the couch.

"Don't come near me! Don't touch me, you son of a bitch!"

"Wilma!"

"I know all about you. Maybe the rest of them roll right over on their back, but you better not get the idea I'm going to."

"What the hell!"

"Hah! A wonderful imitation of innocence, Kirby Winter. I'm glad you're loyal to your uncle, but that doesn't mean I have to respect the *other* things you stand for.

"I knew what you had in mind, setting up those little conferences in that sordid hotel room. We both knew what you were after, didn't we? That's why I was on guard every single moment. I knew that if I gave you the slightest opportunity, you would have been after me like a madman."

"What?"

"I was on guard every single minute. I had no intention of becoming your Miami plaything, Mr. Winter. You got enough of that, all over the world. I used to go to that room in absolute terror. I knew how you looked at me. And I thanked God, Mr. Winter, I thanked God for being so plain you weren't likely to lose control of yourself. And I made myself plainer when I came to that room. Now that it's all over, I can tell you another thing too, something that makes me sick with shame. Sometimes, Mr. Winter, in all my fear and all my contempt, I found myself wanting you to hurl yourself at me."

"Hurl myself!"

"It was the devil in my heart, Mr. Winter. It was a sickness of the flesh, a crazy need to degrade myself. But I never gave way to it. I never gave you the slightest hint."

"All we did was sit in that room and go over the reports and—"

"That's what it *looked* like, yes. Ah, but how about the things unsaid, Mr. Winter, the turmoil and the tension underneath. What about that, Mr. Winter?"

He raised his right hand. "Miss Farnham, I swear before God that I never, for the slightest moment, felt the smallest twinge of desire for—"

He stopped abruptly. He saw anew the neat sterility of the apartment, the plain girl, the look on her face of sudden realization, hinting at the horrible blow to her pride that would soon be evident. And he knew that even if she was slightly mad, he could not do that to her.

He dropped his hand abruptly and gave her a wicked wink. "I guess I can't get away with that, can I?"

"Beg pardon?"

He winked again. "Hell, baby, I used to see you walking, swinging that little round can one sweet inch from side to side and I used to think—uh—if I could just get you out of those glasses and those old-lady clothes and muss your hair up a little and get a drink into you, you'd be a pistol."

"Y-you filthy animal!"

He shrugged. "But, like you said, cutie, you never gave me an opening. You never made the slightest move."

She seemed to cover the distance from the couch to a doorway across the room in a single bound. She whirled and stared at him. Her face was pale. Her mouth worked. "Th-then," she whispered, "if I didn't—why in God's name didn't you?"

In the trembling silence he reached for the right response, but all he could find was his own terrible moment of truth. He felt impelled to meet it. "Because—I'm scared of women. I try to hide it. Women terrify me."

She wore an expression of absolute incredulity. She took a half-step toward him. "But you're so—so suave and so—"

"I'm a lousy fake, Wilma. I run like a rabbit, all the time."

She bit her lip. "I—haven't had many chances to run. But I always have. Like a rabbit. But you!"

"You're the first person I've ever told."

Suddenly she began to laugh again, but he could not laugh with her. He heard the laughter climbing toward hysteria.

"No," he said. "Not again! Please."

She whooped, whirled, bounded through the doorway and slammed the door. He could hear her in there, sounding like a small stampede heading through swamp country. He slowly paced back and forth until the sound diminished and finally died away. He sat in a chair, his back toward the bedroom door.

"Wilma!" he called.

"In a minute," she answered, her voice husky from weeping.

He took the gold watch out. He looked cautiously through the little telescope and shivered. He was studying the intricate monogram on the back of the watch when the bedroom door opened.

"He always carried that," she said. "Always."

"I guess I will. I'll have to wear a vest or get some kind of a belt clip arrangement."

She was behind him, looking over his shoulder. Suddenly he was inundated by an almost strangling cloud of perfume.

"Sometimes he'd look through that little telescope and then he'd chuckle."

"I bet."

"I asked him about it once. He wouldn't let me look through it. He said I didn't speak the language. I didn't understand. Will you let me look through it?"

"I—uh—maybe when—uh—"

She came around the chair. She made a wide circle around it and stood where he could see her for the first time, some eight feet away. He tried to swallow but could manage only half the process. "Bought it two years ago," she said in a grave whisper. "Tried it on once."

She had brushed the brown hair until it gleamed, and for the first time he saw the reddish highlights in it. She was facing him squarely, but she had her face turned away from him. She stood like a recruit who had just been chewed out for bad posture. She was not trembling. Rather she seemed to be vibrating in some galvanic cycle too fast for the eye to perceive. He had the feeling that if he snapped his fingers all the circuits would overload and she'd disappear in a crackle of blue flame and a hot smell of insulation. He slowly began to strangle on the half-completed swallow. She wore a single garment. He could not guess at what possible utility it might have. There was an inch-wide ruffle of black lace around her throat. There were similar visible ruffles around her wrists. There was a third circling her hips, apparently floating in air several inches away from the pale and slender thighs. The three visible bands of black seemed joined together by some incredible substance as intangible as a fine layer of city soot on a windshield. Miraculously affixed to this evanescence, and perfectly umbilically centered, was the pink, bloated, leering face, on some sturdier fabric, of the most degenerate looking rabbit he had ever seen.

He completed the swallow with such an effort, it felt as if he were swallowing a handful of carpet tacks. For a tenth of a second he marveled at the uncanny insight of one Hoover Hess, and with a sobbing sound of guilt, inadequacy and despair, he roared out of the apartment and down the corridor toward the stairs. He heard a howl of frustration, and a long, hoarse, broken cry of, "Oh you baaaaaaas-taaaardddl!" As he clumped down the stairs the corridor fire door swung slowly shut, and he heard those hoots of laughter again, heard them begin to soar upward, and then the door closed and he could hear no more.

Two blocks from the apartment building he suddenly heard himself saying, "For God's sake, Wilma!" and realized he had been saying the same thing over and over for some time. The gold watch was still clutched in his hand. Two old ladies were staring at him with strange expressions. He slowed his headlong stride, put the watch in his pocket and gave them an ingratiating smile. One old lady smiled back. The other one tilted her chin at the sky, braced herself, and with a volume that made every car in that block give a startled swerve, screamed, "Stop thief!"

It panicked him into a dead run, but as soon as he was around the next corner he slowed down, his legs trembling. He stood staring blindly into a bookstore window until his breathing was normal. He oriented himself and discovered he was seven or eight blocks from the Hotel Birdline. Suddenly, for the first time since telling it, he remembered the lie about Uncle Omar's personal records. He remembered how crafty he had felt when telling it. Sober, he knew it was a blundering stupidity.

He went to the Birdline. The one without any space between his eyes was at the desk, the one with the volcanic acne. The clerk leaned into the small office beyond the switchboard and yelled to Hoover Hess. Hess came out, rubbing his hands, projecting the smile of agony.

"Kirb, buddy, you ready to talk business? You can't make a better—"

"Not right now, Hoover. I'm a little too rushed. I was wondering about my stuff you've got here. I thought I'd—"

"Understand, I'm a guy appreciates a sweet gesture, but I told you so long as I got the room down there, the storage was on the house, right?"

"Yes."

"And I'm the kind of a guy wouldn't change the deal on account of you inheriting big, right?"

"But—"

"So what I mean is, I'm touched by the fifty bucks, Kirb. It was a nice thing to do, believe me."

"Fifty?"

Hess looked shocked. "Was it more? Did those slimy bastards take a clip out of it on the way over here?"

"Uh—no. It wasn't any more."

"Rest easy, Kirb. They come and got the trunk and the big wooden case along about eleven this morning."

"Who?" he said weakly.

"The guys from the Elise! In the truck from the Elise! Chrissake, don't you even remember who you sent after it? Look, if you could come in and sit down for just five minutes, Kirb, I could fill you in on the whole picture. The way I figure, in exchange for consolidating the mortgages and bringing it down to an interest rate that makes sense, instead of the cannibal rates I got to pay, what you should have is a piece of it. I even got an inspiration about your name, to go with the place. The Winter House. How about that!"

"Some other time, Hoover."

"Any time you say. I'll drop everything. Everything."

Kirby headed across the lobby toward the pay phone. He had to skid to a stop to let a sailor by. The sailor had considerable velocity. He was skidding across the tile floor, revolving slowly, his eyes closed. He was smiling. He carried on into three short wide men in tense argument over a racing form, catapulted the three of them into a couch and went on over with them as the couch went over backwards.

He dialed Betsy's memorized phone number.

"Kirby! I was about to come looking for you. I tried the hotel a thousand times. Are you there now?"

"No. Look, I think you were right, at least a little bit right anyhow."

"Thanks a lot!"

"Don't be so sarcastic. The way things are going, how am I expected to trust anybody?"

"Why Kirby, dear! Your teeth are showing."

"I think I did a stupid thing. I mean I thought it was shrewd, but I was drunk at the time."

"It's a poor week for it."

"I know. But it worked, sort of. But I've got the idea they're going to be awfully damned mad. And I was supposed to meet her at two o'clock over there. She was going to take me shopping."

"Standard procedure. She has a wonderful way of getting all her men to end up looking exactly alike. They all end up looking like fairy ski instructors. I think it's the tan, the sideburns and the ascot that does it. She's mad for ascots. And it's a long way after two, Kirby."

"I have the feeling it wouldn't be too smart to go over there now. Let me tell you just what—"

"Come on over here. We can talk. I hate phones."

"I'd rather tell you over the phone."

"Come on over here. I'm alone. We can thrash it all out."

"But—but—but—"

"Get over here on the double, you clown!" She hung up.

A little word started bounding about in the back of his mind. It was made of fat little letters, fabric letters, stuffed. NINNY. The fabric, curiously, was the same shade of pink as the face of the lecher rabbit centered on Miss Farnham's gossamer funsuit. He squared his shoulders. He walked carefully around the broiling brutal confusion of cops, sailors and horse players in the front of the lobby, deaf to the resonant tock of hickory against bone, and took the single cab in front.

As they pulled away, the driver said, "Like they got Saturday night on Monday afternoon in there, huh?"

"What?"

"The riot, man!"

"Sorry, I didn't notice it particularly."

After a long silence the driver said, "I don't know what the hell kind of date you got, mister. All I know is I wisht I had it."

He had trouble finding the address. It was a crooked little bayfront street, more alley than street. The building had been added onto in random fashion over the years, and each segment of it seemed to sag in a different direction. Apartment Four, when he finally found it, was one flight up, via an open iron stairway bolted to the side of the building. The door was painted an orange so bright it seemed deafening. Over the bell was lettered *b. sabbith.* He was tempted to press the doorframe with his thumb an inch below the bell, wait ten seconds, then flee down the staircase. "Ninny," he whispered and pressed the bell. There was a tiny porthole in the door. A green eye looked out at him. The door swung open.

"Come in and look at this creepy place," she said. She was in stretch pants again. Plaid. And a sleeveless blue blouse. Barefoot. Cigarette in the corner of her mouth. Toffee hair in harsh disarray.

Most of the apartment was a big studio room. He saw a kitchen alcove and a single door which had to lead to a bath. Glass doors opened out onto a tiny breakfast porch.

She stood, hipshot, and included the whole decor in one wave of her arm. "Observe. Rugs to your ankles. Strategic lighting. Cutie little hearth with, for God's sake, a dynel tiger skin in front of it. Any chair you sit in, you need a helping hand to get out of. That damned bed is nine by nine, and twenty inches high. I measured it. The little library is all erotica. Seventeen mirrors. I counted. Thirty-one pillows. Counted them, too. In the way of groceries, one-half box of stale crackers, one-half box of stale puffed wheat, twenty-one cans of cocktail goodies, two bottles gin, fourteen bottles wine. Make a wild guess, Winter. What is Bernie's hobby?"

"Uh—philately?"

She spun and grinned at him. "You come on slow, but sort of nice, Kirby. I figured you for a fatal case of the dulls. Maybe not. I recommend this couch over here. It's the only thing you can get out of without a hoist. It must have come with the place." She sat down, patted the place beside her and said, "The detailed report, friend."

He told her all, with a little editing here and there. She seemed quieter, more thoughtful than the last time he had talked to her. "What's the stuff you had stored?"

"Just personal junk. Books, records, photographs. Tennis stuff. Hunting stuff. Even a pair of ice skates."

"That's a nice touch. Ice skates. That'll make them very happy. But we are forwarder. Now you know for sure they want something. Uncle's personal records. The clue to the edge he had over the competition. And you say there aren't any records at all. Are you sure?"

"Pretty sure."

"Could the Farnham broad have something tucked away? She sounds desperately loyal."

"I doubt it."

"Charla and Joseph are going to be very irritable, Kirby. But I think they'll think you're still the best link to what they want. And I don't think they know exactly what they do want. But they want it bad. Badly enough so they shouldn't treat you too badly. You sure you didn't give them my address? While drunk?"

"If I had, they wouldn't be trying to find out."

"They don't want us to get together on this. They'd rather deal with a goof, not somebody I've toughened up for them."

"I don't care much for that word, Betsy."

"Oh, for goodness sake, be honest with yourself. If I hadn't planted the seeds of suspicion, Charla'd have you on a leash by now, trotting you around, scratching you behind the ears, tying your new ascots, and giving you the slow strip and tease routine, until you wouldn't be able to remember your name if somebody asked you quick."

"I'm not so sure."

"You just don't know Aunt Charla. Hell, where are we? I think you ought to trudge on back there and play cute. Make out you know what they're after. Admit you tricked them. Say you'll listen to an offer. Maybe then we'll get a better clue as to what they really want, if they know."

"I don't think I'm very good at this sort of thing."

"I *know* you're not very good at it. But hang in there. I think we might get some volunteer help. Bernie's coming down soon with a crew and some models and so on to do some commercials here. Mad ones all. Maybe they'll help us add a little more confusion to the deal."

"Do we need more?"

"Poor Kirby."

"The thing is, in eleven years you get sick of dealing with people you know you'll never see again. I kept wanting to get out. I had this idea of maybe finding a town way off a main road with maybe twenty-eight people in it, so I would know them and they would know me, tomorrow, next year, ten years from now. I could stop trying to remember names and faces. And I'd know where I was before I woke up in the morning, instead of figuring it out afterward."

"With me," she said, "it's a dream of being back in that school. I was there for six years, you know. From nine to fifteen, the longest I've ever been anywhere. And I dream a class is leaving and I have to leave too, and I'm crying. But then they take me out of the line and I know I can stay, and it's the most wonderful thing. All the others are marching away, but they're going to keep me."

"But they didn't."

"Charla came in a car big as a freight engine, with a driver in uniform and an English Lady Something with her who made a horrible snorting sound when she laughed. I was supposed to be in a play at school, but they didn't give a damn. They drove me to Paris and bought me a lot of clothes. We met some other people there, and then we all flew to Cairo."

"Sometimes you have more accent."

"I can get rid of every trace of it when I have to."

"Could Charla have arranged to have my uncle's places—robbed?"

"Why not? It isn't her usual style. It's a bit crude, and probably quite expensive. But she has the pragmatic approach."

"They won't be able to get that letter."

"They can afford to wait a year. And all you got was a keepsake."

He took the watch from his pocket. She reached over and took it from him. "A real grandpa kind of watch." Before he could stop her, she looked through the little gold telescope.

"Happy days," she said in a tired voice. "Don't let Bernie see this. It's all this apartment needs. There's room on that wall for a mural." She took another look. "They make this junk in Japan. A girl in school had a candybox full. Hers were all set in rings." She handed the watch back to him. Just as he put it back into his pocket, she leaned toward him, reached toward him. Because of his humiliating flight from Wilma's apartment, he had resolved to fight fire with fire. He reached toward Betsy. His aim was defective. His palm slid into and across an abrupt nubbin of breast, frank and firm under the blue blouse as an apple in the sun. And he saw a glimpse of teeth in something not a smile, and something flashed and smashed against the left side of his face. The sudden pain filled his eyes with tears. She was a blur. As vision cleared he saw her looking gravely at him as she sucked her knuckles. With the tip of his tongue he isolated the metallic crumb in his mouth, moved it out to his lips, plucked it out and stared at it. It was a piece of filling. It made a small clinking sound as he dropped it into the ashtray.

In the silence she reached for him again, took his cigarettes from his shirt pocket, took one out of the pack and put the pack back.

"Get carried away by the decor?" she asked.

"I just thought—"

"Maybe Charla has warped your values, pal. Maybe with her it's a social gesture, like passing the butter. Or asking for the next dance. Not with me, Winter. I put a higher value on myself."

"She said it was the other way around," he said miserably.

"How many lies are you going to believe?"

"From now on—not very many."

"I didn't mean to hit quite that hard, Kirby."

"I've had better days than this one, I guess."

She got up and moved across the room. Again he marveled at her talent for expression. The stretch pants projected demureness, regret and impregnability. She fiddled with a panel board on the far wall. Suddenly he heard a rising, hissing scream and knew a jet was diving into the building. As he sprang to his feet, the great sound turned into an infantry barrage. She twisted the volume down and it suddenly was Latin music, bongos, strings, a muted trumpet.

"High fidelity is part of the treatment, too. Two hundred watts, maybe, with tweeters and woofers hidden all over the place."

"Loud, wasn't it?"

"The records are down here. There's no activity you can

think of that he hasn't got music to do it by. But I've got it on FM radio now." She moved restlessly across the room, moving to the rhythm, half-dance, half-stroll. "If we just knew exactly what they're after."

"Well—I better go back there and see if I can find out."

"Don't let them know where they can find me."

"I won't. But what would they do?"

"Find a way to keep us apart. It might be something unpleasant."

He tried to think of Charla doing something unpleasant. But when he thought of Charla, the air seemed to get too thin. He saw her, vividly, wearing Wilma's smoky wisp, smiling at him, and the image was combined with the tactile memory of Betsy's small firm breast against his hand. Betsy came over and stared at him. "Do you have some kind of seizures?"

"Me?"

"Try cold showers, deep breathing and clean thoughts, Winter. Now take off, so I can take a nap."

Chapter Six

He arrived at the Elise at quarter to five, and though he went directly to his room without stopping at the desk, the phone began to ring ten seconds after he had closed the door. It rang and it also flashed an imperative red light at him.

"Couldn't you have let me know you'd be delayed, dear?" Charla asked.

"I'm sorry about that."

"Do you have anyone with you?"

"No."

"That seems very odd."

"What's odd about it?"

"Don't public figures usually have a swarm of people around them, eh?"

"Public figures?"

"Kirby dear, you're so lovably obtuse. You better scoot right down here before the sky falls on you. Down the hall, dear. To the suite. I guess we're lucky we didn't try to do any shopping. We'll be lucky if we can make it to the *Glorianna*, dear. She got in this morning."

"What are you talking about?"

"Dear God, don't you really know?"

"No."

"Didn't you stop at the desk?"

"No."

"Then you better hustle down here and let me tell you about it."

She hung up. As soon as he hung up the phone began ringing again. He answered it. A tense male voice said, "Kirby Winter?"

"Yes?"

"Look, fella. I won't horse around. If nobody's got to you,

twenty-five hundred bucks on the line for a twenty-four-hour exclusive. This is Joe Hooper. Remember that name, hey? And I'll see you get protection from everybody else until this time tomorrow. Is it a deal?"

"I don't know what you're talking about."

"Don't be coy, sweetie. You got to move fast. You sneaked by pretty good, but word got around and they're on their way up there now."

"Who?"

"Are you Kirby Winter, for Crissake?"

He heard a commotion in the hall, and people began pounding on his door. "Excuse me, but there seems to be somebody at the door."

"That's *them,* you nut! Is it a deal?"

Kirby sighed and hung up. He started toward the door and hesitated. It sounded like a big crowd out there. Suddenly there was a sharp rapping on the locked interconnecting door at the other end of his room, and a muffled voice. "Kirby?" He recognized Charla's voice. He went over to the door and answered her. "Open the latch, dear," she said.

He opened the door. She smiled at him and tilted her head and listened to the commotion in the hall. "My word, they gather quickly don't they?" She wore a yellow mandarin coat over white Bermuda shorts, and she was wearing huge opaque sunglasses.

"Who?"

"All the news people, lover. All jostling and pushing and despising themselves and each other and you, their nasty little strobe lights and pencils and tape machines all aimed and ready. I thought it might be like this, so just in case, I had Joseph pick up this room in between you and the suite. These interconnect so this whole oceanside can be turned into a big suite. Joseph had to get a dear little honeymoon couple moved out of this room to arrange it."

"What do those people want?"

"Don't stand there like a ninny, dear. They sound as if they might actually break the door down."

He went with her through the extra bedroom and into the suite. She closed the interconnecting door behind them. In the suite she handed him an afternoon edition of the Miami *News.* They had a two-column picture of him on page one.

It was an old picture. The head said, MYSTERY NEPHEW IN KREPPS TAX DODGE. He sat down very abruptly.

"At noon today Walton Grumby, Executive Vice President of Krepps Enterprises revealed that serious estate tax problems are anticipated in the Omar Krepps estate because of the refusal by Kirby Winter, nephew of the late Krepps, to reveal the whereabouts of approximately $27,000,000 diverted over an eleven-year period from Krepps Enterprises into a mystery company known as O.K. Devices, entirely owned by Krepps.

"Grumby told reporters that O.K. Devices occupied a small rental office in the Fowler Building, employing only a Miss Wilma Farnham of Miami, and Kirby Winter. The day after the death of Krepps, Miss Farnham, either on her own initiative, or on the advice of Winter, destroyed all the files and records of O.K. Devices and closed the rental office. Grumby stated that Krepps was always highly secretive about the operations of O.K. Devices, and it seems possible that the company was merely a device for draining off the liquid assets of Krepps' other ventures and placing them out of the reach of the Internal Revenue Service.

"Grumby stated that Winter traveled to all parts of the world on confidential orders from Krepps, returning infrequently to Miami. Earlier today, Winter refused to disclose his confidential activities to Krepps Enterprises executives or to state what had happened to the $27 million. The Farnham woman also refused to reveal any details of the operations of O.K. Devices or to state on whose instructions she had burned all the records.

"Grumby told reporters that in view of these indications of conspiracy, it seemed possible that Winter and the Farnham woman may attempt to flee the country. At press time neither Winter nor the Farnham woman had been located for comment."

"Good Lord," Kirby said, staring blankly at Charla.

She came and sat close beside him and took off the sunglasses.

"Do you see all the implications, dearest?" she asked.

"I guess they're anxious to talk to me."

"That figure has a horrid fascination. A million dreary little people are absolutely vibrating with the vision of all that money hidden away in the romantic corners of the world.

They hate you for having it. And they have a sneaking admiration for you for grabbing it all as soon as your uncle died."

"But it wasn't that way!"

"Does that make any difference, really?"

"But if I explain the whole operation in detail—"

"Without any documentation at all? And you *did* tuck a little bit away here and there for yourself, didn't you? Don't look so indignant. If you didn't, you are an idiot, of course. Didn't Miss Farnham intercept a little? How can you be sure? But it isn't the news people you have to worry about."

"What do you mean?"

"Dear Kirby, the world is jammed with animals who would happily put you and your Miss Farnham on a double spit and roast you over coals for just one per cent of that much money. All of a sudden, dear, you two are very tasty animals in the wrong part of the jungle. And I think you might find out how sharp the teeth are if you walk out that door." She had been edging close to him and he had been trying to move away, inconspicuously. Now he was at the end of the couch and the satin weight of one breast was on his arm.

"You need us more than ever," she said.

"Huh?"

"The *Glorianna,* dear. Don't be so dense. Either we smuggle you away, or the world tears you to pieces, believe me. And I really don't know why we should even dream of helping you, after that nasty trick you pulled on us. Ice skates, indeed!"

"I was just checking."

"Joseph was livid with rage, but I told him it served us right for underestimating you. It was quite clever, really. But I imagine you wouldn't have been so wary if Betsy hadn't given you a lot of wrong impressions about us."

"But—I guess you do want something."

"Of course, dear! Isn't it refreshing to have it out in the open? We can all stop playing games, can't we?"

"I guess so."

"No secrets?"

"I guess—that depends."

"On what? Darling, if you're thinking of being so crude as to require some sort of agreement, you might spoil things for us, don't you think? I couldn't promise to be your absolute slave. But it might turn out that way, once we're at sea. I wouldn't really strike a whore's bargain, no matter what is at stake. It would make it all so terribly ordinary. And we want it to be extraordinary, don't we?"

Thinking of Betsy, he chose his words carefully. "I think, instead, I'm thinking in terms of a different kind of bargain. How my end of it will come out. And what the safeguards are."

She was so close he could see a tiny amber wedge in the gray-green iris of her left eye, and see the exquisite detail of her lashes and brows, the individual hairs like gold wire.

The eyes narrowed and she took a deep breath and held it. "Then you have it!"

"Have what?"

"Just don't get too bloody clever, Mr. Winter. You could bitch it for yourself, you know."

"How could I?"

"All of a sudden, pet, your dead uncle has put more pressure on you than we ever could. Now I think you're going to have to make a deal. Maybe you won't have any choice."

He was feeling his way. This was a new and rather deadly Charla, a confirmation of Betsy's description. "Just suppose, even with all that pressure, I don't need you."

"Indeed?"

"Just suppose a goodly chunk of that money did get stashed. Where I can get to it. And suppose I have the idea you people are a little crude."

"Crude?" she said thinly, shocked.

"Ransacking all Uncle Omar's little hideouts."

She studied him for a long time. "So you're a good actor too. I think that makes you twice as dangerous as cleverness alone, you know. When the stakes are high enough, it's worth making a direct move sometimes. It could have worked. Then who would need you?"

"But it turns out you do."

She tilted her head. "And why the aw shucks, gee whiz, Huckleberry Finn reactions to my little—attentions, Kirby?"

"I like to be disarming."

"Dear Jesus, you *are!* So what makes you immune? Is Farnham that good?"

"Probably."

She got up to pace slowly, frowning. He noticed she had

lost some of her accent in the past few minutes. "Very nice," she said. "Set the mark up and when you get to the kill, he second-cards you to death. I suppose you are thinking in terms of a partnership."

"Not particularly."

"Is it in the same place the money is?"

"Is what?"

She stamped her foot. "Don't be so damned coy! Certainly you know we could have done it the other way at any time. You drank whatever I handed you. And we could have gotten you to a place where screaming wouldn't matter. Joseph hasn't got the stomach for it, but I have, friend. I have. I find it very interesting."

He swallowed a sudden obstruction in his throat. "So I guess that must mean it wouldn't have done you any good."

"It wouldn't do *you* any good, dear."

"I guess you have to assume I know what I'm doing."

She nodded, reluctantly. "I'm beginning to think so. But what the hell was your uncle thinking of? He must have realized this would happen."

"If this is the way he planned it."

She gestured toward the newspaper. "If you brought this down on yourself, you must have a lot of confidence, Kirby."

"I didn't make any public statement." He went over to the phone. He looked at his watch. "I want to see if I can get Grumby at home by now."

"Better let me place the call for you. Knowing where you are would be worth money to the girl on the switchboard."

He looked up the number. Charla placed the call. When she had Grumby on the line, she handed the phone to Kirby.

"Interesting press conference you held, Mr. Grumby."

"Ah, Winter! You must understand that we have to protect ourselves."

"Then you'll understand my statement when I make it."

"I don't think I follow."

"All I can say is that I was an underling. Uncle Omar certainly didn't leave me anything. All I can say is that O.K. Devices was some sort of tricky corporate thing I never quite understood. It never made sense to me, using all that money to buy property and securities abroad and then putting the deeds and certificates and a lot of cash into Swiss banks in your name and the names of your associates. But I did it because I was paid to do it. And I can tell them that Miss Farnham is baffled too, because she burned the records at your request."

There was a long silence. In a rather rusty voice, Grumby asked, "What is the purpose of all this, Mr. Winter?"

"I am going to try to avoid making any statement at all."

"A statement like that—fictitious one might destroy us all."

"In the absence of any documentation, it could get sticky for everybody. I'm just suggesting that you don't try to get any cuter."

"We may have seriously underestimated you, Mr. Winter."

"You can't retract the statement. But you can avoid making any more. I have all the trouble I need right now." He hung up.

Charla looked at him approvingly. "You can be quite a serpent."

"At heart I'm a ninny."

"It's an effective disguise. Omar did look like such a sweet, baffled old man. We should have assumed you'd take after him."

The phone rang and she answered it. "Who? Oh, yes, of course. What is that? Oh, no, my dear. My brother and I hardly know the young man. Seen with him? You must be mistaken. Not that I would mind, you understand. It's really quite exciting being in the same hotel, actually. Even the same floor, I understand. He must be a *very* interesting chap. All that money. My word! I'm sorry my brother and I have to leave this evening. It would be amusing to stay here and watch the fun. No, of course not. You're very welcome."

She hung up. "A bright girl, that one. Playing percentages, bribing the help, I imagine. Possibly the bellhops who carried you upstairs last night. I tried to stay well out of it, but those boys are quite observant. Well, darling, you might as well bring your suitcases in here and we'll leave it up to Joseph to plan a good way to get you out of here tonight and onto the *Glorianna*. She'll be refueled by now. And it's just what you need, you know. The dramatic, mysterious disappearance."

"That's all I need."

"We'll do our bargaining at sea, Kirby."

"Will we?"

"Dear boy, give me credit for *some* intelligence. If you

weren't interested in making a deal, you wouldn't be hanging about, would you?"

"I guess not. I—uh—think I'll shower and change."

"Take your time, dear. We won't be out of this for hours and hours. Want your back scrubbed?"

"No thanks."

"Don't look so severe. Any other little service you can think of?"

"Not right now. I'll let you know."

"I'm sure you will, you lovely serpent."

When he was back in his room with the door bolted, he went and listened at the corridor door. He could hear a murmur of voices in the hall, and some laughter. He walked back and forth, biting his lip, smacking his fist into his palm. He remembered her words, "a place where screaming wouldn't matter." It made him feel sweaty and chilled.

At seven-thirty he stood on the exposed landing with the green eye looking out of the porthole in the bright door at him, shadowed by the dusk.

"It's me," he said in a squeaky, muffled, breathless voice. "Me!"

Betsy opened the door and let him in. "Dear Lord," she said softly. "Anybody follow you here? No, I guess they wouldn't."

He undid the jacket and belt of the hotel uniform and took the hotel pillow out. He pulled the wads of tissue out of his cheeks. He collapsed into a chair and said, "They sent up a fat one."

"A fat what?"

"A fat waiter. I called from the honeymooner's room."

"From the whose room?"

"I haven't hit anybody since I was thirteen years old. He put the tray down and turned around and—Pow. I left a fifty-dollar bill in his hand. Then I walked right through all of them."

"All of who?"

"Why would they have uniforms this color? Salmon and emerald?"

"Kirby, I heard all about you on television, on the six o'clock news, and I could guess that the thundering herd is after you, but really, you'd better start at the beginning.

Unless you start somewhere near the beginning, I am going to all of a sudden start screaming."

"She said something about screaming, and it was very nasty."

"Kirby!"

"All right. All right." And he told her. There was, for once, no need for in-process editing. She listened carefully, thoughtfully.

"So she finally showed her teeth, did she?"

"My God, the last place I ever want to be is on that yacht. And it's a damn strain to talk to somebody and not really know what you're talking about."

"I think you are a sweet lamb and I think you did very well. But where are we? Now she thinks you know what it is she's after. But you have no idea what it is?"

"Absolutely none."

"But now she knows she's either got to be awfully damn cute to get it away from you, or awfully rough, or pay your full price, or come in as a partner. What does it sound like, whatever it is?"

"All I can think of, I swear, is some sort of an invention."

She nodded gravely. "That's where I've been going too. Years and years ago, he *did* try to invent things. And suddenly he became rich and powerful. He got an edge, a gimmick, something that works. I think that Charla and Joseph reasoned it all out by inference. Maybe they don't even know exactly what it is. But they could guess it could be written in his personal papers."

"And they think I know exactly what it is."

"Maybe it would be awfully useful right about now if you could lay your hands on it, Kirby."

He closed his eyes. "You know, I'm just about whipped. Everybody in the world thinks I've got twenty-seven million dollars squirreled away and they all want it. Just six people know I gave it all away. You, me, Wilma, Wintermore, Charla and Joseph. And I gave Charla the idea I'd kept some. But they want something else, and I don't know what it is, and you don't, and you seem to think they don't either."

"Leaves Wilma, doesn't it?"

He opened his eyes. "Could she know?"

"Maybe she could know without knowing she knows. Maybe she could have it without knowing she has it."

"Guess I better phone her."

He phoned Wilma. A man answered. He had a precise, high-pitched voice. "Who wishes to speak to her, please?"

He hesitated. Betsy was listening too. She nodded. "Kirby Winter."

"You wouldn't mind proving you're Mr. Winter?"

"How do you expect me to—"

"Just a moment, please. I must get the questions she wrote down. You can prove you are Mr. Winter by answering them correctly." He was gone for twenty seconds. "Are you there? Good. First, please give me the name of the man you were dealing with at the time of your uncle's death."

"Uh—Manuel Hernandez y Gomez."

"And the name of the man in Rangoon in December?"

"Oh. Dr. Na Dan Boala."

"Thank you, Mr. Winter. I suggested this precaution to my sister. She was in such a state of horrible emotional shock, she wasn't thinking with—her customary precision. I am Roger Farnham. She hoped you might call. Now, thank God, I shall be able to leave also. The harassment is sickening, as I guess you must have learned by this time. I must say, it is a grim reward for my sister's years of loyal faithful service to your uncle."

"I didn't have anything to—"

"I realize that, of course. And there is much about this I can't pretend to understand, sir. Wilma will tell me very little. But I do know, of course, she is—uh—incapable of hanky-panky."

"Yes. Of course."

"I'll doubtless be followed when I leave here, but I'll have the satisfaction of knowing I won't be leading them to Wilma. Do you know that the reporters actually badgered her into hysterics?"

"That's too bad."

"It took considerable guile to get her hidden safely away."

"I can imagine."

"And it would be a shame if you led the world to her hiding place."

"I'll certainly try not to."

"She's too delicate for this sort of thing. I'm leaving it up to you to do the right thing, and find some way out of this for her. Someone should be sued for the filthy hints they put in that interview."

"I don't think they'll be doing any more hinting."

"The damage is done, apparently. At any rate, sir, I have a home, a family and a profession to return to. Please tell her I cannot be expected to damage my own life in some vain attempt to assist her."

"Where is she?"

"You will be careful about contacting her? She does want to see you."

"I'll be very careful, Mr. Farnham."

"I smuggled her to the house of one of my associates, Mr. Winter. He is on a sabbatical leave in France, and he left the key with me. Unfortunately the phone is disconnected. Have you a pencil? Two-ten Sunset Way, Hallandale. It has considerable privacy due to the plantings Professor Wellerly arranged with that in mind. A small pink house. She has food and water, and she should be quite safe there, from the rabble and the curiosity seekers. But she is upset, naturally. Give a long ring then a short and then a long, and she will know it is either you or me, sir. She will open the door to no one else. And I believe I am right in saying we are both depending on you to do something to clear up this unfortunate situation."

"Thank you."

"Not at all, sir. It's my duty to my sister. Good evening."

"Well now!" Betsy said as he hung up. "How cozy you'll be! In your wittle pink housey."

"So how do I get there?"

"I can't say that I really care how you get to Hallandale, friend."

"In this uniform?"

"Bernie Sabbith is almost your size, and there is a whole closet loaded with stuff. Be his guest."

"She wouldn't think of letting me stay in that house with her."

"You're kidding!"

"I mean it. She's a very—she's sort of an odd girl. Uh—very proper."

"Even under emergency conditions like this?"

"I wouldn't want to risk it. Really, it would be a terrible

risk for me to leave here. Any cab driver might recognize me."

"Well, my friend, you can't stay here. I'm a very odd girl too."

"Is it or is it not important to you to help me?"

"Indeed it is, but there are some kinds of help—"

"I was thinking, Betsy, I could write a note to her telling her to trust you. You know, she really doesn't think much of my judgment. Then you could go out there and stay there with her tonight and talk the whole thing out and maybe you and she can figure out what it is that Charla is after. I can reduce the risks by staying here alone. Then you can come back tomorrow and if you've learned anything we'll know what to do, and if you haven't, then we can try to figure out the next step."

At first Betsy was reluctant, but at last she agreed the idea had some merit. She made drinks while he wrote the note. Then, having laid in some stores during the day, she cooked ham and eggs in the tiny kitchen corner. Just before she left, a little before nine, she showed him where the television set was. She crawled on her hands and knees to the intricate headboard of the enormous bed, flipped the switch that moved a ceiling panel aside exposing the picture tube built into the ceiling. The other controls were next to the switch.

"If Charla locates the place, ask her to watch TV with you, Kirby."

"If I can arrange my life properly, I'll never see that woman again."

"What's the matter. Scared of her?"

"Totally."

Betsy gave him a wan smile. "Frankly, so am I."

Chapter Seven

After checking again to be certain the door was locked, and after a lengthy hunt for the final elusive light switch, Kirby Winter crawled to the middle of the giant bed. There was a troublesome fragrance of Betsy about the pillow. It was a warm night, with a murmurous traffic sound, a ripped-silk sound of far off jets, the adenoidal honk of boat traffic. The ten-o'clock news had displayed other pictures of him, still shots, grinning like an insurance salesman. And there was one picture of Wilma Farnham, looking severe. The newscast made them sound like the master criminals of the century. Informed sources believed that Winter and the Farnham woman had already fled the country. They had both made mysterious disappearances under the very noses of the ladics and gentlemen of the press. One could see them chummed up on Air France, snickering, tickling, getting bagged on champagne, heading for that stashed fortune and a simple life of servants, castles, jewels, furs and tireless lechery.

He wondered about Betsy and Wilma. By now they would be deep in all their long talking, and he blushed to think of Wilma, distrait, uttering all her shy girlish confidences. "And all the time he really was terrified of women. You should have seen him run from me in absolute horror."

He was physically exhausted, but he could not slow his mind down. He knew he would not sleep, but suddenly he was down in the jungly world of nightmare. Wilma, giggling, opened zipper compartments in long cool pale thighs to show him how solidly stuffed they were with thousand-dollar bills. Charla had little gold scissors, and she smirked and cooed as she cut the ears from little pink rabbits which screamed every time. She was bare and golden, oiled and steaming, and when she turned he saw the vulgar placement of the little tatoo which read "Ninny." He walked into the scene in the little gold telescope and found Uncle Omar there, off to one side, chuckling. Uncle Omar thrust a deck of cards toward him and told him to take any card, but when he took the card it was warm and heavy and moving, and suddenly he was back in an old car in a heavy rain of long ago, and he found the dream blending into a reality of some warm, solid, busy, rubbery creature burrowing against him, snuffling and giggling and snorting, raking him with small claws. In a few moments of night fright, he tried to dislodge it, thrust it away from him, but the very act of clutching at it, the agile roundnesses under his hands, turned fright into a sweet aggression, his mind—standing aside—awed, wringing its hands, finding no way to intercede.

In a vague and troubled way, as he became aware of the helpless inevitability of it, he felt all the responsibilities of literary allusion, of equating it with fireworks, ocean surf, earthquakes or planetary phenomena. At the same time he was remotely, fretfully concerned with identity, wondering if it were Charla, Betsy, Wilma—but soon realizing that particular problem was, as of the moment, entirely academic. He just did not have time to give a damn.

So it transpired without benefit of analogy, or time to create one, aside from the hurried thought it was rather like some sort of absurd, stylized conflict, like a sword fight to music where you duck in time and in relation to the imposed necessities of tempo. As the fight was both won and lost, in a white blindness, he sensed, from a long way off, her vast tensions, some spaced yippings, then a buttery melting of the creature quelled.

And then there was a head beside him, wedged into his neck, tickling him, and a breath making long slow hot whooshings against his throat, and a hand that came up to idly roam his indifferent cheek.

"Hoooo—boy!" she whispered. "Hooooo, *Bernie!* Oh, you the doll of all times. The livin' most."

"Um," he said, pleased that his heart had decided not to hammer its way out of his chest.

"Suh-prize, suh-prize, huh, sweetie? Nice suh-prize?"

"Um."

"Couldn't make the damn key work for hell. Figured on

you changed the lock, and I would truly kill you dead, you'd done that to Bonny Lee one time. Then it worked and I come a-mousing in, felt the bed, looking for two pair of feet. I find two pair, Bernie-boy, there be the gawddamnedest fracas around here you heard ever."

"Uh."

"You doan talk much to a gal missed you so bad, honey. Don't you get the idea now I could be hustling you for any piece of that TV crud, on account if you just use them sick-looking broads you brang down here like always. I come here because you're just the most there is anywhere, and I love you something terrible, and it was real wild and nice, hey now?"

"Um."

She ran her fingertips across his upper lip. "Hey! You gone and shaved it off! Now what in the world you look like, I wonder."

She scrambled away from him. She fumbled with the headboard control panel for a few seconds and then a bright overhead spot blinded him. He shut his eyes tightly, opened them a little bit and squinted at the girl.

She was kneeling, staring down at him, a deeply browned leggy girl. Her brown eyes were huge and round. Her mouth was shaped into a round shocked circle. She had big round brown breasts with a startling white stripe across them. She had a flat tummy, smooth muscles of a swimmer, and under a tight tangled cap of white curls, a lovely, delicate, angelic face, bronzed and innocent.

"Who you, you tow-head son of a bitch!" she yelled. "What kinda smart-ass trick you pulling anyways? I'm gonna rip the face right offen you!" Her fingers curled dangerously.

"Now hold it!"

"For what? What do you think I am anyhow? Where's Bernie?"

"I don't know."

"You were supposed to be him, gawddamn it!"

"I don't know about that."

"Anybody pull what you pulled, mister, somebody ought to take a rusty knife to 'em and plain—"

He sat up and glared a her. "What the hell is the matter with you?" he roared. "I was sound asleep! I didn't know who you were, and I don't know who you are. I was so sound asleep I didn't know even *what* you were."

A corner of her mouth twitched. "You could have got the general idea I was a girl."

"That occurred to me!"

"Don't you roar at me, you sneaky bassar! You woke up, all right, soon enough, and you could have figured it out, being in Bernie's bed, maybe some mistake was happening. But did you say a damn word?"

He stared at her. "When? And what was I supposed to say? My God, girl, it's like a man falling off a building; you'd expect him to tie his shoes and wind his watch on the way down."

Her mouth twitched again. "Real something, wasn't it?" Without warning her eyes filled and she put her hands over her face and began to sob like a child. She toppled sideways and lay curled up, shivering and weeping.

"Now what?" he said with exasperation.

"S-S-Sneaky b-b-bassar!"

"Why are you crying?"

"What you d-done to me. In my whole l-life I never had no affair with s-somebody I din even know. Makin' me feel like a slut girl. Makin' me feel all cheap and r-r-r-rotten. Oh, oh, oh."

"You hush, whatever your name is."

"Doan even know my *name!*" she wailed. "Bonny Lee Beaumont, gawddamn you!"

"My name is—" He hesitated. "Uh—Kirk Winner." He pulled her right hand away from her face and grasped it and shook it. "Now we're introduced. For God's sake, stop blubbering."

"But I din know you *then!*"

"But if you'd known you didn't know me, then it wouldn't have happened would it?"

She stopped abruptly and looked up at him, sidelong and wary. "Huh? How does that go?"

"As far as you were concerned, I was Bernie. Right? So there's no reason to blame yourself, is there?"

She was silent for a moment. Then she sat up, snuffled once, nodded at him. "I guess I got to think on it the way you say. But I broken a secret vow to myself, made when I was fourteen, how never in my whole life would I sack out with no man I din feel love for. Even it's an accident, it still counts, sort of. I even feel funny you lookin' at me, and it never bothers me with no man I love. But I get dressed, that's funnier yet. I doan know what the *hell* to do, mister. What's your name again?"

"Kirk Winner."

"Friend of Bernie's?"

"A friend of a friend."

"You down on the television thing?"

"No."

"Married?"

"No."

She tilted her head. "You're not such a bad *looking* fella anyways."

"Thanks so much."

She wrinkled her clear young forehead into a thoughtful scowl. "What bothers me, it was so real *fine*, Kirk. I mean I had the idea there had to be love, so when it's fine with a stranger, it makes me out some kind of animal like."

"You were expressing the love you feel for Bernie. That's what made it right, Bonny Lee."

She grinned. "You talk things out good for me. You'll be having me coming around with all kinds of problems, hey?"

"Any time."

"I keep wondering now how Bernie would look without the mustache. Gawddamn it, I thought I was going to get to see."

"How old are you, Bonny Lee?"

"Twenny, practically."

"Dear God. You live with your folks?"

"My folks! You some kind of a nut or something? My folks, they're farmin' on shares, South Carolina, and I was fourteen, went into a beauty contest you were supposed to be sixteen, and I sure God looked sixteen or better. I didn't do good on the talent part, but the prize I got was one of the judges taken me to New Orleans and I never been back since. Married one time and it was a mess and I shucked him fast, man played clarinet and drank shine. Then I got to singing around, and now I'm working a place, Rio's, up North Miami, singing and sort of stripping some, but not down to raw, and a bongo thing I do too. But what's coming on for me good now is a career, and that one marriage was plenty I can tell you, and Bernie he's been good to me, starting last year.

So I have a ball, it saying on my work card I'm twenny-two, and my own little car and all, and friends enough, but Jesus I didn't count on walking into nothing like this here. I tell you true, it has plain upset the hell out of me, Kirk."

She swiveled and moved off the bed in a leggy stride, moved out of the bright area of the light. She was in a shadow area then, where the only visible things were the bright hair and the two pale areas of bikini.

"Folks!" she said and snorted. "I swang that hoe enough under that hot sun, and I stayed, I'd be wore down with nakedy kids by now, cause there you don't have your first young by fifteen, you got to be looking like a toad frog, and I sure didn't. And don't."

"No, you don't."

"Took that little judge's wife seven weeks to hunt him down, and then she bust every dish in the apartment. On him, and me going out the back way with the little bit of money he had left by then. That taking the money is the only thing I ever did shamed me until this night, Kirk."

Moving slowly, she picked her clothes off the floor, shook them, hung them over an arm of a chair. She came back toward the bed, picked up a white purse and sat on the edge of the bed, toward the foot of the bed, just out of the cone of light, facing him.

"Glaring on you," she said. She got up and switched on a low lamp in a far corner, turned off the overhead prism and sat on the bed again. She took a small brush out of her purse and brushed the fitted cap of white curls. She was partially silhouetted against the light. She lit two cigarettes and stretched toward him and handed him one.

"Well, hell," she said wistfully. "You can't win 'em all."

He had begun to realize how remarkably good he felt. He wanted to ride a chrome bike down Main Street, no hands, waving all the flags of the Americas. He wanted to get a reasonably good start and run right up the side of a few tall buildings. He could do a tireless handstand and twirl batons with his toes. This was indeed a splendid girl. He was very fond of her.

"What's so gawddamn funny?" she demanded.

"Sorry. I didn't realize I was laughing."

"What you do for a living, sugar?"

"I—I'm sort of between jobs."

"What's your trade?"

"Sort of—investments."

"And the investment was three kings against a lousy little full house. That's how it goes, sugar."

"Uh—Bonny Lee?"

"Yay?"

"You—uh, you said it was—pretty fine?"

"You were there, weren't you, brother? You weren't all that much sound asleep, and that's for sure. You want a medal of honor or something? I swear to God, some day I hope to meet a man doesn't want to be told he's the best there is. What is it with men anyhow? A girl, she just wants to be lovin' and wanted, and a damn man, every time, it's like he wonders if he can make the Olympics. You all scared you haven't got it? Y'all go round provin' it often enough, then swaggering around like you'd done something special, like as if it was something any mink couldn't do quicker and oftener. Big deal. I give you a passing grade. Okay?"

"Sorry I mentioned it."

"So am I, sugar. So am I. There's one thing bores me damn near to death, it's talking about it. Folks get hungry and have a fine steak, they sit over the bones and talk about it? They get thirsty and have a big cold drink, they sit around peerin' down into the glass a-wonderin' what temperature it was, for Gawd's sweet sake. The way I figure—"

"I said I'm sorry I brought it up!"

"Shees marie, you don't have to beller at me, sugar! You know, you got a temper onto you?"

"I'm a very mild guy! I always have been! I *never* lose my temper! Get off my back, will you?"

"Kirk, sugar, you're real edgy. There anything to eat?"

"Some cold ham. Rye bread."

"I'll just whomp up sanwiches, make us both feel better. You know it's three in the morning?"

She went into the kitchen corner and turned on the bright overhead fluorescence. He propped himself on the pillows so he could watch her. Her long legs were so tanned they looked carved out of redwood, shaped lovingly, sanded to sleekness, polished. As she bent and moved and worked, he admired the smooth clench and slither of the young muscles of haunch and back and shoulders. And he felt the vast contentment of what he knew could be no more than a momentary ownership, and he wanted to find a heavy stone and chunk himself in the head with it for having deprived himself for so long of this kind of fatuous, arrogant smugness he had not realized existed.

She began to hum and then to sing. Her singing voice was an octave deeper than her speaking voice. Both the song and the phrasing were tantalizingly familiar.

"Billie!" he said suddenly.

She turned and grinned at him. "God rest her soul. Played all them records til nothing left but a scratchy hiss, then boughten some more and played those out too. Withouten Lady Day, I'd have hardly no career at all, sugar. There any one of hers you like special?"

"God Bless the Chile."

She clapped her hands with delight. "Damn *all,* Kirk honey, that there is *my* song. Seven thousand times I sung that, all alone and for the people, and not one time it wasn't like my heart turning over slow. I can *cry* to that song, thinking of that poor lost broad and how the world broke her down. After this here ham, I'll sing it to you good, and you shuten your eyes, you'll think she's come on back for sure. Say, here is some of that burgundy red wine all fizzed like a sof'drink, like I had here one time before. You want some tall with ice?"

"I'd like that, Bonny Lee."

She brought the wine in tall glasses, and thick sandwiches on white napkins, all on a teak tray. Nothing had ever tasted better to him. "I'm night people," she said, chewing busily. "Three o'clock, four o'clock, I could gnaw the ears off a gallopin' horse."

"But you get out in the sun."

"Set my alarm for noon, usually. Swim fifty lengths, five at a time, bake myself in between. Keeps me tightened up nice, you think so?"

"Very nice, Bonny Lee."

She took the tray out and brought back more wine. When it was gone she put the glasses aside and said, "Now close your eyes and hear Billie."

She did it beautifully, her tone smoky, gentle. Midway he opened his eyes. She was singing with her eyes closed, swaying slightly. "—rich relations give crust of bread and such. You can h'ep youself, but doan take too much. . . ."

After the last note was gone into the silence of the room, she opened her eyes and they were shiny.

"You liking that, Kirk sugar, knowing about Billie and all, asking for that one—it's somehow something starting out all dead wrong and swinging around right. You feel that?"

"Yes, Bonny Lee."

"And it could set that first time all the way right if I was to know it was you, maybe. But I don't want you thinking wrong, this being the first time in my whole life knowing a gentleman friend such a short little time. But time got messed up kind of for us."

"I wouldn't think wrong."

She went over and turned out the light and came back. In a little while she said, "Kirk sugar, what for you shaking so?" In another little while she said, "You know, you're hands are like *ice!*" And in another little while she said, "Sugar, is it really meanin' all this much to you, honest?" And when she knew it did, she whispered, "Then it's meaning ten times as much to me too. Which I am now to let you know. Shees marie, here I am tumblin' into love again, and a damn tow-head, cold-hand, evil-temper yankee, a gamblin' out-a-work man, and so gentle-sweet I can start crying any minute, and nobody does any more talking from here on in."

Chapter Eight

There was a hornet big as a sea gull perched on something right in front of his face. It had a wide nasty little face, gray-green eyes, long heavy milky hair, a puffy mouth heavily lipsticked. It smacked its evil little mouth and swung its stinger back and forth. It had big veined wings which looked as rigid as plate glass. At intervals the wings would vibrate for several seconds, becoming almost invisible, making a harsh resonant burring sound.

The hornet was gone. A phone was ringing. He sat up, lost in space and time, still half wary of the hornet. He was in a huge vague bed in a shadowy room, with a dawn slant of sun coming in from the breakfast porch. As an orderly part of his mind picked up the count on the ringing of the phone, he turned and saw a tousle of curls sunk into a pillow at the far edge of the bed, four feet away, and a brown nape of tender neck, a silky V of white hair against it, and a deep brown shoulder, and a pale blue sheet, draped, molding the long girl-shape of the rest of her—incredible ornamentation to an unknown morning. Memory was suddenly an avalanche, pouring into the dry arroyo of the stunned and empty mind. He felt a stab of delight so unexpected it was more like pain than joy. He felt as if somebody had suddenly thrust a hollow needle into his heart and pumped it full of spiced molasses.

. . . thirteen, fourteen, fifteen, and the phone went on and on. By the simplest deduction, it had to be Betsy Alden. Anybody else would have given up. By letting it ring and ring, she was letting him know who it was.

. . . nineteen, twenty, twenty-one . . .

He found the phone on the shelf to the left of the headboard.

"Yes?"

"Good *morning,* Kirby," Joseph said, the rich voice almost gelatinous in its baritone flexibility.

"Uh—how—"

"You've really been *very* tiresome lately, Kirby. But all will be forgiven if you can give us a little co-operation now. You are really in all kinds of trouble now, you know. The vicious assault on that poor waiter was a stupid mistake. But you seem to be reasonably ingenious, so we think you can probably devise some way of getting from that apartment to the *Glorianna* without incident. Listen carefully, my boy. She is tied up at the Biscayne Marina, E Dock. Please be aboard by ten at the latest."

"What time is it?"

"Twenty after seven. It should give you ample time."

"But I don't—"

"Filiatr—Betsy, rather, is a very silly, stubborn, emotional child. She tried to be clever. Let's just say it isn't wise to attempt a fool's mate against the queen's gambit. Perhaps she was counting upon a sentimentality which doesn't really exist. Or trying to play us against you. It's rather hard to tell at the moment. She's no longer very coherent. I must congratulate you upon not confiding in her completely. Because she really became very eager to confide in us. We did learn you two young people have become quite fond of each other in a very short time. And, of course, where to get in touch with you. And with Miss Farnham. Charla is wonderfully eager to talk with Miss Farnham too, and they should be bringing her here any moment. But we won't start asking her tiresome questions until, say, ten o'clock."

"What are you trying to—"

"I'm urging you to join us, old boy. I'm counting on your sense of responsibility for Betsy. And your sentimentality, I suppose. She's really too high strung for this sort of treatment, you know. Also, unless you've suddenly become irrational, you must realize that with the way things have developed, you need us quite badly. We'll be expecting you, Kirby."

The line was dead. He hung up and looked at his hand and noted that his fingers were trembling. He got up and put on his shorts and went around to the other side of the bed. He sat on his heels and looked at Bonny Lee's dear sleeping face and thought his heart would burst with the wonder of it.

It was dark against the pillow, lips parted, a face of absolute innocence. Her hand rested near her face. It was a lean, tanned, muscular hand, very like the hand of an active boy in his early teens. In the reflected glow of the early sunlight he saw the white hairline outline of a scar on the back of her hand shaped like an L. He wondered where she had gotten it.

He put his hand on the warmth of the bare shoulder and shook her gently. "Bonny Lee, darling. Hey! Bonny Lee!" Aside from a faint frown that disappeared immediately, there was no response.

He shook her more violently, spoke more forcefully.

"Wurrow!" she said, a small, irritable squalling sound, and flounced over onto her other side. He rolled her back over and shook her.

Finally she opened her eyes and slowly focused on him. She glowered at him. "Middla ni'," she mumbled. "Middla ni'. Lemmilone." And she was gone again. He pulled the sheet off her, pulled her legs out of bed, took her by the shoulders and sat her up. She sat with her chin on her chest, shoulders slumped, mumbling and growling at him. When he took his hands from her shoulders, she toppled onto her side and gave a small, purring snore. He sat her up again, took her wrists and started to pull her into a standing position. When he realized he would merely be pulling her off the bed onto her face, he reached and took her around the waist and stood her on her feet about two feet from the bed. She started to sag, then braced her legs. She peered at him, her eyes slightly crossed. As soon as he let go of her, she made a slow half-turn, took one step and dived face down across the bed. He stood her on her feet again and began to walk her. She leaned heavily against him, staggering, cussing him, groaning. He released her suddenly, ready to catch her if she fell. She wobbled around, caught her balance, shuddered violently, combed her fingers back through her curls and focused on him.

"So what the *hell* you doing, Kirk? Gawd!"

"Please wake up, Bonny Lee."

She squinted toward the porch. "Dawn!" she said despairingly. "Sonuvabitch!"

"I would have let you sleep, but I need your help."

She looked at him with venomous suspicion. "I tell you, sugar, it better be important."

"It is."

She shuddered again. She turned and blundered toward the bathroom. He heard the shower begin. He went over and examined her clothing. Lime slacks, a white blouse with a yellow figure, a little yellow jacket, white sandals, two blue-green wisps of nylon. He put her clothing on a chair just outside the bathroom door. The shower stopped. The door opened wide enough for her wet brown arm. "Fetch m'purse, sugar!" she called. He put it into her hand. He checked Bernie's wardrobe, laid out a gray sports shirt and dark blue slacks.

In a little while she stuck her head out, started to say something, saw her clothing, smiled at him and took her clothes into the bathroom. The protocol was slightly confusing. Apparently one could move about as unself-consciously naked as a tenpin until morning ablutions began, at which time modesty set in.

She came striding out, brushed and lipsticked, giving a little hitch at the waistband of the lime slacks, tossing her jacket and purse on a chair, smiling at him. "Once you're up I guess it isn't too terrible. I been told I'm a little hard to wake up."

"You bounced out of bed the first time I whispered your name."

"You're next in there. I'll neaten up some. What you staring it?"

He realized his expression was probably rather strange. Looking at her, he had been reminded of something a teammate had said about Mickey Mantle. "The more he takes off, the bigger he looks."

Clothes changed Bonny Lee. She looked taller and thinner. It did not seem plausible that all of that well-remembered abundance of breast and hip, all the fecundities, the armsful and handsful of sweet sighing weight could have disappeared into such a compacted trimness, into the tailored litheness of a clothed and pretty stranger.

Her smile disappeared and her brown eyes widened. "Oh, Gawd, you never seen me in clothes afore!" She blushed violently, deepening her tan to redness and making her face look moist. "I wanna fall right smack through the floor, sugar."

"It's all right. We understand how it happened."

"Sure enough, but I'm thinking on how it would *sound* to somebody. Shees marie, how the hell would you explain it?"

"We don't have to try."

"You rushing me out of here on account of somebody coming?"

"No."

"Just who is this friend of Bernie's that's a friend of yours?"

"She's an actress."

"Oh, great!"

"Uh—Bernie's in love with her, I think."

"Anything in a skirt, Bernie's in love with it. Take your shower."

When he came back out in the gray shirt—too snug across the shoulders—and the blue slacks—too high above the shoes—rubbing a jaw made raw by the only razor blade he could find, he smelled coffee. She'd made the bed. She moved slowly toward him, her jaw belligerent, her fists on her hips, her brown eyes narrowed. The waiter's colorful uniform was behind her, on the foot of the bed.

"You wearin' Bernie's stuff, Kirk. You maybe been a waiter at the Elise? Just what the hell is going on?"

"Bonny Lee, I just can't explain right now—"

"Right now is when you do, mister, or it's going to be like you was wrapped in bob wire and spun like a top toy."

He made two forlorn beginnings, then said, "My name is really Kirby Winter."

She tilted her head. "You say it like it meant something."

"I thought it might."

"Kirby Winter? Sounds like I know of you somehow. You talk nice. School educated. Some kind of actor?"

"I'm—sort of in the news. Starting yesterday."

"I don't pay much attention to—" She stopped abruptly and put her hand to her throat. She peered at him, shocked and incredulous. "Sugar, you *him!* Twenny-seven million bucks! You the one stole and hid all that money!"

"I didn't steal it. I haven't got it."

She shook her head wonderingly. "You kin to that Kroops."

"Krepps. Uncle Omar."

She moved back to the bed and sat down limply and stared

up at him. "You and some little old school-teacher-lookin' gal tooken it, and like the whole world looking for you all over hell and gone, and you cozied up in bed here with Bonny Lee Beaumont, herself."

"I didn't take a dime."

She studied him for a few moments. "Kirk, sugar. I mean Kirby. I surely know you didn't. I know the rough kind and I know the sly kind, and once in ever' long while, the sweet kind, which you are and which there's not enough of, and I wouldn't say you tooken it at all, so why don't you go turn yourself in and say how it came about?"

"I can't. There's so many reasons, there isn't time to tell you, but I just can't. I just hope—you'll be willing to help me, even though you know who I am."

"Even though? Don't you make me cross now, sugar. On this here big crazy old bed you learned me who you are, and what you want of me, I will do. But let's put a cigarette and coffee with it," she said and got up.

They took the coffee out onto the breakfast porch. There was a sun-glare on the bay. "You said you've got a little car?"

"Down in the alley. A little old yalla Sunbeam thing."

"Do you know where the Biscayne Marina is?"

"Sure thing. I knew a boy kept his boat there one time."

"I'd like you to drive me there, Bonny Lee."

"Then what?"

"Just leave me off there."

"That's all? Not much favor to that, Kirby."

"A lot of people know my face. A lot of people are looking. It could turn into a mess."

"You running away by boat?"

"I—I expect so."

"Can't put the top up on the car on account it doesn't have a top any more. You could kind of scrunch down, I expect. Let me see what I can find." She went into the apartment. He heard her opening and closing drawers. Music began to play. She came back out with a wide-brimmed planter's hat and a pair of dark sunglasses. "Should be news any time now. Here, you try these."

The hat was a little small, but he could pull it down far enough.

She nodded. "You look like anybody and ever'body.

Camera a-hangin' round your neck, you'd be invisible any place in Florida entire. No need of scrunching."

"Aren't you going to ask if taking me there is going to implicate you in anything?"

"Implicate? That mean messed up in? I love a somebody, Kirby, I do like he asks me."

He took the glasses and hat off and stared at her. "Love?"

"You weren't listening in the bed, sugar?"

"Well, yes, I was, but I thought it—was sort of a manner of speaking."

"Hell yes it was, and I'm speaking it again. You got something against it?"

"No. I just mean that—well, I mean you seem to accept the fact I'll go off in a boat—and you don't know if we'll see each other again, and you don't seem to—well, to really care very much—and I thought—"

"You know, you could be, like they say, over-educated."

She wiped her lipstick onto the paper napkin, came smiling around the table and bent over him, put her hand on the nape of his neck and began to kiss him with considerable skill and energy. He groped for her and turned her and brought her into his lap. Within minutes they were trembling and gasping and giddy. She pushed his hands away from her and sat bolt upright, her hands on his shoulders, head tilted, smiling. Her eyes looked drowsy.

"I love you good, Kirby. And love is a pretty thing. See how fast all worked up we gettin'? That's the good of it, sugar. Going to bed is happy and it's fun. It's the way you get the good of it with none of the bad. It's like everybody has forgot that's all it is and all it was ever meant to be. People got to mess it up, it seems. Cryin', moanin', clingin' onto one another, all jealous and selfish and hateful. We love each other on account of we give each other a lot of happy fun, and if it comes round again, we'll take some more, and if it doesn't, we got this much already anyhow. But no vows and pledges and crap like that, hear? That's what people do because they got the funny idea it's the right thing to do. And before they know it, the fun part is gone, gotten itself strangled on the fine print, like it was a deed to some land. I live free and simple, Kirby, and I look on myself in the mirror and say hello to a friend I like. The day I stop liking her, I change my ways. So this is who loves you, and that's what the word means, and I got friends would die for me and me for them. What I say, you run onto a hell of a girl."

"I did," he said. "I did indeed."

"Any man *using* me," she said intently, "he gets a kick turns him soprano. I'm eager, but I'm no gawddamn free lunch counter for any bassar prowling for kicks, hear?"

"I'm not."

"Don't ever get to be. Hey! That's the news starting."

They went inside and sat on a couch. After the national news, Kirby was the first item on the local news.

"State, Federal and local authorities have joined in the hunt for mystery man Kirby Winter and his accomplice, Wilma Farnham. Last night Arturo Vara, room service waiter at a Miami Beach hotel, swore out an assault warrant against Winter. As the police reconstruct it, Winter, hemmed in by reporters in the corridor outside his hotel room yesterday, broke into an adjoining room, placed a call for room service, then, when Vara arrived, slugged him, donned his uniform and made his way through the reporters to the elevators and escaped from the hotel. He has not yet been apprehended."

Bonny Lee turned and stared at Kirby and raised one eyebrow in question. He nodded, guiltily.

"Dr. Roger Farnham, Associate Professor at Florida Eastern, elder brother of Wilma Farnham, disclosed that after a brief unfruitful interview with the press yesterday, Miss Farnham left the apartment where she lived alone, taking a few personal possessions, and has not been seen since. Police have established that Miss Farnham and Winter held clandestine meetings at a Miami hotel during his infrequent returns to this area from various foreign countries.

"The question which is on everyone's lips is what could have happened to the missing twenty-seven million dollars turned over to O. K. Devices by Krepps Enterprises at the direct order of Omar Krepps, international financier, who died suddenly last week. It is believed that Winter and the Farnham woman carefully planned the huge embezzlement over a period of time, including the destruction of the files and records and, according to police theory, including plans to leave the country, plans they may have consummated last night.

"In addition to the assault charge, Winter and the Farnham

woman face embezzlement charges lodged by Krepps Enterprises. At midnight last night K.E. posted a reward of ten thousand dollars for any information leading to the apprehension of either or both of the fugitives. They are also bringing civil suit against both Winter and the Farnham woman. Both the tax and immigration authorities are anxious to serve summonses on both Winter and the woman.

"Winter is described as being six feet, one-half inch tall, weight about one-ninety, sandy hair, dark blue eyes, age thirty-two, small crescent scar on left cheekbone, clean-shaven, polite, soft-spoken, highly intelligent, disarming."

Bonny Lee went over and turned off the radio. She came back to him, shaking her head. "You now a celebrity, man." She touched his cheek. "Where'd you get the scar?"

"A little girl hit me with a rock when I was about six years old." He grasped her hand, touched the scar he had seen. "How about this one?"

"I swang back-handed at a little old buck-tooth boy pinched me when I was about eleven."

"You need ten thousand dollars?"

"Hope to God I never do need it so bad, sugar. Can you think of anything at all they *don't* want you for?"

"Armed robbery."

"Keep trying. Maybe you'll get lucky. Sugar, I better get you onto that boat before anybody tracks you right to here."

"Or before I get too scared to walk out the door."

He put on the hat and the glasses and checked his pockets. He went and got the gold watch off the shelf near the phone. Thanks for everything, Uncle Omar, he thought.

"How far to that Marina?"

"Ten minutes, about."

Before they went out, he kissed her. They held each other tightly for a few moments. She looked up at him. "Fun?"

"More than I can say."

"I could get a little weepy over you, Kirby. Let's go."

The Sunbeam roadster was, he guessed, about three years old, dinged, dirty and beginning to rust out. But the engine roared immediately, and she yanked it around a corner like a toy on the end of a string. He clapped his hat back on just in time. It was almost nine o'clock. She drove with her brown hands high on the wheel, chin up, eyes slitted, cigarette in the corner of her mouth. She shifted up and shifted down, and danced in and out of the lines of morning traffic with what at first seemed like terrifying abandon, but he soon recognized as such skill that he felt entirely safe in the noisy little yellow car.

She cut through to the waterfront, turned north and went three blocks, and when she began to downshift he saw the big Marina sign and all the pleasure craft at the wide docks. Suddenly she gunned it and went on by, and he saw the prowl cars at the curb and saw the uniformed men on the dock. She turned the next corner, braked, and tucked the little car into a parking slot.

"That door there is shut and locked," she said.

"I don't know what the hell to do!"

"Just sit tight and let Bonny Lee find out for sure. What's the boat?"

"The *Glorianna.*"

She found a newspaper under the seat and handed it to him. "Hide behind this, sugar. Be right on back."

She was gone for a full fifteen unbearable minutes. Then she piled into the car and drove away away from there. She headed west, found a shopping center, parked amid the other cars.

"It took me a time, Kirby, to single me out a cute cop and get him a-coming over to me to show off how big he is. That *Glorianna,* she took off twenty minutes ago and those cops got there ten minutes too late. Now as near as I can tell, what happened is they found out a lot of your stuff was moved out of some cruddy hotel, and it took time to track it down, and they found it got took to that Marina and put aboard the *Glorianna.* So they figure you're on it and they got you nailed good, because they got the Coast Guard looking already and they'll pick it up any time. It's a big old son of a gun the man there said. You know, they got the idea that twenty-seven million got put aboard, and they're all standing around so sweaty they can't hardly stand it. It wouldn't hurt me a bit to know what did get moved onto it, sugar."

"Personal junk. Total cash value, maybe two hundred tops. There's even a pair of ice skates."

Her eyes looked startled. "Shees marie. *Ice* skates!"

"I've got no place to turn, Bonny Lee."

"I should truly like to hear from the beginning. Should we go back to Bernie's?"

"I'd rather not go back there."

"All we need is a place to talk, for now. And the last place they'd look I'd say is a public beach. Okay?"

"Okay, Bonny Lee."

The noise of the little car eliminated any chance of conversation. She drove over to the beach and headed north. By ten o'clock they were on a cement bench in a small open pavilion, looking out across a wide beach toward the curl and thud of the blue Atlantic waves. Though it was a Tuesday morning in April, there were hundreds of people on the beach. He was beginning to feel depressed and helpless.

"You load it all onto me, sugar, and then you get a new opinion."

He told her. He droned a leaden parade of facts, without color or hope. And in the telling of them, he disheartened himself even more. He took it from the first legal conference after the funeral right up to the morning phone call from Joseph.

He stared woodenly at her. "Think I should go try to explain?"

"Who the hell would believe you? Gawddammit, Kirby, they'd start looking for the needle marks in your arm."

"Do you believe it?"

"I'm this girl loves you. Remember? I do. But it is sure God an effort. Not loving you. That's right easy. Believing all this stuff comes hard. Charla. What the hell kind of name is that? Sugar, after those three broads, you sure got a change when I hopped into bed."

"What should I do?"

"You ever get a cake with a hacksaw in it?"

"I was afraid you'd say something like that."

"If both them girls were on that boat, the Coast Guard got them by now for sure. And that Charla and Joseph are maybe jammed up as bad as you."

"I doubt it."

He took Uncle Omar's gold watch out of his pocket. He fiddled with it, absently. He wound it, pulled the stem out, set it to correspond with his wrist watch. It had an hour hand, a minute hand and a sweep second hand. It had a fourth hand motionless at twelve o'clock, silver instead of the gold of the other hands. He wondered what it was for. He pushed the stem in again, and suddenly discovered that by pushing it in and turning it, he could turn the silver hand back to a new position.

In the instant he did so, the world turned silent and his vision clouded. His first thought was that he was having a heart attack. There was such an utter silence he could hear the murmurous sound of his own blood in his ears. Any speculation as to what might have happened was drowned in a total, primitive, unreasoned terror. To known hazards, the human animal can react with fear bleached with reason. The unknown drops him back into the cave nights, into the sabered terror, awash in adrenaline, the sphincter precarious, muscles knotted for the sideways leap, the head-down whimpering run.

He sprang to his feet, gasping, trembling, and yanked the sunglasses from his eyes. He felt a strange resistance as he jumped up, as though a wind he had not felt or heard pressed against him. All the world was still. With the sunglasses off, the world was a pale, unpleasant red. He had seen the world look like that before, when he had looked through the prism of a single lense reflex camera with a red filter on the taking lense. But through the camera he had seen the normal unending movement of the world. Now he was in a pink desert, or a garden of savage sculpture, or inside a painting by Dali filled with the horror of a timeless motionlessness.

A single wave, the length of the beach, curled and did not fall. The gulls of pink stone hung from invisible wires. He turned and looked down at the girl. The color of her face was unpleasant, and her lips looked black. She was caught in that eternity, hand half-raised in gesture, lips parted, tongue touching the edge of her front teeth. She had the merciless stillness of a body in a casket.

He closed his eyes tightly, opened them again. Nothing had changed. He looked at the gold watch. The gold hand that marked the seconds was motionless. He looked at his wrist watch. It, too, had stopped. He looked at the gold watch carefully, looked at the silver hand and at last was able to detect the tiny movement of it as it crept up toward twelve. He held the watch to his ear and thought he could hear a tiny sound, a faint, sustained musical note. He had set the silver hand back to ten. It was at seven minutes to twelve. It seemed a fair assumption he had been in the red world of silence for three minutes.

He took two experimental strides. Again he felt the odd resistance against his body. And his shoes felt as if they weighed twenty pounds each. It was difficult to lift them, to move them forward through the air and then to push them back down again. They had a strange weight and inertia, as though he walked through glue. And the pressure against his body seemed caused by an equivalent inertia in his clothing. He bent down and picked up a discarded paper cup. It was like lifting a cup made of lead. He felt the weight and resistance of it when lifting it, but when movement stopped, it seemed weightless. All the normal muscle-to-brain signals were distorted. Cautiously he released the cup. It remained suspended in the air, exactly where he had released it. He reached out and pushed it. He could move it through the air, but its motion stopped the instant he stopped exerting pressure against it. In this red world a body in motion did not tend to stay in motion. He grasped the cup and squeezed it. He could crumple it, but it was like crumpling a cup made of heavy lead foil rather than thin cardboard.

He looked at the watch again. Three minutes to twelve. He looked down the beach at the hundreds of motionless people. He looked toward the drive and saw the frozen river of traffic. Far over the city a jet was pasted against the sky. Fifty feet away was a small boy halted in the act of running, horridly balanced on the ball of one bare foot.

Cautiously he pressed the stem of the watch in, thinking he might turn the silver hand back to twelve, trying to believe that if he did so the world would be the same again, knowing he could not endure another three minutes of the red silence.

When he pushed the stem in, the silver hand, like the hand of a stop watch, snapped back to twelve. The noise of the world crashed in around him and the redness was gone instantaneously. The wave struck, the cup fell, the boy ran, the flying things flew.

"Think you could—" Bonny Lee said and stopped, stared at him, stared at the bench, looked at him again, swallowed, and said, "You can sure God move fast, sugar! Wow! You're in better shape than I thought."

He looked at her and laughed. He laughed until the tears ran down his cheeks, and until he began to hear an edge of hysteria in his own voice. She tried to laugh with him and then stopped, staring at him with concern.

"Kirby! Kirby, dammit!"

"I'm in great shape," he said, gasping. "I've never been in better shape!"

"You losing your damn mind, sugar?"

He dialed the gold watch back to the red world. He wanted time to think, time to control the helpless laughter. But laughter was easy to control. It sounded too hollow, too ghastly in the silence. She was again frozen, this time looking directly into his eyes.

He shuddered, shaking himself like a wet dog. He looked at the watch. He had set the silver hand at quarter of twelve. Fifteen minutes, if he wanted all of it. Or just depress the stem and let the world snap back to life. No. That was a distorted version of reality, an invitation to insanity. The world was the same. It was continuing. He had merely stepped out of it. Everything had stopped but the vibrations of light itself. And the dingy red look of the world might mean that light itself had slowed in relation to him. More logically, he had changed his objective relationship to time, so that perhaps one hour of red time would be a fractional part of a second of real time. Of course, that could lead you into conjecture as to which one was "real" time, a philosophical route to the same goal—insanity.

Using that premise, he considered the phenomenon of the paper cup. The feeling of weight would, in that event, be the product of its natural inertia multiplied by the extraordinary speed, the "real" world speed with which he had lifted it. And when he had released it, it had dropped back to the speed of the real world, which in the red world was an objective motionlessness. When he had crumpled it, he had stopped the invisible upward motion. It had begun to fall, imperceptibly, and when the world had returned to normal he had seen, out of the corner of his eye, the rest of the fall.

Suddenly he knew why Uncle Omar had been so extraordinarily deft at amateur magic. And he knew what had happened at Reno. He could see the plump, nervous little highschool teacher with the shabby clothing, with the tense smile, watching the dice coming to rest on the green table and, at the very instant they stopped, moving into the red world, circling the table, reaching through the silence to turn one die to the proper winning number, returning to his place, and instantaneously catapulating himself back into the "real" world.

And he could guess where all the rest of the money had come from, and why so much had been given away. And he knew he had received his inheritance. It was as if he had been looking through a kaleidoscope, turning it aimlessly, looking at the meaningless patterns of the fragments, then had by accident turned it just so and had the bright bits form a realistic image. He marveled at the control, the caution, the life-long guile of Omar Krepps.

He reached out and touched the girl's cheek with his fingertips. Her cheek felt neither warm nor cool. It seemed to have no discernable temperature. And it felt unhumanly firm, as though fashioned of some dense but very slightly resilient plastic. He touched the pale curls and they had the texture of iron wire. When he bent them, they stayed in that position.

Again he found himself in danger of making the subjective error of assuming the world had changed. He found himself glad he had been forced, by Uncle Omar, to take the courses in Logic. Bonny Lee was in "real" time. Through her eyes he was merely movement far too fast to leave any retinal image, his touch on cheek and hair, too brief to leave any sensory impression.

He suddenly perceived one of the rules Uncle Omar must have followed all his life. You must return to the real world in the exact space where you left it. Otherwise you can drive men mad. In spite of all the caution of Omar Krepps, he had been considered most odd and most eccentric by the rest of the world. Perhaps there had been some carelessness from time to time. Now he knew the reason why Charla and Joseph thought of him with an almost superstitious awe. In international financial intrigue, the gold watch would give Uncle Omar the insuperable advantage of a one-eyed man in a world of the blind.

This was the edge! This was what they wanted, yet could not specifically describe. It made him feel cold to think of this device in the hands of Charla.

Ten minutes more. He resolved he would let the time run out and see if, when the silver hand reached twelve, the result would be the same. He started to walk, but the inertia of the shoes made it a slow and difficult effort. He took them off. When he dropped one, it remained in the air. He started to push it down to the sand, then realized it made no difference to leave it there. He could walk more easily, but he had to press against the inertia of his clothing, and knew that if he was naked he could walk freely. His feet did not sink into the sand as far as he would normally expect, but he did leave curiously perfect shallow footprints. He wondered about it and realized that the soft sand had begun to fall back into the prints but, in the red world, the motion was too slow to be visible. He walked by the eeriness of the red statues, all the way to the water's edge. He stepped into the water. It offered resistance, but his foot sank into it. It was like stepping into firm jello. When he pulled his foot out, the impression, inches deep, remained. Drops of sea water hung in the air, perfect spheres, pink in the red light of the world. One was as high as his face and, on impulse, he leaned and took it into his mouth. It was like a firm little blob of gelatine. He chewed down on it and swallowed it. It left a salty taste in his mouth.

Five minutes.

He walked back through the people. He made himself stop and look into their faces. He came upon a little girl feeding gulls. The hurled morsel of stale bread was a few inches from her fingertips. The gulls were poised. A yard from the back of the little girl's head there was an object frozen in the silent air. It was a toy sand shovel. He looked and saw a fat boy several years older than the girl, his face bloated with hate and rage, ten feet behind the little girl, frozen in somewhat the attitude of a big league pitcher when the ball is halfway to the plate.

Kirby reached out and put his hand against the tin shovel and pushed. He moved it several feet to the side. The fat boy wore swim trunks and a baggy T shirt. Kirby walked in front of the little girl and reached up and put his hand around the body of one of the gulls and pulled gently. He pulled it down and walked it over to the fat boy. He pulled the boy's T shirt away from his bare stomach. It was like bending metallic mesh. He pushed the gull up under the T shirt and bent the bottom edge of the shirt back in.

Two minutes.

He hurried up the beach to the pavilion. He put his shoes on and positioned himself as before, and discovered he had time to spare. On playful impulse he took a cigarette out and placed it carefully between her parted lips. The silver hand moved closer and closer. . . .

The bright morning was like a light turned on.

She gave a great leap of surprise and took the cigarette out of her mouth. "What the *hell!*"

"A trick my uncle taught me," he said. He turned and looked down the slope of the beach. Gulls dipped. A bright shovel had spun harmlessly into the sand. A fat boy had gone mad, howling, leaping, whirling, until a gull, crying alarm, darted up, leaving some white feathers floating down. The perfection of his footprints was gone, and the footprint in the water.

Bonny Lee's face looked strained. "Tricks are fun, but I din like that one worth a damn, Kirby. Make me all cold and queasy."

He sat on the cement bench beside her. "I'm sorry."

"Honess, Kirby, first you act like the end of the world is here, then you're laughing like a nut, then you do some spooky trick. I thought I had you figured, but now I—"

"Something important—suddenly happened, Bonny Lee."

"I don't get it."

"I want to do—a sort of experiment. Look right at this spot here on the bench between us. Look at it very carefully. Then tell me what happens and tell me how you feel about what happens."

"You know, I'm getting terrible nervous about you, sugar."

"Please, Bonny Lee."

He twisted himself back into the red world, this time turning the silver hand further than before. He turned it all the way around to twelve again and there it stopped and would not go further. This, then, was the limit of the red world, one hour of subjective time. He put the watch down and carefully, cautiously let go of it. Nothing changed. So it was not necessary for actual contact to be made throughout the red time interval. He saw a piece of broken shell a few feet away. He picked it up and placed it down on the cement right in Bonny Lee's line of vision. He picked the watch up and pressed the stem with his thumb. The silver hand snapped all the way around back to twelve, and he was back in the bright movements of her world.

She started. She looked gray under her tan. She closed her eyes and swallowed and then reached and touched the fragment of shell. She moved it a few inches and shivered. She stared at him, and sounded close to tears as she said, "You gotta stop this kinda tricks, Kirby. Please."

"What happened?"

"You saw it! Gawddamn it, you *did* it! All of a sudden, a hunk of shell is there. It didn't grow or fall from any place or—it was just *there!*"

"How did you feel?"

"Terrible!"

"I mean, what did you feel?"

"Whattaya mean, sugar, *what* did I feel? I'm just looking where you say and then—" She stopped and peered at him and looked angry. "I get it now, you spooky bassar! You're hypnotizing me! You're not supposed to be able to do it to anybody doesn't want it done. And I don't like it. So cut it out, hear?"

"I'm *not* hypnotizing you, and stop getting sore. Now I want to try something else. If it works, it might frighten you at first, but—"

"No more, Kirby!"

"Didn't you say you wanted to help me?"

"Sure, but—"

"And you love me?"

"I guess so, but—"

"Then let me try this, and I swear it won't hurt you in any way, and I'll explain it to you if it does work."

She looked at him sullenly, dubiously, and then gave a nod of agreement. He moved over close to her and put his arm around her. He held the watch in both hands in front of her. "Put your hands over mine."

She did so and said, "What has that old gold turnip watch g—"

The world was red and she was frozen, unyielding. Maybe you couldn't take another person into the red world, take someone out of "real" time. He snapped the silver hand back.

"—ot to do with it?" she said.

"Try touching the watch this time."

"Make up your mind," she said. Again she was a statue in the redness.

He came back to reality. "This time, get your fingers like this, your thumb right against the stem, and now as I press down, you press down too and give a little turn and—"

He was alone on the bench, his arms holding a girl no longer there. The watch was gone also.

He had the immediate memory of closeness, of the lithe warmth of her. She had winked away into nothingness, and in its own special way, it was a nastier, more gut-wrenching shock than his initial foray into the red and silent world.

No, two could not go.

Kirby sat stunned with the realization of what he had done to her. She had neither the maturity nor the background to cope with the silent horror of that other world. He stared into distance and did not see her. Her primitive mind, shrewd though it was, would shatter under such an impact. He had a horrible thought. Perhaps, believing the watch to blame, she would hurl it into the sea. It would stop, and leave her forever trapped in that red time, where no one could see her or hear her, where all the rest of her life might pass within, perhaps, a half-hour of real time.

He sat dazed by guilt, by the enormity of what he had inadvertently, stupidly done to Bonny Lee Beaumont.

Chapter Nine

Not until Kirby stood up did he see, beyond the end of the concrete bench, a little pile of clothing—a pair of lime slacks, white sandals, a white blouse with a yellow figure, a yellow jacket, a white purse. He picked them up and put them on the bench. The items missing were the blue-green nylon bra, the matching panties.

Her voice came from ten feet behind him. "Hey! Hey, sugar, this is more damn fun!"

He spun and saw her there in the sunlight, brown and beautiful, winded, glowing with excitement. The sun glinted on the gold watch in her hand. She put her fingers on the stem of the watch. "Give it to me!" he yelled, but she was gone before he could say the last word.

He heard thin cries, almost but not quite like the yelping of the gulls. He looked far down the beach to the north where the crowd was the thickest and it seemed to him that all the people down here had gone mad simultaneously.

He squinted against the glare and thought he saw Bonny Lee appear and disappear again in the middle distance, but he could not be certain.

He began to realize that he had made a poor estimate of her response to the red world. Bonny Lee had a totally pragmatic mind. She would not give a damn for theory. All that would concern her was that it worked, and he had given her the clue as to how to make it work. Though—from the viewpoint of his limited experience—she had given him ample, skillful and luxurious proof that she was a woman grown, and even though she had devised a philosophy of existence which seemed to suit her and seemed to work for her, he remembered that she was but "twenny, practically," that there was a child inside the woman, and the child had never had much chance for the games of childhood, and that she was a hoyden, reckless, irreverent, comical and inventive. He remembered, too, that she was in bursting health, firm, fleet and tireless.

He squinted at the people running to and fro in the distance, yelping, and he wondered if he had not inadvertently loosed upon them on this pleasant Tuesday morning something just as fearful as a playful tiger. He remembered the mischief and the satisfaction of tucking the gull under the fat boy's shirt. He had astonished himself with that act. Surely Bonny Lee would go a good deal further than that before astonishing herself.

He wondered if he should walk down the beach and see what was happening. But Bonny Lee would expect to find him at the bench.

He saw two figures coming up the beach at a dead run. They seemed more energetic than fleet. He stared at them as they went by. First one would hold the lead and then the other would overtake her and pass her. They seemed to be heading for the parking lot. They were a pair of young women of rather generous construction, naked as a pair of eggs.

An elderly tourist who had been walking by came to a dead stop near the bench and stared at the running women. He wore a Truman shirt, Bahama hat, Bermuda shorts, blue sneakers. He watched them make the sweeping curve toward the parking lot and disappear. He turned and stared questioningly at Kirby.

" 'Til this very minute, son, I prided myself on twenty-twenty vision."

"Sir?"

"Mind telling me what just run by?"

"Uh—two young women."

The man moved closer. "Son, what would you say they were wearing?"

"They didn't seem to be wearing anything."

The old man peered at him. "If I was your age, son, I'd be right with 'em, running like a deer. You don't seem even interested. You sick?"

"I—was thinking of something else."

"I got down here from Michigan day before yesterday. Maybe I got the wrong idea. Maybe that ain't so unusual a sight around here."

"Well, I wouldn't—"

"Good day in the morning, here comes another one!"

She was a small sunburned redhead, with a transistor radio in one hand and a thermos bottle in the other. She was near the end of her endurance, wobbling from side to side as she cantered along.

After she, too, was out of sight, the old man sighed heavily. "One thing I give you, son. You picked the right place to set. Is it a new fad, you think?"

"I don't know."

"I hope it catches on." He shaded his eyes and peered up the beach.

Suddenly Bonny Lee was close enough to touch and there was a pile of paper money on Kirby's lap. It spilled onto the bench and onto the sand. She laughed once and was gone.

The old man whirled around. "Son, you got a high laugh on—ain't you spilling something?"

"Oh, this?"

"Money, ain't it?"

"Yes," Kirby said heartily. "It certainly is." He grabbed at the bills that started to blow away.

"I think the sun has got to me," the old man said. "I think I better get the hell out of it." He plodded away.

Some other people had moved near, staring curiously at the money. Kirby gathered it up quickly. She hadn't bothered with one-dollar bills and there were only a few fives. It made a wad so thick that after he had folded it once, he had difficulty putting it in the side pocket of the borrowed slacks. He picked up Bonny Lee's clothes and walked away from the bench, north along the beach, knowing that she could always find him. While she was in the red world, he would be motionless to her. He became aware of a vast traffic jam in the drive behind him. He heard sirens in the distance. He came upon a man walking in a slow thoughtful circle, hitting himself in the forehead with his clenched fist.

Suddenly Kirby had a new pipe in his mouth, a bouquet of roses tucked under his arm, a gold ring with a big yellow diamond on the little finger of his left hand, and Bonny Lee in her pretty undies striding along with him, chuckling. He made a frantic grab for her, but she danced back, fiddled with the watch and flicked out of his world. He looked at the place where she had disappeared and saw blurred shallow footprints heading north. The fact that they were blurred and now perfect meant she had already reappeared somewhere else. He realized that inasmuch as his world was static to her, in relation to his time, she had to reappear somewhere else the instant she disappeared in front of him.

Later he was to learn that, during the fifteen minutes she was on the loose, she spent, as near as she could remember, about four subjective hours in the red world, four hours until she tired of the games and could think of no more.

Later he was to learn, in more detail, of the bewildering calamities which befell all those unfortunates among the thousand and a half people enjoying that stretch of Atlantic beach.

As Bonny Lee told him, "There they were, all them broads, naked as the law allows, strutting it around to work up the guys, and I figured it would be a lot more honest they should unwrap the merchandise entire and see how the guys reacted then. That's before I was working it so good, before I learned you can do it okay one-handed, just push down with your thumb and give it a little bitty twist. So all the ones in the right positions so I could get at their suits and halters and stuff, I went to work, where they were gathered thickest, and honess, sugar, I worked like a horse, maybe a half-hour, peeling that stuff off them and carrying it down and tossing it out over the water—pushing it out. When everything is red, you can't throw anything. It kind of stops."

"I know."

"Nine outa ten, I swear, they looked a hell of a lot better with the suits on. A lot of those guys got a bad shock. Anyhow in that one patch of beach I got maybe forty stripped entire, and got the top half off I guess twenty more. And what good is a joke you can't see it, hey? So, seeing how I was dressed, I thought I should sort of hide, then I realized compared to them sixty broads, I was *overdressed*. So I just went to a spot where nobody was looking right at me and pressed the dingus."

"How did you find out about doing that?"

"Anybody smart enough to make a cute thing like that is going to make it so you can use it and not be waiting around for the time to run out. So I tried turning it and tried pushing it and found out how."

"Oh."

"Shees marie, Kirby, you shoulda seen! Out of sixty, maybe three or four took it cool. The rest went straight up in the air, screeched like to bust your ears, scrabbled around for towels, but I'd got rid of them too. Then they tried to find something to hide behind or under. But a beach is damn empty, you know. Those guys had their mouths hanging open and their eyes bugged out, and the broads milled around, yelping, and then all the ones could swim, like those lemming things somebody told me about once, they went into the ocean on the dead run, maybe seven guys with good reaction time right after them. And the ones couldn't swim, they headed every which way, the smart ones heading toward where I hadn't gathered the towels and stealing them from other folks. I laughed until I had the hiccups, and then two guys started closing in on me so I went back into the red place, put two big sand buckets over their heads and took off."

"How about the money?"

"The money?"

"The money you dumped in my lap."

"Oh. That. Oh, that's from when I went over into all those stores over there. Ever' time I went by a cash drawer, I took some. But carrying stuff is a drag. You gotta kind of push it or pull it along. In the department store I found a hell of a thing, you know? An old lady had tripped or something right at the top of the escalator and there she was, tilted way out, her hands out in front of her, her face all screwed up. That's when I found out you can move people, too. I went behind her and got her around the waist and braced myself and first I thought I couldn't. But if you give a real steady pull, they come along. I pulled her back and straightened her up and there she was, about eight inches off the floor. So I got in front of her and pushed her about six feet, and pulled her back down onto the floor. Then I picked her packages out of the air over the stairs and put them in her arms. I had her holding them funny, but I didn't want to try bending her arms. I was afraid I'd break something. So then I went to the racks and got a dress and put it on and went back and stood by her and turned the world back on. She gave a big jump and dropped all her packages. She wore the damnedest expression, sugar. She stared at the escalator and then she picked the packages up and stared at the escalator again and dropped them again. Then she picked them up and shook her head and started walking toward the elevator. It was right after that I found out something else funny."

"What was that?"

"In the sports part—I was still wearing the dress off the rack—there was a little bit of a boy throwing a basketball to a clerk. It was in the air. The clerk had his hands out, grinning. The ball was in the air and in my way, so I just shoved it toward the clerk as I went by. A second later time ran out on me. I forget all about time in a store anyhow. And I heard this thud and this horrible gagging sound and something falling. I looked around and the clerk was rolling around on the floor hugging his stomach, and making them sounds, and the little boy staring down at him, and the little boy's mother."

" 'Honey, you threw it too hard,' she said to the little boy. They helped the clerk up and his face was a terrible color. The woman said she was sorry her little boy had thrown it so hard. The clerk told her she was missing a great opportunity. He said she should take the little jerk out to spring training and by October he'd be in the series, making big money. The woman started yammering and the little boy started crying and the clerk started yelling, so I turned the whole thing off and got out of the damn dress and got rid of the purse I took to carry your money in, and came back. I think it was right after that I got into the softball game."

"The softball game?"

"No. First I took car keys. Gawd, sugar, it's funny walking in those cars knowing if you push the dingus, they're suddenly going like hell. I was going to reach into those and take the keys, but I didn't rightly want I should get nobody killed, so I took the keys out of the cars stacked up for the red light. There was a big convertible so I climbed into the back and turned the world on, after I pushed all the keys into the trash basket on the corner. Every yuk in the world starts blowing his horn and nobody can move. The guy at the wheel looked around and saw me and I smiled pretty at him and he shut his eyes and turned pale white. So before he could open them, I turned everything off again and went and got all the keys out of the cars stacked up the other way, since the light had changed. Everybody in such a damn hurry, sugar, it's good for them to take a little time out."

"I'm sure they enjoyed it."

"Then I got into the softball game, way down the beach. A big old muscly lunk was showing off for his girl, busted into a ball game of little kids, smacking that ball way down the beach. So I found me a girl way off and took her cute little short shorts and her little halter and come back and practiced some until I could stop everything when that ball was just out in front of the plate, and then I'd go out and push it up six inches or down six inches, and the little boy pitching turned out having the biggest-breaking curve strike you ever see, and the big bassar—he like to sprained his back swinging, his girl laughing at him—got so mad he slang the bat at the little pitcher. But I stopped it in time, pushed it back toward him too hard I reckon, and he hadn't ducked would have whomped his head clean off whistling by. He shaky like an old man, his girl leading him away."

"You kept busy."

"I would have said it got to be way late in the middle of the afternoon, but a little bit of time here goes a long way there. Took food I wanted offen a picnic, taken it to a quiet place and ate fast. Found me a brute man cuffin' his little wife around, and I sure God played hell with him." She smiled in fond reminiscence. "Park fellas painting a restroom close by. Ended that brute man up buck naked, painted bright green, mouth packed full of sand, sobbing like a big old fat baby."

"Good Lord!"

"Found me a big-jaw, mean-eye wife blasting her little husband for staring at girls, him lying on a woolly blanket nearby looking heartsick, so I give her something to work on for sure. Towed over a mess of pretty little girls, one at a time, and like to clean covered him up. Turned the world back on and that woolly blanket was like onto a bucket of worms afore they could all get untangled and take off ever' which way. She screamed for sure, but I don't think he heard a word, just sat there wearing a funny little smile. Got up and walked clean away from her, still smiling. Never had so much fun in my whole life entire."

But all that came later. At the time she gifted him with the pipe, the ring and the roses, he wasn't certain he'd ever see her again. And that very probably wasn't what Uncle Omar had planned for him—if, indeed, the old man had arranged things in some pattern he had yet to discern. He put the ring in his pocket, flipped the pipe into some plantings and jettisoned the roses in a trash basket. The continuous blare of horns from the expanding traffic jam was making the day hideous. There seemed to be a lot of women in swimming, screaming instructions to people on the shore. Suddenly he realized that an impressive number of police had begun to appear on the scene, blowing whistles, yelling at each other and expressing confusion.

As a tall young officer came hurrying by, Kirby turned away too quickly. The cop stopped abruptly and came toward him, staring at him intently. "Take off them glasses, buddy," he said.

"But I'm only—"

An ugly-looking revolver was suddenly poised, aimed at the middle of his chest. "Hand over some identification, real slow and easy. Make me nervous and I twitch. My whole hand twitches something awful. Trigger finger and all."

Kirby placed his wallet in the cop's hand, very, very gently. The cop flipped it open, took one quick glance at it and began to grin and bounce up and down on his toes. "Oh, you fine handsome ten thousand bucks! Oh, you pretty package, you! What you say is that Corporal Tannenbaumer collared you. You keep mentioning that, hah? Promise me now, or I bust those teeth off at the gum line. Can you remember the name?"

"Corporal Tannenbaumer."

"Now grab the back of your neck with both hands. That's nice. Harry! Hey, Harry! Come see what *I* got!"

Harry, too, was lean and bronzed, with that look of eagles marred only slightly, as was Tannenbaumer, by a minor look of adenoidal vacuity.

Harry glanced at the wallet identification and said, "Honest to God, Tanny, you could fall in a sewer and come up wearing a gold bridge. Want I should go get the Sergeant?"

"No, Harry. For one grand you ignore the Sergeant. For one grand we take him in all by ourselves, and let the Sergeant worry about all this other crap."

"For two, Tanny."

"One and a half tops."

"We got to walk him a hell of a ways, Tanny."

"So cuff him to me."

"Why not to me?"

"Because for ten grand, Harry, you would sap me and leave me face down here in the cruddy sand, so don't squirrel around with me. What's going on down the beach there anyhow?"

"The report said there was a lot of naked broads, Tanny, and there are a lot of naked broads. And the other report said like forty guys lost their car keys in traffic, and the tow trucks are working on it. And there is one guy painted green they're still trying to catch. But the way it figures, some smart-ass crowd set up all the confusion so as they could clean out them stores across the way. The hell with it, Tanny. We got a good day's work right here."

"I got a good day's work. You got one and a half, after I get mine. Hustle them cuffs, Harry."

Tannenbaumer moved beside Kirby and held out his left wrist. Kirby, by instruction, held out his right wrist. Harry got the cuffs out and looked at Bonny Lee's clothing on the sand. "What's that stuff?"

"Girl clothes, for God's sake. So what? Maybe he was figuring on disguising himself. Are you stalling for the Sergeant to get into the act? He'll take the full ten and give us a couple cigars and a day off. Hurry!"

Harry made as though to snap the cuffs on the two wrists and suddenly he was standing there with both his own wrists handcuffed. Tannenbaumer stared at him. "How the hell! Harry, you cruddy thief, you're stalling!"

"What are you arresting him for?" Bonny Lee demanded.

Harry and Tannenbaumer turned and stared at her. Tannenbamer said, "We got an ordinance underwear ain't allowed on any public beach in Dade County. You go get some clothes on, kid, or you get took in."

"Get these off me, Tanny," Harry said plaintively. "The key's in my shirt pocket."

"You run while I'm busy, Winter, and I blow one of your knees into a bag of pebbles."

Tannenbaumer unlocked one of the cuffs, and then it was on his own wrist. "My hand musta slipped," he said apologetically. "Where's the key?"

"You got the key, Tanny."

"I had the key."

"It musta fell in the sand, huh?"

"Harry, I think the Sergeant is headed this way. You, kid, you got to go get out of that underwear."

"I'm not bothering anybody," Bonny Lee said.

"I wasn't so busy, Tanny, she'd be bothering *me*. How about you?"

"Shut up. Look, Harry. What we do now is, we cuff him to my other wrist, and we go in like this."

"Won't it look a little funny, Tanny?"

"We can't help that."

"How will we drive the car, Tanny?"

"We'll all sit in the front. Hold your wrist out, Winter. Harry, I hand you my gun?"

"You didn't hand it to me, Tanny. Hey, girl, you see him hand me the gun?"

"Leave her out of this. Give me your gun, Harry."

"Hell, they musta both fell in the sand. Tanny, we're not making this arrest very good, you know?"

"If they fell in the sand, where are they?"

"We been moving around, Tanny. Maybe we kicked sand over them."

As they were both looking behind them at the sand, Bonny Lee sidled quickly over to Kirby, put the watch and chain into his hand and said swiftly, "Carry me outa here, sugar. I can't carry you."

Tannenbaumer turned around and yelled, "Get away from —" And was suddenly a red statue in the eerie light of a dying sun. Kirby looked at the watch. He had flipped the silver hand back twenty minutes. He was impelled by a feeling of haste until, by an effort of logic, he realized he was occupying an instant of no-time, and thus had all the time wanted to take. He stuffed the watch into his pocket and bent the pocket back around it. He put his arms around Bonny Lee's waist. She felt like a stone statue covered with a layer of tough rubber. With a slow and steady effort he was able to lift her off the ground. He lifted her a couple of feet into the air and released her. He went around behind her, braced both hands against the rounded rigidities under the blue-green nylon and, his feet digging into the sand, moved her a dozen feet away. He was gratified to know he could get her away from there, but it was a rather disheartening effort.

He left her there and reviewed the situation. A natural

caution made him wary of leaving a nothingness for the two cops to stare at. There might be a reduction of future trouble and future questions if he could give them a chance to talk each other into it being a case of mistaken identity. He walked to where red statues stood by a red refreshment stand and walked among them and selected a girl first. She was Bonny Lee's size, and blonde, and would have been very lovely except for her deplorable lack of chin. The less inertia, he decided, the easier she would be to manage. She had on a wraparound skirt, and taking it off was like unwinding sheet tin from around a fence post. The halter top was a little more complicated. She had been caught in a frozen toothy smile. The underthings were lacy black below, uplift white above. By the time he had covered the fifty yards with her, he had, by trial and error, discovered the easiest way—to arrange her horizontally, hug her feet into his armpits and tow her. He stood her where Bonny Lee had been, rewarding Harry and Tannenbaumer with her dental smile. He remembered to leave his shoes behind when he went and selected a man. The effort was like pulling something which was being simultaneously pulled from the other direction. The moment effort stopped, the forward motion stopped. By the time he'd reached the scene with the stranger who resembled him in size only, his breath was creaking and his legs were weak with effort. He rotated the man and positioned him. He went wearily over to Bonny Lee and turned her into a horizontal position, ready for transit. He rested and reviewed the details. He recovered his wallet from Tannenbaumer's shirt pocket, inserted one of his cards in the stranger's wallet and put it in Tannenbaumer's pocket. He picked up Bonny Lee's clothing and wedged it under her arm. He shoved her purse and shoes and his shoes into the front of his shirt. He grasped her feet, hugging them under his right arm, and, leaning far forward, began to tow her toward the parking lot, two hundred yards away. He rested several times. Finally he tried to make the job easier. He pulled her feet apart, carefully bent her legs at the knees, then hooked her legs over the tops of his shoulders, plodded on, holding her wooden ankles in his hands.

Suddenly the world went bright. Bonny Lee slammed him with a tremendous impact, seat first, right against his shoulders, and banged him headlong into the sand and went tumbling end over end beyond him, with a yelp of pain and fright and a welter of flying garments. He sat up, spitting sand, and looked back. The chinless girl stood screaming, and the manacled cops were in tandem, chasing the substitute.

"Whyn't you watch it!" Bonny Lee shrilled at him.

"Are you hurt?"

"You didn't do me any good, you silly bassar! What the hell are you—"

He spun her into red silence. He got up, saw that he had given himself a half-hour, arranged her for transit again, and took her to the parking lot. He found a small maintenance building with a wall screening it from the road. The building itself stood between them and the beach. He straightened her legs and stood her against the wall. The look of indignation and anger was frozen on her face. He tried to brush the sand out of her hair, but the small particles remained in the air near her head. He looked in all directions to be certain they were safe, then pushed the watch stem.

"—trying to do?" she said, catching her balance. She looked around. "Oh."

"The time ran out on me."

"You shoulda checked, Kirby. You could get somebody hurt. You move something and then turn the world on, and it goes like hell. I seen a fella comes to Rio's and gives me a bad time, just walking out of the ocean, so I give him a good lift up and back, like to sprain a gut, then pushed that dingus and he went on up like out of a cannon, roaring and going end over end and landing back in the water fifty feet out."

"Are you hurt?"

She fingered her shoulder and her hip. "You like to brush-burn half the hide off me, sugar. What do we do now?"

"Let's start by you putting your clothes on."

"Fair enough. Shees marie, I'm pooped for sure. Where's the cops?"

"Chasing the wrong guy."

"You put another guy there?"

"And a girl."

"Lot of work, wasn't it?"

"Yes, but we shouldn't be careless with it, Bonny Lee. If too many things happen which can't be explained, somebody is going to figure out that—"

She buttoned her blouse and slapped the rest of the sand out of her hair. "What you don't know about people, Kirby, anything they can't explain, they make up something suits them. If suddenly a guy can fly just like a bird, he'd know for sure it was clean living and deep breathing." She opened her purse and fixed her mouth. "Sugar, let me have that big old watch a minute."

"Sorry. We're getting into the car and getting out of here."

"Getting bossy, hey?"

They got into the little Sunbeam. The parking lot did not exit on the same street as the traffic tie-up. She stopped at the exit to the lot, the motor running. She frowned at him.

"What's the matter, Bonny Lee?"

"I was figuring out something. Don't mess with that watch while we're moving, sugar. The car would stop cold dead and you'd keep on going. I'd have to clean you off the dash and the windshield with a sponge."

"Uh—thanks. What were you doing that was making all that confusion?"

"Lots of things. Tell you later."

"Where are we going?"

"We need a safe place, don't we? I'm busting my biggest rule. No man was ever going to set foot in my place. Ever'body knows about it, and you can sure get in without being seen."

"How?"

"Sugar, sometimes you're right stupid."

"Oh. Of course. Sorry."

"What time is it?"

"Twenty after eleven."

"In the *morning*!"

"In the morning, Bonny Lee."

She had a garage apartment in an old part of the city, behind a stately old house of Spanish-Moorish design which, she told him, had been cut up into small apartments and was occupied almost exclusively by old ladies with small incomes. "Coming and going at all hours, and the kind of work I do, I give 'em something to cluck over," she said. "But it keeps the men scared off from bothering me here, and I get along with them, most of them. And they bring me cakes and stuff."

She explained how he could get in, and dropped him off a

block away. He gave her ten minutes and spent the time strolling along the narrow quiet street on a shady, overgrown sidewalk. He leaned against an iron fence and, when he was not observed, he stepped into the red world. It was easier to carry shoes than to wear them. He went back to the house she had pointed out. In a lawn across the street a sprinkler made a static pattern of shining pink droplets hanging in the silent air. A small dog paused for its moment of forever, staring intently up into a tree, ears forward.

He walked along the driveway. Three old ladies sat at a metal table in the back yard in the shade of a beach umbrella, mouths ajar, knitting needles rigid. He went into the open door of the garage and turned to the right as she had told him, and up the stairs. Pulling the screen door open at the top of the stairs was like opening the weighty door of a vault. Indoors, the redness seemed more oppressive, but he could see that by normal light it would be a tiny cheerful place with bright draperies, straw furniture, gay rugs and pillows. There were framed publicity pictures of her on one wall and he peered at them with approval through the bloody murk.

She was in the small bedroom, sitting on the dressing table bench. She had pulled her blouse down from her right shoulder and was stopped in the moment of rubbing something into the abrasion from her fall. The room had a three-quarter bed, ornamental iron bars on the window, a deep window seat, a bamboo chaise, a vase of wilted flowers. He stood behind her and started to pop into her world and then hesitated. He had almost fifteen minutes left. And too much had been happening too fast. Her head was turned sharply so she could see her shoulder. He kissed the side of her throat. In this world it had the rigid somewhat waxy texture of polished wood. He went over and sat on the bed. The unyielding rigidity of it startled him for a moment before he remembered that in the redness everything was fibrous, toughened, yielding reluctantly to forces and pressures.

He looked at her, sitting erect, six feet away. Her back was arched, her shoulders good, the waist slender, the lime slacks plumped to the pleasant tensions of her ripeness. There was a tantalizing familiarity in the back of his mind and after a moment he identified it. He had seen a television play—two years ago?—a fantasy about a department store dummy, played by a blonde actress—Ann Francis?—and after she had been free for a little while, they had forced her back into the store, and in the final scene she had become rigid and waxen again, frozen in position, displaying a summer frock.

Bonny Lee seemed just as unreal, just as unalive, but he could move his thumb a quarter of an inch and bring her to glowing life. He had not had time to think about her, actually. But now he could take time which was no time at all, because it was time the world was not using. He felt toward her a vast and tender gratitude. She had cut briskly through a thousand dreads and fears and mysteries and had brought him joyously to his delayed maturity. It would be all too easy, he sensed, out of his new-found confidence and arrogance to devaluate the gift, to use cheap and easy words—shallow, ignorant, amoral, much as the swaggering adolescent feels obligated to jeer at the girl he so clumsily seduces.

The revelations of Bonny Lee gave him a new perspective on himself and on the world. Having thought himself uniquely inadequate, he now wondered how many other Kirby Winters there were, milling about in the world, winking at the right times, laughing at the punch lines, handling the little flirtations very well indeed, but poised to run in terror if it appeared the lady was trying to say yes.

He remembered the sound of the rain on the tin roof of the old Hudson, and the feral graspings and gabblings of Hazel Broochuk, and how weeks of plotting and importunings all came to a ghastly inconclusive end in the incredible clumsiness of those few minutes. He could have gotten as much excitement and almost as much pleasure by falling into a hay baler. And he remembered her thin pocked face in the faint light, twisted with contempt as she wriggled back into her skirt, and remembered the dreadful words which had remained forever in his mind, written in a puckering of scar tissue. "You not worth a goddamn, boy. You done me no good. Owning a hammer don't make nobody a carpenter, boy, so you better leave me off down in the middle of town. I'll say where."

And there had been no one to hustle the crashed pilot into another aircraft, and the nerve was gone, and he spent thirteen years on the ground—until Bonny Lee erased the myths, peeled the scars away, showed him the bed was a picnic shared, rather than a lonely stage, where instinct was the only value and the only necessity.

Five minutes remaining.

He hefted the watch in his hand. It was the only object in the red world which did not have that odd sticky drag of inertia. And he felt an overwhelming awe at all the things it represented, at all the temptations implicit in its ownership. Here was absolute power, and total corruption. Here was a freedom so complete it became not freedom at all, but enthrallment to the witchery of being able to dislocate time itself. Here was invisibility, voyeurism, invincibility, wealth—in fact, all the night dreamings of adolescence, in one-hour subjective packages. Here was, in a specialized sense, immunity.

The possibilities of it gave him a sense of reckless, dizzy elation, yet at the same time made him distrust himself. The obligations implicit in the possession of such a device were severe. Use of it had to be related to some responsible ethical structure. And a good part of the responsibility was to conceal the power and the purpose of the device from the world.

Suppose, he thought, there were fifty of these in the world, or five hundred? Chaos, anarchy, confusion and fear. It would be as though a new mutation had occurred in mankind, a time of the superman, making privacy meaningless, making all ownership conditional.

Suddenly he was filled with an awed respect for Omar Krepps. For twenty years he'd had this edge, this advantage, and he had kept it as quiet as possible. Had he displayed the abilities this gave him, other men might have conducted research in this same direction. Apparently Uncle Omar had decided that this device would turn the world to a shambles were it released. He could see a pattern in the things Omar had done. He had quieted the publicity about his gambling winnings by returning and purposely losing an amount almost as great as the amount he had first won. He had made amateur magic his hobby—to help cover any slip he might make. He had avoided all personal publicity. And he had hidden behind great wealth, acquired quickly—yet so short was public memory, it was as though Omar Krepps and his ancestors had been rich since an earlier century.

The noise and brightness and movement of reality came into the room, and within the first two seconds he turned the silver hand back, halting reality. Bonny Lee's hand had moved higher on her shoulder. Her head had turned slightly.

He had sunk into a sudden softness of the bed and then it became rigid again, but in a more comfortable contour.

How then, had Uncle Omar acquired the money? Wealth, he realized, is a strange abstraction concerned with the exchange of bits of paper, signing them, filing them, recording them at the right times, in the right places. Stock manipulation would not be too difficult, once the procedures were understood. He could imagine Uncle Omar trotting busily through a red hour, inserting the proper orders in the proper files, using the red time to give him the same advantage as hindsight. Once acquisitions had been made, control could be turned over to Krepps Enterprises, and money had a knack of multiplying, when there was enough of it.

But if Omar Krepps had been so aware of the potential menace of the device he had created, why hadn't he let it die with him?

The reason, possibly, was a kind of egotism. Someone had to know. And, long ago, Uncle Omar had apparently selected Kirby as the inheritor of this fantastic power, had judged him capable of using it well, had seen to it that Kirby acquired the academic background which would enhance a judicious use of the device. The courses which his uncle had insisted he take, and which had seemed so impractical at the time now made increasing sense. Sociology, psychology, philosophy, ancient history, comparative religions, ethics and logic, anthropology, archeology, languages, semantics, aesthetics. And then eleven years of the exercise of judgment in a context which required no competitive instinct, and made secrecy, reserve, evasion and rootlessness a habit of life.

He now sensed that it was an ideal background for the new owner of such absolute power. It created a minimum risk of the device being used for violent, random, frivolous, acquisitive purposes. It directed the new owner to use it for the maximum good of mankind.

But, in that case, why had Uncle Omar not explained the whole situation long ago? Perhaps because Uncle Omar had thought him lacking in strength and resolution, had been impatient with him, had even told Mr. Wintermore that his nephew was a ninny. And then, after the warning attack, Uncle Omar had apparently prepared for death by setting up a curiously random situation. The watch first and—a year later—the letter. He knew the letter would relate to the watch.

What if he had put it in a drawer and forgotten it? What if he had been in a moving vehicle, a car, train or plane when he had fiddled with the silver hand? Why had Uncle Omar so instructed both Kirby and Wilma Farnham that immediately after his death they would be in grave difficulty? Surely Uncle Omar could have anticipated what would happen.

It all seemed to be some kind of a test, but he could not see any consistent pattern in it.

For the first time he examined the watch with great care. The ornate initials OLK on the back were worn thin. There was a catch near the stem so the back could be opened. He hesitated, put his thumbnail against the catch and snapped it open. There was a second case inside, of smooth gray metal, with absolutely no way to open it. On the interior concavity of the gold back was engraved something else, almost as ornate as the initials, unworn. He translated, with some difficulty, the Latin words. "Time waits for one man." It had that ring of slightly sour humor so typical of Omar Krepps. He snapped the case shut and for the first time he began to wonder about the power source. It would seem plausible to assume that distortions of space, time and energy could be achieved only through expenditures of vast power. The watch seemed to be permanently sealed. It had an old-fashioned bulkiness. Certainly the distortion of time could not be achieved through purely mechanical means. He held it to his ear and again thought he heard the faint musical note, in a minor key, like a faraway wind in high tension wires. And he wondered if its capacities could be used up, if it would work only for so long, or for so many times. That sort of information would probably be in the letter.

What if Wintermore had fiddled with the extra hand?

He felt exasperated at his uncle. It did not seem possible Omar would have left so many things to chance.

What next? The watch, properly and carefully used, with sufficient advance planning, would enable him to solve the problems of the various criminal actions and civil actions. But it would have to be done in a way which would quiet public interest rather than enhance it. A total notoriety—as Uncle Omar had realized—would make life impossible. One would be sought at the ends of the earth by nuts, monsters, shysters, maniacs, fanatics, reporters.

He knew he had started badly. Letting it get into the hands

of Bonny Lee had been an inadvertent violation of the implied trust and responsibility. It should be treated with as much gravity, care and respect as a cobalt bomb. Four times he had tried to escape from Uncle Omar's control into a life of normality, of the small goals and pleasures of the average life. He knew that chance was gone, unless he denied the responsibility by smashing the watch, or dropping it into the sea. That was one possible decision, but he could not make it until he had used the watch to remove all pressures, regain anonymity.

Again there were five minutes left. He looked at Bonny Lee and felt a great galloping rush of desire for her. But electric as the urge was, there was a strange placidity about it, an assured and comforting smugness. In Rome last year he had desired the woman named Andy just as much, but there had been no flavor of happiness to it. And because it had made him wretched, it had distorted desire into too significant a thing. So now something new had been discovered. Frustration bloated the role of sex, kept it in the center of the stage and gave it all the lines. It had stunted the other aspects of his life through its false importance. Release had suddenly put it in proper context. It was dwindled, and could now share the lines with the other actors—essential to the play but not obsessional, suitably dramatic but linked to reality, capable of comedy as well.

I was a legless man, he thought, and watched everyone in the world walking and running and climbing, and the attribute of leglessness colored every reaction to some degree. I pretended I had legs, so no one would notice. Now I have legs, and though walking is a joy, legs are now just a part of living, and the awareness of them comes and goes. I accept the fact of having legs.

He went over to Bonny Lee, bent and put his lips against the rigidity of her mouth and pressed the world back to life. The warmth and softness came in a twinkling and she gave a convulsive leap of fright, a small squeak of dismay. The brown eyes narrowed.

"That's right sneaky," she whispered. "Like to jump clean outa my skin, you bassar. It's not a kind of thing anybody is ever going to get used to, sugar."

She wiped her fingers on a tissue and went into the other room and closed the heavy plank door and bolted it. She moved casually into his arms, kissing him lightly on the chin and gave a huge, shuddering yawn. "I'm pooped entire, Kirby." She trudged over and sat heavily on the bed and yawned again and knuckled her eyes. "Don't you go near the window so any of those biddies can see you."

"I've got a lot of problems to think about, Bonny Lee."

She kicked her sandals off and stretched out on the bed. "Can't think of a thing until I get some sleep. Aren't you bushed too?"

"Yes, I guess I am." He went over and sat on the edge of the bed and leaned over her and kissed her with considerable and lengthy emphasis.

She chuckled. "Man, you're not as sprung as I am."

"Bonny Lee?"

"No, sugar. It would be a waste of talent for sure. Please let me sleep, sugar, and then we'll see. You oughta sleep too. Whyn't you go on out on the couch where you can quieten down nice?"

"I shouldn't waste time sleeping, with all that—"

She silenced him with a sudden gesture, bit her lip and said, "Gimme the watch, sugar."

"I really don't think you ought to—"

"I wanta try something, stupid! I'm not going to get cute. I'm too gawddamn tired to get cute. You gotta trust me, or we are going absolutely no place at no time. Hand it over."

He hesitated, gave it to her reluctantly. She grasped the stem of the watch. In something that seemed like a flicker of movement just a little too fast to be visible, she was in an entirely different position, the watch on the bed a few inches from her slack hand, her eyes closed, breathing slowly, deeply, audibly through her parted lips. He spoke to her and she did not answer. He shook her and she whined. When he shook her again she reached for the watch. An instant later she had flickered into a slightly different position, and she was completely bare. One instant she was wearing her clothes. The next instant they were in midair beside the bed, falling to the floor. He woke her again and she mumbled and growled and took the watch and flickered into a different position. He touched her shoulder and she came awake quite easily. Her eyes were slightly puffy with sleep. She yawned and stretched luxuriously. With the awakenings, the entire procedure had taken just a couple of minutes.

She smiled at him and said, her voice soft and husky, "Three whole hours. Mmmmm. Now you." She wriggled over to the wall. "Get comfortable first, sugar, cause the damn bed and pillow get hard as a stone. Better strip on account of clothes feel sorta like cement."

He stretched out and turned the world red. He made the full twist, turning it back the maximum of one hour. She was sculptured of smooth dark red wood, propped on one elbow, smiling at him. He was in the rigid hollow in the bed his weight had made. He tried to go to sleep, but the clothing was oppressive. He got up and tried to take it off, but it was as stubborn as thick lead foil, so he clicked back into the world and stripped rapidly, his back to her, his face hot with the confusion of modesty, of a daylight intimacy he had never known before. In haste and an awkward confusion he stretched out again and flipped into redness and soon drifted into sleep. Suddenly he was awakened and her head was on the pillow, facing him, a few inches away.

"Take another hour, sugar," she whispered. "Take two. I can wait."

He went back into redness and into sleep, and was awakened with her smiling at him as before. "Doesn't it work good?" she whispered.

He yawned, marveling at her quick instinct for the utility of the device. It was something he would never have thought of—or at least not for a long time.

"That was one strange thing about Uncle Omar. Sometimes he seemed to be able to get along on no sleep at all. We wondered about it sometimes."

"That old man had it made, Kirby. It's like only a couple of minutes since I woke up for the last time. You want a little more sleep?"

"N-Not at the moment."

"You know, I din think so, somehow," she whispered. "This must be my day for breaking all the rules there are." She moved closer. She hooked a warm firm silky leg over his. She was so close all he could see was the single huge brown eye, moist and bright, feel the heat and weight of her breath. "It's so nice to love you," she sighed. "Because you're sorta shaky and scared, kinda. And sweet. What you do, you make it *important*, Kirby. And that makes me go all funny, like marshmallows and warm soup, and my heart is way up here going chunk chunk chunk, and I almost wanta cry, and let's make this time all slow and sweet and dreamy and gentle and closer than anybody ever got to either one of us, and be talking to me. Be saying the nice things, and I shall say them back, ever' one."

Chapter Ten

Kirby Winter and Bonny Lee Beaumont made love, took naps in the red world, showered together with a playfulness, with small mischiefs and burlesques, bawdy comedies over soap and shared towels—a playtime so alien to his own estimates of himself that he felt as if he had become another person. He had strode in lonesome severity past all the fiestas, thinking them flavored with evil and depravity to be righteously condemned. But suddenly he had been invited in, where all the warmth and the music was, and had found himself caught up—not in depravity, not in decadence, not in wickedness—but in a holiday flavor of a curious innocence, a wholesome and forthright and friendly pursuit of quite evident pleasures.

In any plausible use of aesthetic theorizings, she had contours, textures and colorings which made her, as an object at rest or in motion, highly pleasing to sight, touch, taste, and hearing. Through the very process of appraising her as not only an individual, but also an object of aesthetic value, pleasing to him, he was able to achieve an inversion of that logic and assume that he, in kind, was also, to her, an individual as well as an object which pleased her. And this brought him to an objectivity which altered his prior attitude toward his body, changing it from something ludicrous, something so grotesque as to merit concealment, to an object meriting that pride which was a reflection of her pleasure.

He was pleased to be tall, grateful for a muscularity in part inherited and in part developed, perhaps, as a byproduct of many sublimations, distressed at a roll of softness around his middle, particularly after Bonny Lee's soapy, derisive, painful pinch, and was resolved to become as taut as she, knowing it would please her. Though at first the physiological mechanisms of desire had a distressing obviousness, targeting him for saucy jokes, he achieved acceptance of the inevitable and then progressed to a degree of self-satisfaction bordering upon the fatuous.

Yet throughout the whispered soapy games, in spite of his years of inadvertent continence, he could guess she was a rare one, precisely suited to bring him back into the race of men with minimal delay. He sensed that had there been any trace or trick of self-consciousness about her, any contrived modesties or measured reservations, had she in fact struck any other attitude other than that of a happy, exuberant, exhibitionistic, inventive, gamboling, young, coltish creature, he would have tumbled back into ackwardness, irrational shame, dismay and the puritan persuasion that anything so delicious must, of necessity, be evil.

There was a pattern in the love play, little times of promising to stop all this nonsense, and then an instinctive awareness of whose turn it was to become the aggressor, to be repulsed playfully, or with mock solemnity, or with wicked reprisals, and sometimes the sweet and momentary acceptance, abandoned quickly by one or the other before it went on beyond any chance of stopping it.

She sat on the edge of the blue tub and he scoured her hair dry with a big maroon towel and watched it spring back to damp tight ringlets. Suddenly the games were over, with no need to explain it to each other, with only the need to carry her to the bed and, with all the accumulated tensions, quickly, strongly, boisterously, strenuously, joyously take it so quickly over the edge that in her completion she made sounds like a slow, strange laughter while, with an astonishing strength, she held him absolutely motionless.

They listened to the two o'clock news with astonishment and incredulity. After the fifteen minutes ended, there was a special fifteen-minute bulletin on Kirby Winter—the adventures of.

When the final commercial came, she turned off the little transistor radio and placed it on the night stand beside the bed.

"Even crazier than the news, sugar, is it being the two o'clock news. My head is out of joint. All these naps. It should be tomorrow, almost. No more naps, Kirby, because you know what'll happen for sure. Get all rested and want each other again and take more naps and—hell, we keep this up the only way you'll leave is on a stretcher, or float out the window."

"I can't understand how Betsy Alden—"

She sat up and frowned at him. "Say, did your Uncle Omar look a lot older than he was?"

"What?"

"A day is got to have twenny-four hours, sugar. Lemme see. You know I stuck maybe an extra eleven onto this one? Time and a half, like. I bet if I had the same kinda day every day for ten years, I'd all of a sudden be thirty-five insteada thirty. Was he old-lookin'?"

"I guess he was. I guess he looked older than his age."

She lifted a long brown leg and flexed it. "Hefting them people around on the beach and all, I wore myself down. So there's wear and tear, but now there's just a little sore, like the day *after* you do too much."

"Didn't you hear the broadcast?"

"What kind of a smart-ass question is that? Surely I heard it. They've all gone nuttier than ever."

"So they made a positive identification and so then I overpowered two policemen, disarmed them, handcuffed them and lost myself in the crowd. So now I'm armed and considered dangerous."

She giggled at him. "Eliot Ness'll be coming after you, sugar. Anyways, what could those cops say? You know, I'm about to starve, sugar. I got some steaks. How you want yours?"

"Medium."

"You want it medium, but you get it rare, sugar. I'm to be taken care of you, hear?"

He remembered the money, the confusion on the beach, the pipe, the ring and the roses, and asked her what she'd done. She put the steaks on and came back and told him some of it, went and turned them over and came back and told him more, then went and brought in a tray, with the steaks and glasses of milk and a big stack of French bread and a bowl of sweet butter. As they ate she told him all the rest of it.

He went and got the wad of money and the ring out of the borrowed slacks. She watched him silently as he counted the money. He stared at her and said, "Sixty-six hundred and twenty dollars, Bonny Lee!"

She shrugged. "Geezel, sugar, it din seem like stealing it, but I guess it was. Nothing I did seemed real. You know. But you heard what the radio said. Twenny thousand. Hell, they're all adding it all on for the insurance."

"How about the ring?"

"Oh, that. Over near the bathhouses I see a fat ugly bassar with two of his buddies, got a guy backed against a wall looking for some way to run. I din like three against one, so I froze them still and wrapped the belt off one of them round his ankles, tied a necktie on the ankles of another one and gave the littlest one a big push. I guess I only tilted him over an inch. I worked the ring off the pinkie on the fat one, and I went fifty feet off, sorta behind a bush. The little one went ass over teacup into a cactus patch and the fat one went down backwards and the other one went down sideways, and the little guy against the wall took off like he was a deer." She took the ring from him and scratched her empty milk glass with it. "Diamond, all right," she said. "Big sonuvabitch, huh?"

She glanced at him quickly enough to catch his fleeting grimace.

"Don't talk so sweet and pretty, do I?"

Her perception startled him. "I don't mind, Bonny Lee."

She tossed the ring onto the tray. "Maybe you do. Maybe I do, too. But maybe there isn't a gawddamn thing neither of us can do about it, sugar. I got to be a woman entire afore I learned up on being a lady. I had four year of schooling, all told. You want you a tea party lady, you just go get yourself one, hear? Go grab one offa the P.T. and A. You and she can talk up a storm on art and culture and such, Kirby, then you try taking a shower with her and hustling her into the sack and see how things work out, see if you don't have to sign contract papers forever with a guarantee income afore she'll even step down offa her high heels."

"Bonny Lee!"

"Oh, don't look at me so gawddamn pitiful, you sonovabitch! I get along fine and I don't need you nor anybody." She hurled herself face down on the bed and began to sob, making sounds like a small boy punished. He patted her and soothed her and held her.

Finally she got up and went in and bathed her face and came out, grinning somewhat shamefacedly, snuffling from time to time. "All a damn lie," she said, "and you know it. You being schooled makes me feel funny. I want to do better, but what the hell chance have I got? Shees marie, I work six nights a week and that's when they got night schools, even if I could get in. Sorry, sugar. I don't crack up so much. It's on account of this being such a goofed up day, maybe. I'm just a share-cropper girl outa Carolina, cheap, ignorant and fun-lovin'."

"You low rate yourself too much. You're bright and quick."

"So is a she-fox. Let's drop the whole thing."

"You're the same age as a college kid."

"Compared to a college kid, I'm a hunnerd n'ten."

He picked up the wad of money and dropped it beside her. "You took it. So use it, if you mean what you say. Use it until it runs out, then go back to work."

She looked thoughtful for a few moments, then looked side-long at him. "Say, didn't you hear that broadcast? First things first, Kirby."

The news had been peculiarly distressing. The *Glorianna* had been intercepted down near Dinner Key and had put in there and tied up while the Metro police had made an investigation. On the yacht had been a skeleton crew of three, Mr. Joseph Locordolos, a Spanish national and a developer and speculator in hotel and resort properties, his sister, Mrs. Charla O'Rourke, a Greek national and member of the international set, and Miss Betsy Alden, Mrs. O'Rourke's niece, a nationalized citizen of the United States who had worked in New York and Hollywood as a bit-part actress on television. The yacht was registered in Panama. Mr. Locordolos was very agitated at being halted in such a pre-emptory fashion. All the papers were in order. He explained that they were taking a short shake-down cruise of several hours to see whether the newly installed radar was working properly. Both he and his sister explained that, while staying at the Hotel Elise, an establishment partially owned by Mr. Locordolos, they had made the acquaintance of Mr. Kirby Winter, nephew of Omar Krepps whom they had known slightly over the years. They said Mr. Winter seemed quite depressed and, because the boat was roomy enough, they had suggested he come along with them to Nassau, and he could then fly back from there. Mr. Winter had said he would think about it, and they had assumed he would not be joining them until the trunk and the crate arrived aboard. They had been unable to contact Mr. Winter to ask him about it, but they assumed it was his intention to go with them to Nassau, perhaps for a longer stay than he had indicated would be possible. Perhaps, as soon as they heard of the huge embezzlement, Mr. Locordolos admitted, they should have contacted the police. Instead, as he explained, he investigated the contents of the two containers and found nothing of any importance in them. He had given up, of course, any idea of permitting Mr. Winter to accompany them, and had merely been waiting until Mr. Winter put in an appearance, at which time he was going to have the containers moved onto the dock at the Biscayne Marina and wash his hands of the whole matter. Though the police had a search warrant, Mr. Locordolos felt that it might not be properly applicable to a vessel of foreign registry, however he volunteered to overlook the legal considerations and asked for a complete search on a voluntary basis. The police impounded the items Mr. Winter had shipped to the yacht, and found nothing else of any pertinence to the Winter case. They had previously impounded the suitcases discovered in Winter's temporary quarters at the Hotel Elise.

During the search of the boat they had an opportunity to interrogate Miss Alden. She was in bed in one of the staterooms. Mr. Locordolos and Mrs. O'Rourke had explained that the young actress had suffered a minor breakdown from overwork and they were taking her on a restful cruise. Miss Alden, in a weak voicc, had confirmed all aspects of the explanation given to the police.

In the meanwhile, Winter having been definitely identified as being still in the area as of eleven that morning, all exits from the city were being watched. So many pictures and descriptions had been circulated, it was not believed he could remain long at liberty. It was entirely possible the Farnham woman had already departed for some planned rendezvous with her co-conspirator, and once Winter was picked up, it was entirely possible he would disclose where the Farnham woman could be found. With both of them in custody it seemed possible that recovery of the secreted millions might be undertaken.

Grumby, in yet another public statement, had warned all authorities involved in this complex matter that Kirby Winter, once apprehended, might very possibly attempt to confuse the picture by falsely implicating others. He asserted that despite periodic pleas, Mr. Krepps had never revealed the use that was being made of the twenty-seven millions diverted from Krepps Enterprises to O.K. Devices. He stated under oath that they had never seen a dime of this money, had no idea what had become of it, and assumed that it was properly covered in the Krepps will in that portion which spoke of the bulk of the estate which should be established as the Krepps Foundation. In an accompanying statement, the District Director of Internal Revenue stated that all appropriate income and gains taxes had been paid on the twenty-seven millions prior to their disappearance into the mysterious operations of O.K. Devices. He said that in the absence of any other records, the twenty-seven million could now be considered a part of the estate and taxed as such. If during the interim period additional values had accrued, then doubtless capital gains taxes would be due and payable in the event the assets of O.K. Devices were found and liquidated. However, in view of the unusual aspects of this situation, he was prepared to wait and find out what had happened. If the executives of K.E. were indeed blameless in this situation, as they appeared to be, then possibly some adjustment might be made to avoid punishing them financially for the wrongdoing of another.

Mr. D. LeRoy Wintermore, of Wintermore, Stabile, Schamway and Mertz, made yet another statement, saying that in view of the cluttered situation, he was exercising the option of delaying the assessment of the total estate until one year from the time of death. He hoped that things would be more orderly by then. He said it would delay the establishment of the Foundation, but it might well make the tax computations easier for all concerned. In closing he said that he felt that Kirby Winter had neither the cleverness nor the resolve to engineer such a vast malappropriation of funds, and wondered aloud if the whole thing might have been more logically planned and executed by the Farnham woman.

Winter, meanwhile, was wanted for assault, resisting arrest, theft of police weapons and carrying concealed weapons without a license—all this in addition to the summonses, the subpoenas, and the formal charges of embezzlement, tax evasion, conspiracy and fraud.

The morning disturbance on the beach was neatly accounted for. It seems that a large rowdy band of teen-agers had run amuck on and near the public beach, yanking the beach costumes off women, snatching the keys from parked cars, racing through the stores and grabbing money, and playing other cruel and grotesque tricks upon the innocent. County officials believed them to be under the influence of some sort of narcotic which had turned them into a large pack of reckless animals, and said it was possible they might be part of the spring college group down from Jacksonville, Daytona or Lauderdale, or even on their way back to school from the Bahamas.

"I am a large, rowdy band of teen-agers," Bonny Lee said happily.

"They have a description of one of the gang. You heard him. Several people reported her. A short-haired, deeply-tanned blonde in pale blue underwear."

"Aqua."

"The same one Tanny and Harry saw, you know."

"Uh-huh. I know."

"I replaced her with an item in black panties and a white bra."

"Stacked?"

"Best I could find on short notice."

"Blonde?"

"Natural."

"Beautiful?"

"Completely."

"You tryna be a bassar?"

"Except she had an unfortunate profile. An almost perfectly straight line from the edge of her upper teeth right down to the base of her throat."

"*That's* better. Enjoy the undressing bit?"

"I was too nervous to notice."

"That's good too, sugar. That's right sweet of you."

"I'm damned worried about Wilma."

"Who? Oh, the one looks like a priss. From what he said on the phone, that Joseph guy, they were bringing her to the boat. So was she hid someplace aboard?"

"I don't think so. Charla told me they had a crew of five. The news account said there was a crew of three. So I think it's a safe bet two were sent after Wilma and didn't get back in time. Joseph got some news flash about the cops checking on my things that were moved out of the hotel, and he got nervous and took off. Maybe they got to the dock with Wilma in time to see the boat chugging away."

"Or maybe they came and saw the cops like we did."

"So what would they do?"

She shrugged. "That's an easy one, isn't it? She was in a safe place, until Betsy told Joseph about it. So they can't walk the streets, and I suppose a crew would live on a boat, so why not take her on back where they got her and stay there with her until Joseph gets in touch, huh?"

"It's logical, I guess. But it might be a long wait, you know. If they didn't buy what he said all the way, they'll be watching him."

"You said there's no phone there. Where is it?"

"Ah—two-ten Sunset Way, Hallandale."

"We could find it, you know."

"But the big straw hat and the glasses didn't work so well, Bonny Lee. That cop wasn't fooled."

"Because you flinched. Remember? You tried to ask him what was going on, he'd never looked twice, believe me. You be okay, sugar, just head up and ready to spit in their damn eye. I'll get me some clothes on."

It was a quiet street of small ugly stucco houses on the sizable plots of pre-war Florida, their ugliness softened by the tropic plantings which had grown up in almost vulgar profusion. Professor Wellerly's house, tinted a faded pink, was more obscured than the others on the street. It was a hot, sleepy afternoon. A power mower made an angry snorting sound several houses away. Birds were yelping, raiding a fresh store of berries on the tall bushes lining Wellerly's driveway.

A laundry truck passed them. Bonny Lee slowed and, when the truck was out of sight, she turned into the weedy shell driveway of a boarded-up house.

She turned toward him. She had changed to a black and white checked shirt, a white crisp skirt. "Sugar, I don't wanna be no nuisance woman, but how about you show up right here? I mean so I'll know nothing is messed up."

He nodded, gave himself the full hour just in case. It seemed odd to him that it was easier to get used to the redness than to the silence. The abrupt silence was so absolute it was like being enclosed in a padded vault. He slapped his thigh just to assure himself he had not lost the power to hear. He took off his shoes and walked back three houses to the Wellerly house. After he got beyond the screen of plantings he saw the blinds were closed. When he went around the corner of the house a mockingbird startled him. It hung there motionless at the same height as his face. He circled it and saw the back bumper of a car parked behind the house. He realized Bonny Lee's guess might be absolutely correct. He looked at the car. It was a newish cheap dark sedan, and might logically be a rental car. There was a dark blue baseball cap on the front seat.

He circled the house and found it was completely closed up. He tried several ways to gain entrance and was stymied by the leaden inertia of all objects in the red world. Remembering what Bonny Lee had told him of the odd behavior of objects, he picked polished stones out of a big planting pot. They were the size of plums and lifting them was like pulling them up through heavy glue. He released nine of them in midair, properly positioned, five in front of the back door, four in front of a back window. He then gave each of them a lusty push toward target, aiming them at latches and hinges and frames and locks. They stopped the moment pressure was taken off them. He remembered his promise and hurried back to the car where she sat, looking up at him with the unchanged expression of concern he had seen on her face in the instant of departure.

He clicked back to normal time, and heard a distant thudding, crashing, splintering, tinkling of glass.

"What in the world are you—"

"Back in a minute," he said and turned her off along with the rest of the discovered universe.

He hurried back and hid behind the car and turned the world on, then thought better and turned it off immediately. The shattered door hung from one hinge. The window was completely gone. He went into the kitchen and discovered that the stones had gone through the door and window and across the kitchen and into the dish cabinets and cupboards, and he suddenly felt ill to think of what could have happened had Wilma been standing there. A new lesson learned.

They were in the living room. Two beefy young men were

stopped in the middle of a card game. The room lights were on. Apparently, back in the normal world it was hot in the room. They were shiny with sweat. The big one with light hair had his shirt off and a hand towel draped around his neck. He had intricate faded tattooing on his forearms and biceps. The other was shorter and wider, and burned dark by the sea. Both of them had long sideburns, coarse, thickened features, that impenetrable look which is a combination of slyness and animal hungers and a taste for brutality.

The dark one held a card poised. Both of them were looking toward the kitchen with startled expressions. Wilma Farnham stood by a book-lined wall near the small coquina rock fireplace, books from floor to ceiling. Her brown hair, in an unkempt cascade of wispy strings made her small face look smaller. Her glasses were crooked, her blouse half out of her skirt, her mouth oddly slack with surprise as she too stared beyond him toward the kitchen. The drink in her hand was tilted and, as she stood off balance, a dollop of it was stopped halfway to the floor.

He went to work. It was difficult work, but in its special way, enjoyable. Within fifteen subjective minutes he had the tattooed one and the dark one neatly arranged. He had found it easier to work on them when they were suspended horizontally in the air a yard above the figured rug, but it had taken every ounce of his strength to bend them, straighten them, hoist them into that position. He'd wrapped their wrists and ankles with heavy twine which, in the red world, reacted like thick copper wire. He'd stuffed their mouths with toweling and tied it in place. Finally he had sheathed them in bedsheets, wrapping it like foil, then wound them from ankle to shoulder in clothesline. Bending it around them was like wrapping them in copper tubing. He had to grasp the rope at some distance from them in order to get that leverage which made the task easier.

He hurried back to the car. Bonny Lee looked startled when he reappeared.

"What's this little delay, hah?"

"Sorry. Look, I got to get back there in a hurry, but you can come in there now. Through the back door. Bring the car in and turn it around, facing out."

"Okay."

He twisted the stem and walked back through the deadness

of the silence. Wilma had used the several seconds to move closer to the two mummies, and again she was spilling as she stared at them. Kirby felt mild regret at missing the chance of seeing them fall simultaneously, side by side. At first he was going to appear, carelessly, thoughtlessly, in front of her. Just in time, he went back to the doorway off to one side and slightly behind her. He stepped into normal time and normal space and said, "Wilma!"

Suspended liquid fell onto her bare instep. She swung around, took one uncertain step and peered at him. She pushed her glasses into place and said, "Loanbeehole, Sir Lanschlot, as I live and bree!"

"Are you drunk!"

She tottered toward him, smirking. "Za skunk, cutie bug. Bessa my life in selfless devotion a duty, 'n you know what I get? Pleece looking for me. An that Bessy girl asking me things I don't know'nything about. Ol' Omar's stone cold dead, 'ny got no job, 'na hole thing's giving my dear brother a nervous stomach, 'n you, you silly man, I popo—propozizhun you, firse timin my lousy wretched choked-up life I gotnuff guts. 'N whattayou do?" She put her nose inches from his chin and looked up at him cross-eyed. He could hear the Sunbeam snoring into the drive. "Whattayou do? Run! An then—" She backed off slightly. "An then here I am, poor incent girl at the mercy of those two sailors an all they want to do is play cards. *Course* I'm drunk, fren! Firse time." She burped herself slightly off balance, recovered, beamed at him and said, "I like it!" She turned vaguely and stared at the shrouded figures. They were both making small helpless spasms and smothered grunting sounds. "What happened alluva secon to Rene and Raoul?" she asked plaintively.

Bonny Lee came in and stared at Wilma. Wilma swung around again and held Bonny Lee in an inquisitive squint, pushing her glasses back against the bridge of her nose. "Who you, pretty fren?" Wilma asked.

"Wow!" Bonny Lee said. "I figured in your picture you looked like a school teacher. Excuse me all to hell."

Wilma peered at Bonny Lee, pulled herself together with precarious effort and said, attempting precision, "Ektually, my dear, I yam more the cerebral type."

Bonny Lee sighed. "You want to talk to her, I guess, don't you, sugar?"

"If possible."

"Who's in the packages?"

"Rene and Raoul, seafaring men."

"They look like they'd keep. See what you can do about some coffee, Kirby." Bonny Lee gave a hitch at her skirt and marched toward Wilma. It was as though she had rolled up her sleeves and spit on her hand. She marched Wilma, wailing protests, sputtering with indignation, into the bedroom wing.

All Kirby was able to find was some instant coffee of an unfamiliar brand. But it looked dark and smelled strong, and the label said nothing about how it would improve sleep. In the other end of the small house were the distant sounds of conflict, yelpings and the roar of water. He went in and checked Rene and Raoul. They were still until he checked their bonds, and then they began thumping and grunting again. He could hardly blame them. It must be very uncomfortable in there, he thought. The sheets were getting wet with sweat and beginning to cling. It was very muggy inside the house.

He filled a big pottery mug with strong steaming coffee and took it into the bedroom. The bathroom door was ajar. Wilma's clothes and Bonny Lee's clothes were on the bed. He put the mug on a table and walked back out. Bonny Lee seemed to be winning. All he had heard was the rushing roar of the shower mingled with a heartbroken whimpering. He fixed the knots more securely and went over and studied the bookshelves. Professor Wellerly apparently acquired books in every field of human knowledge, providing the title was dull enough and the binding sedate. He gathered up the spilled cards, shuffled them and dealt random poker hands. The gold watch would considerably simplify poker. He evolved various methods and decided the most useful one would be to freeze the scene in the instant the dealer was reaching to pick up the deck which had just been cut. Take the cards and arrange for three or four strong hands, and give the others nothing so they would fold. Give yourself the best hand, by a narrow margin. Like four little threes against three pat hands, a flush, a full house—aces up, and a high straight. Put the sorted deck back under the reaching hand, sit back and wait for the action.

"Kirby, sugar!" Bonny Lee called. He went in. Bonny Lee

was dressed again. Wilma sat huddled on the edge of the bed wearing a man's summer robe that was like a tent on her. Her hair was darkened and flattened and she looked sullen and drowned. She stared down at the floor.

"Sip the nice coffee, sweetie," Bonny Lee ordered.

"No thank you," Wilma said in a precise but muted voice. "I think I might be going to be ill."

"Sip the pretty coffee, sweetie, or we strip again and I trot you in and wedge you under that cold water and I take that big brush and I scrub off all the hide you've got left."

Wilma hunched slightly and humbly sipped her coffee.

"You know, she's not really so bad, except how she don't even try, for God's sake. She's got a real cute figger."

"Figure."

"Figure," she said carefully.

"Hell, I'm sorry, Bonny Lee."

"I'm not. Not at all. You keep it up. Anyhow, she *has* got a real cute—figure, sorta like boyish, but not enough so anybody's going to get confused. But geezel, them wire glasses and that ratty hairdo and them Salvation Army clothes—"

"I have no urge to be cheap and obvious," Wilma said.

"Stay snotty and I'll stomp your spectacles, sweetie. You're not obvious for sure. All the men in the world are in a big candy store, and you're out there in the dark knocking on the window with a sponge. You ever hear a whistle in your life? Ever get pinched?"

"Thank you, no."

"Do you some good, sis. Makes you stick out on top and swing on the bottom. I'd put bright green contacts on you, give you a Cleopatra beehive, put you in something too tight to sit down in, and four inch heels, and learn you to be walken slow, with your shoulders back and your belly in and your butt stuck out, dangle earrings and musky perfume. Not my style, but in gear like that, sis, you'd make strong men cry."

"Cleopatra beehive?" Wilma asked shyly.

"Not exactly beehive. The Egypt bit, like Liz."

"Liz?"

"Oh for God's sake," Bonny Lee said. "You talk to her."

"Betsy brought you my note?"

"Yes, Kirby."

"And you talked to her?"

"All night, just about. She kept trying to make me remember things about your uncle. She thinks there's something special hidden. I don't have it. I don't even know what it is. Your uncle was a very unusual man. He was so smart, Kirby, he didn't need any special kind of thing. His great mind was enough. I did just as he told me to do, and no matter what they do to me, I'll never, never—"

"I understand your loyalty, Wilma. Out of that loyalty could you be denying the existence of something you know exists somewhere?"

"I swear I'm not, Kirby. I swear it. She told me where you were. Why would you hide in the apartment of a cheap person like that, Kirby?"

"As I don't know the man, I'm not ready to pass judgment."

"Would that be how you met this trashy girl? Who is this girl, Kirby?"

"Bonny Lee is a good fr—excuse me. Bonny Lee is a girl I am in love with."

"Oh dear," Wilma said.

Bonny Lee winked at Kirby. "Y'almost flunked out, friend."

"That was a lie, wasn't it?" Wilma asked in an almost inaudible tone, "When you told me you were frightened of women. You were saving my face, weren't you? How you must have laughed after you got away from me!"

"I told you the truth. I ran in pure panic, Wilma."

"But right now you seem—different. You don't seem scared of anything in the world—anything."

"I'm scared of a lot of things."

"But he's gettin' right brassy around the broads lately," Bonny Lee said and giggled at Kirby's look of annoyance. "I hear tell he undressed one right on a public beach. Din' even know her name."

Wilma looked horrified. "Kirby! Are you well?"

"I'm perfectly all right," he said angrily.

"Didn't she struggle?"

"Poor dear little thang couldn' move a muscle," Bonny Lee said.

"*Please,* Bonny Lee! Please."

"Sure, sugar. I'll be good."

"Wilma, have you been keeping track of the news reports?"

"I think I heard it all, but parts of it I can't remember very clearly. About that yacht and your things being on it, and about you escaping from those policemen this morning, and taking their guns. It just—didn't sound like you."

"When did Betsy leave here?"

"Very early. She said she was going to go race a bluff. That doesn't sound quite right. Run a bluff? Yes, that was it. But the expression is unfamiliar."

"I guess you must realize her bluff didn't work."

"I don't understand what happened. I guess it was almost three hours later when those sailors got here. They rang the bell properly, so I assumed it was Roger or you or even Betsy coming back. They forced their way in. They seemed quite—cordial in a rather unpleasant way. When I started to be severe with them, Rene, he's the big one, but I didn't know his name then, smiled and took my wrist and turned it slowly until I was finally down on my knees with my face against the carpet. It was absolute agony. My arm still feels odd, you know. Then I knew I had better go along quietly. I couldn't understand who they were. I was afraid they were some thieves who had hurt Roger and made him tell where they could find me, and then they were going to force me to reveal the location of that money, that absurd money that's all gone. But I gathered they were taking me to a yacht, the yacht they worked on, and that Betsy was there waiting for me. They made me sit on the floor in front with my head back under the dash. It was very hot and dirty and uncomfortable. Then suddenly something was very wrong. They became cross with me and with each other, and they argued about what to do and then they came back here. From what they said, I gathered the boat had left without them. They were most surly and rather apprehensive until at last we heard the news about the yacht. But they said Betsy had been taken ill. She seemed a very tense and excitable person, but I did not guess she was close to having a breakdown."

"Sis," Bonny Lee said, "you kill me. You really do. Those bassars grabbed that Betsy girl and took her onto that boat and hurt her until she said where they could find you and find Kirby here, and made Kirby promise to come on account of being maybe able to help Betsy and to keep them from doing you like they done her. This thing you don't know what it is, they want it bad."

Wilma stared solemnly at Bonny Lee. "*Hurt* her?"

"Sweetie, of a Saturday night in the wrong part of New Orleans, you can get you crippled for a lifetime for a cruddy seven bucks, so why should this make you bug your eyes? Where you been livin'?"

"This is terrible!" Wilma said. "Your uncle would have agreed, Kirby. We must find out what it is they want and see that they get it, or prove to them no such thing exists."

Bonny Lee gave a laugh of derision. "We know what they want, and they don't get it."

"What is it?" Wilma demanded.

"Bonny Lee!" Kirby said warningly.

"No sweat, sugar. Even if I wanted to tell her, she just isn't ready yet and I can lay odds she never will be. What'll we do now?"

"Get her out of here."

"But where? Oh. My place. Hells bells. At least it's the one address those people don't know already."

Wilma stared at Kirby, her unpainted lips parted. "Did you —overpower those two sailors, Kirby?"

"Watch it, Winter," Bonny Lee said. She turned to Wilma. "Sweetie, you don't drink so good."

Wilma flushed. "It seems that I just—I just stopped giving a damn about anything. Life had become too confusing to be endurable."

"Surprise hell out of you, sis, how much more complicated life can get for a drunky broad. Get out of here, Kirby, and I'll find some damn thing to put on her."

"I have clothes."

"I know, sweetie. And glasses. And your picture in the papers."

Kirby got up and walked out of the bedroom. As he took the first step into the living room, the side of his head blew up. As the floor came toward him, he seemed able to observe the phenomenon with a remote, clinical interest. It was the way they blew up a cliff. First you saw the flash and then the dust and the rumble and tumble of boulders. He heard a remote screaming of women as he fell into velvet.

Chapter Eleven

Kirby came up from far places, like blundering up cellar stairs in the dark toward the edge of light at the kitchen sill. He opened his eyes and the light was like a spray of acid. There was a slow regular pulsation over his ear, like a child trying to get a balloon started.

Somebody took hold of his chin and shook his head roughly, and he marveled that it did not come loose and fall off.

He squinted up into the oversized face of the big one, Rene.

"Look at some good knots, buddy," Rene said jovially.

Kirby was sitting in an armchair. He looked down. There was a single strand of clothesline lashing both arms together, just above the elbows, pulling his elbows tightly together, making him hunch his back awkwardly. His hands, slightly numbed, were not restrained, but the arc of their movement was limited. A second strand lashed his knees together, just above the knees. Both lines were fastened with a single, competent square knot.

"Learn something every day, buddy. Never tie wrists. Never tie ankles. See them knots? You can't get anywhere near either of them with your fingers or your teeth, and you got no way to wiggle out. You don't know a thing about knots."

"I guess you got loose," Kirby said dispiritedly.

"And got Raoul loose. He was nearly loose anyway. So I got by the door and pow!"

"Yes indeed," Kirby said. "Pow." He looked around the empty room. "Where's Miss Beaumont? And Miss Farnham?"

"Beaumont? That was the blonde, huh? She decided not to hang around." Rene looked and sounded annoyed. He had a makeshift bandage on his wrist and long deep scratches on his throat. "When we tried to grab her, she went off like a bomb. Bit hell out of me. Scratched like a tiger. Kicked Raoul good, belted him one in the eye and went out the back, through the door you busted all to hell."

Kirby struggled to force his mind into paths of logic. Rene sat on the couch. He seemed perfectly relaxed.

"Aren't you afraid Miss Beaumont might summon the police?"

"Her? Nah. She won't. She run right into the boss and a couple boys he picked up local. One good thump on top of the head settled her right down."

Kirby moved his arms and was able to see his wrist watch. It was twenty minutes of five. "What's going to happen now?"

Rene shrugged. "We just wait. The boss is figuring some kind of deal to get you and Wilma onto the *Glorianna.* Maybe they'll take off with all the right clearances, then anchor off someplace, and we'll get out to her in a small boat."

"Oh."

"It made the boss real happy to see you, Winter. I guess you're the jackpot in this thing. The boss thinks everything is going to work out just fine from here in. It got pretty messed up for a while. Too much publicity. The boss hates publicity on a business deal. If, like they say, you got twenty-seven million hidden away someplace, I guess you're worth a lot of effort."

"Where would they take Miss Beaumont?"

"I don't know. I don't know if too many people are still interested in the boat. They'd have to take her someplace else, and if the boss has gotten some more help lined up, maybe there's another place lined up too. How about that twenty-seven million, Winter?"

"What about it?"

"That's what the boss is after, hah?"

"I wouldn't have any idea."

"Anybody steals that much, they're a pigeon for the first people that can get to him. Money like that isn't any good unless you can keep it a secret."

"I'm happy to have the benefit of your expert advice."

Rene came slowly to his feet, walked over, leaned, reached and with calloused thumb and finger gave the end of Kirby's nose a forceful quarter turn. It was contemptuous, degrading and astonishingly painful. The tears ran down Kirby's cheeks.

"Talk nicer when you talk to me," Rene said. "We got a long wait. You can make it easy and you can make it rough."

Rene went back and sat down and began to pare his ridged nails with a pocket knife. After a few minutes had passed, Kirby said, "Excuse me, but did Joseph say when we might be taken away from here?"

"Who?"

"Mr. Locordolos."

"I ain't seen him. Just the boss was here. Mrs. O'Rourke."

"Oh."

Rene shook his head sadly. "And that Wilma got very snotty with the boss. That wasn't so smart. The boss gave her a shot. A Syrette thing like out of an aid kit. Thirty seconds and she was snoring like a bugle."

Raoul came wandering in from the direction of the kitchen. His left eye was puffed. He was spooning something into his mouth out of a can held in a big brown fist.

"What you got now?" Rene asked disgustedly.

"Beans."

"More beans for God's sake?"

"Good."

Raoul sat in a chair and finished the beans. He set the can aside, wiped his mouth on his forearm, stared blandly at Kirby for a few moments, then turned to Rene and began to speak in a language Kirby was able to identify after a few moments as the vulgar French of North Africa, larded with Spanish, Italian and Arabic words. Though he could follow it very imperfectly, he suddenly realized Raoul was suggesting to Rene that he be permitted to go into the bedroom and cure his boredom by amusing himself with the scrawny little sleeping chicken. Raoul accompanied this request with winkings so convulsive they distorted half his face.

To Kirby's horror, Rene did not react with appropriate violence. In fact, he seemed bored. He asked some casual question Kirby did not catch. Raoul said something about who was to find out, in any case. And what harm could it do? It would pass the time.

As it seemed that Rene would shrug and nod approval, there was a curiously muscular convulsion in Kirby's mind, like a gagging in the throat. The fat watch—the golden edge—had pulled reality too thin, had made it too easy to think of the submissive world as a stage for low comedy, for tricky effects, for narrow triumphs of virtue over the brute. The watch had dislocated the world, had made temptingly feasible all the traditions of fantasy, but here would be no slender triumph of virtue. Here, for Wilma Farnham, all the games could end, and he would be powerless to stop these two. For Kirby Winter the world settled suddenly back into its ancient grind of blood and pain, of small lonely disasters in the hearts of men.

He caught the sense of Rene's next remark, something about waiting, something about how, if they had to stay here the whole night, then, orders or no orders, they would share the chicken, wait until she wakened and could be suitably instructed in obedience, and then cut cards for her.

Raoul shrugged and yawned and said that inasmuch as he had already lost money at cards, maybe now they could play again and this time make the chicken part of the stakes. For later.

Kirby's eyes had finally stopped watering. The end of his nose felt as big as a biscuit.

The two men moved over to the coffee table. As Rene shuffled the pack he stared at Kirby and said, "How'd you put us out and tie us up?"

"I had help," Kirby said.

"That figures. Did you use some kind of a gas, maybe?"

"Something like that."

"The boss wondered. She'll want you to tell her all about it. Anything she can use, she wants to know about."

"Deal," said Raoul.

The cards made small flapping sounds in the humid silence of the room. From all evidences, Kirby felt that it was a reasonably good guess that the watch might still be in the right hand pocket of the borrowed slacks. He bent his cramped back further, shoved his lashed elbows down beside his right thigh and ran his left elbow along his thigh. He felt the round bulk of the watch and thought he heard a tink of the heavy chain against the case.

"Don't get smart," Rene said, suddenly alert.

"Just trying to work a cramp out of my shoulder," Kirby said humbly.

Raoul spoke in the crude patois of the African port cities. Kirby missed much of it, but he caught the essence. Don't exercise yourself about the clerk type, my friend. He is too weak and scared and helpless to make problems for us.

The helplessness, Kirby realized, was the greatest danger.

The gold watch could as easily have been a mile away, for all the good it could do him. Helplessness froze the mind, preventing any kind of creative scheming. It made one believe that Charla would manage to arrange everything just as she wanted it, in spite of the police search, in spite of all the alarms and publicity and public fascination with an amount of money beyond any rational comprehension. And in spite of anything he might do, he would find himself on the *Glorianna* with the crew of five and the three shattered young women. Or perhaps, all impudence gone, Bonny Lee was at this moment falling all over herself in her eagerness to tell Charla about the mysterious powers of the inherited watch. Soon they would come for it, test it, and perhaps quietly and efficiently crack the skulls of everyone connected with the venture and drop them off at the edge of the Gulf Stream, with suitable wires and weights.

The awareness of defeat, the anticipation of defeat, was like a sickness. He had only pride to fight it. This is the time, he thought, when I must become whatever Uncle Omar thought I could become, hoped I could become—or give up completely.

He wondered if Bonny Lee's little car was still out there. It would seem logical that they would leave it behind. It was rather conspicuous. For Charla, Bonny Lee would be a new factor in the equation. But he sensed that Charla adjusted with maximum speed and efficiency to all new factors. He was doubly grateful he had told Bonny Lee about the whole mess he was in. She would be in a better position to anticipate Charla's moves. He hoped Bonny Lee had the good sense to play absolutely dumb. If there was the slightest hint she knew anything of value, Charla would not rest until she had found out what it was—as unpleasantly as possible.

If Bonny Lee's little car was out there, one could assume the keys were in it, as Bonny Lee had known the probable necessity for leaving quickly.

Rene and Raoul were arguing over the play of one hand. Raoul seemed to feel he had been cheated.

"About that twenty-seven million," Kirby said.

They both stared at him. "Yes?"

"It's very boring and uncomfortable just sitting here. Maybe there's some game three could play. For some of the money."

"You've got no money," Rene said. "We took it. We split

it. Twelve hundred." The rest of it, Kirby remembered, was tucked under Bonny Lee's mattress.

"I could give you an I.O.U. against the other money."

Rene looked contemptuous. "And the boss would pay us off on your I.O.U. Winter?"

"She wouldn't. I would."

"You won't be doing anything."

Here was the special moment of truth. Defeat was implicit in the length of clothesline around his arms, biting into his flesh. He smiled at the two men. "Don't you wonder a little bit why I'm taking all this so calmly?"

Rene looked mildly uncertain. "You're not like a lot of the jokers the boss has clobbered. I figured you'd try to make a deal with me. I wouldn't buy, even if you did. But maybe I wonder why you don't."

"Deal," said Raoul.

"Shut up. Winter, I don't see how you got any edge at all. Three days aboard and you'd sign over your sister, if she asks you. She'll pick you clean and then she'll keep you for kicks or throw you away, and there isn't a damn thing you can do about it."

"Deal," Raoul said again.

"The best Mrs. O'Rourke can get from me is a partnership deal."

"That's going to surprise hell out of her."

"I expect it to. I've got it all tucked away in photo and thumbprint accounts."

Rene stared at him dubiously. "Thumbprint?"

"They're number accounts, of course, but there's no draw against them except on personal application. Six hundred different accounts in nine different countries, all set up the same way."

Rene thought for a minute. "So if you dropped dead, what's the deal to get it out then?"

"There isn't any. Any time five years passes with no activity in any account, it's automatically closed and the net is delivered to whoever I nominated, whichever person or organization in each case. So I'm no good dead to your boss, and there's nothing she can force out of me that'll give her access to what she wants."

"But she doesn't know this?"

"Not yet. And when she finds out, she's going to have to

treat us nicely, me and Miss Farnham and Miss Beaumont, and even Miss Alden."

"What if they haven't been treated so nice already?"

"Then I'll reduce Mrs. O'Rourke's participation, as a sort of penalty for greed and bad manners. You see, my friend, I'm going to end up in pretty good shape—assuming Mrs. O'Rourke is a logical woman."

Rene stared at him with a corrugated brow. "So why hassle with her the way you been doing?"

"Why should I split with anybody? But now that she's won this round, I might as well cut her in. There's enough to go around, I'd say, wouldn't you?"

Rene grinned like a yawning dog. "One half of one twenty-seventh would do me good for the rest of my life."

"I wouldn't gamble for that much. But whatever I did gamble for, I guess you can see I'd be in a position to pay off, if I should lose."

"She say keep tied," Raoul said. "Deal."

"We can keep him tied, Raoul, and still bring him into the game."

"Don't like it," Raoul said.

Rene switched to the rough argot, and reminded Raoul of what he had said about Kirby being no cause for worry, and reminded Raoul that they would be playing the stranger only for money, that they would keep a separate record of winnings and losses to determine who would have the little chicken first. Raoul shrugged his acceptance.

Rene came over and picked Kirby up, chair and all. It was a shocking demonstration of raw power. He set the chair in front of the coffee table. With a flick of the seaman's knife he severed the line around Kirby's arms. With more line he deftly lashed Kirby's left arm to the arm of the chair, put a fairly snug loop around Kirby's throat and tied that to the back of the chair. Though it was pleasant to be released from the previous cramped position, Kirby realized he had gained less than he thought. His right arm was free, but it would be awkward, obvious and too slow to stick his right hand in the trouser pocket and hope to manipulate the watch in time. And even if he did, he would be almost as helpless in the red world. He had learned enough of the behavior of inanimate objects to know that the rope would become like stiff cables.

"All you need is one hand loose," Rene said. He put two

hundred dollars in front of Kirby. "You owe me two hundred, pal."

"Want it in writing?"

"I can make you remember it."

"I'd rather put it in writing. Have you got a piece of paper? I think I've got a pen right here." With difficulty he put his hand in the side pocket of his borrowed slacks.

"Hold it!" Rene yelled.

His fingers touched the watch stem and he pressed and turned. The world was a murky red. They were caught in the cessation of time, staring at him. He took the gold watch out. He placed it on the table and tried to undo the knots binding his left arm, but knew he could not budge them. It was a strange impasse. Even if he could get hold of a knife, he doubted that he could saw his way through the rope. Objects had an obdurate toughness in this subjective space where time stood still. The silver hand moved. The gold hands of the watch were motionless at quarter to six.

He knew he would have to set himself up for a better opportunity, but did not know how he could manage it. But the watch would have to be in a more convenient and accessible place, yet without any impression of any blur of movement which would make them suspicious. He suddenly had a reasonable idea, and tucked the watch under his thigh, chain out of sight, stem pointing out. He put his right hand back in his pocket and, through the fabric, reached the stem of the watch with his middle finger and pressed it.

"I thought I had a pen but I guess I don't," he said and slowly took his hand out of his pocket and showed them it was empty.

"We don't need it in writing. Stay away from pockets," Rene said.

"He got nothing on him," Raoul said.

"Neither did that guy had a razor in his hat brim, and he cut you up pretty good," Rene said.

"Shut up and deal."

They agreed on five card stud. Kirby held his own. Raoul lost steadily. He was the eternal optimist, confident the last card would solve all his problems.

"Your friend is very lucky," Kirby said to Raoul.

"Deal."

Kirby licked his lips and said, "And he has very quick hands."

Raoul tensed. He leaned toward Rene, and spoke the argot with a speed Kirby could not hope to follow. Kirby let his right hand fall casually near the watch. He could hope for some small change, some small opening, but did not know what it might be. At the end of his gunfire warning, Raoul slapped a knife down on the table beside him, not within Kirby's reach. Kirby had not seen him take it out or open the blade.

As Rene began protestations of innocence, Kirby thumbed them to murky stillness. He remembered what he had learned from Bonny Lee regarding the behavior of objects in motion. He leaned forward as far as he could. The loop bit painfully into his throat. He could not reach the knife. He took a playing card by one corner and found that by extending it, he could touch the knife. He began to scratch at the knife with the edge of the card, bringing it a millimeter closer each time, pausing to lean back from time to time to take a breath. At last he could grasp it. He released the card and it remained in the air. He took the knife and worried it, point first, blade up, under the double strand that held his left arm to the arm of the chair. When it was in position, he pulled up on it as hard as he could. It made no impression on the strands of line. He brought the watch over and put it in the fingers of his left hand where he could manipulate it as quickly as possible. He pressed, and when the silver hand jumped back to twelve, he turned the stem back immediately. In the instant of reality he heard a loud fragment of one word from Rene and felt a tug at his left arm. Now the knife was two feet above the level of his head. The strands had been sliced and were slightly apart. He peeled them back and freed his left arm. He put the watch in his lap and worked the stiffness out of his left arm. He pushed the loop out and was able to slump in the chair and work it up over his head, not without some further attrition to his bruised nose. He reached up, recaptured the knife and used the same procedure on the line around his legs just above his knees. Before he thumbed the watch stem, he looked at Rene and Raoul. Their glance had swiveled toward him and the first faint indication of astonishment was beginning to change their brute faces.

He worked it more quickly than before, freezing the knife

at eye level this time. He peeled the rope back and got up and paced around the room, feeling the familiar drag of the inertia of his clothing, slipping his shoes off after tiring of the effort of moving them about. There were two heavy masonry pots on either side of the fireplace. Whatever had been growing in them had died and withered to naked sticks. With great effort and by degrees he positioned the two pots in midair, and, after estimates of the forces involved, about seven inches above the heads of the two men.

It would not do, he realized, to give the impression of having suddenly disappeared, not in front of two witnesses. So he got back into the chair right in their line of vision, before thumbing the watch stem. His discarded shoes clumped to the floor. The card fluttered down. The knife chunked deeply into a cypress beam overhead. The pots fell, thudded against thick skulls, smashed on the floor. Rene slumped sideways on the couch. Raoul bent slowly forward and bounced his forehead off the coffee table.

As soon as he ascertained they were both breathing, Kirby, profiting by experience, tied them precisely as he had been tied, finding it easier to operate in the brightness of real time, where materials were not as stubborn. Realizing they might untie each other, he added the refinement of the rope loop about the throat, fastening Raoul to an iron eye in the front of the fireplace, and Rene to a sturdy catch at the base of a window across the room.

Wilma was still in the oversized robe, face down across the bed, her head hanging over the edge. She snored rhythmically, insistently, beautifully. After ten minutes of proddings, slappings, pinchings, and an attempt to walk her, he knew that all he could hope to achieve was a temporary interruption of the snoring sound. She was a limp, warm, loose-jointed doll, and the most infuriating thing about the whole procedure was that she seemed to be smiling.

But, with or without her co-operation, he knew he had to get her out of the house. He had already given up more hostages than he could afford. He felt less regard for Wilma, but more responsibility. He pulled the robe off her and tried not to stare at her more than was necessary as he dressed her. Compared with Bonny Lee, as well as the girl on the beach, Wilma seemed to wear extraordinarily practical underthings, opaque and designed for long wear. She kept slipping away, toppling over and picking up the rhythm of the snoring again.

After a few attempts to brush her wild brown hair, he looked in bureau drawers until he found a bright scarf. He put it around her head and knotted it under her chin. He noticed that someone had stepped on her glasses, bending the frames and powdering both lenses. This place was not safe, but he could not think of a place which might be. In any case, he would need money.

Rene stirred as Kirby was recovering the money from his pockets. He opened blurred eyes, shook his head, winced.

"How the hell'd you do that?" he asked weakly.

"I had help."

Rene closed his eyes. "You seem to get it when you need it."

Kirby found the rest of the money and the keys to the rental car in Raoul's pockets. Raoul kept sleeping. Kirby found his pulse. It felt solid and steady. He thumbed Raoul's eyes open. They were crossed. He wondered if that had any special clinical significance.

He went in and picked up Wilma and hung her over his left shoulder, his arm around her legs. As he walked back into the living room, he thought he heard a sound outside. He darted his hand into his pocket and made the world red, made it safe for a quick reconnaissance. He eased out from under Wilma's folded figure and made a quick tour of the area and found nothing amiss. The Sunbeam was in the drive. The keys were in it. He was hidden from the world by all the Wellerly's tropical shrubbery. Just as he was about to bring reality back so he could move the car out of the way, he remembered Wilma. He hurried back in. It would have made a strange and awkward fall for a sleeping girl. He fitted his shoulder into her middle and once again brought the untinged world back.

"Mrs. O'Rourke isn't going to like this at all," Rene said.

"My friends sneaked up on you. What could you do?"

"She'll think of something we could have done."

He took Wilma out and put her on the floor in the back of the rental sedan. He backed the Sunbeam around the sedan, out of the way. He got into the rental car, put on the sunglasses and the baseball hat and drove out. He drove swiftly east to Route 1, a half-mile away, and parked at the first convenient motel.

There was an old man at the desk. He had a ground floor vacancy.

"You and the missus, aye?" He peered beyond Kirby. "Whare is she?"

"Taking a nap in the back. She's very tired."

Kirby signed the register and paid cash for the night. He drove to the unit, parked close, unlocked the door and went back and lifted Wilma out. When he got her into his arms and turned, the old man was standing there. "She sure God *is* tired, mister. Wouldn't be sick, would she?"

"She's just a heavy sleeper."

"I don't want nothing funny going on. I run a nice place here. Where at's your luggage, mister?"

"In the back end."

"Now I just want to see you got some luggage."

"Let me take her in first."

"Better set her down, because you got no luggage, you're not bringing her into my place."

Kirby propped Wilma on the seat. He had to admit that the look of her didn't inspire confidence. She looked drugged. And was.

He went to the trunk and unlocked it and, as with his left hand he began to raise it, he twisted himself out of normal time. Forty feet away a man was unloading his car. He had put a row of suitcases on the paved parking surface in preparation for carrying them inside. Kirby went over and took two of the smaller items. He pushed them back to the sedan, shoved them into the trunk. He took the same position as before, lifted the trunk lid the rest of the way.

"I like for everybody to have luggage," the old man said in apology.

"Sure," Kirby said. He went to pick the girl up again. This time she slipped her arms around his neck.

"Soooo sleepy," she mumbled. "Sooo terr'ble sleepy."

The old man carried the bags in. Kirby plumped Wilma onto the nearest bed. She began to snore immediately.

"Sure a sleeper," the old man said.

After he was gone, Kirby held the door open and turned the world red and silent and took the small suitcases back. The man stood in an attitude of perplexity, finger pointing, obviously counting the items of luggage. Kirby pressed them against the ground behind him and went back into the room.

When he thumbed the stem of the watch, the door swung shut. He took off Wilma's shoes. He wrote a short note to her. "You are safe here. I'll come back when I can. Don't leave the room and don't phone anyone under any circumstances. Put the chain on the door. I'll knock five—pause—three, rapidly."

He brought the room key with him, and made certain the door was locked. He drove to a public phone booth in a shopping center parking lot, phoned the police number in the front of the book and reported that it sounded as if somebody was trying to break into 210 Sunset Way, at the rear, and the Wellerly's were out of the country. When the first question was asked, he hung up.

He drove south toward Miami. It was quarter of seven. He had the feeling he was wasting too much time. And he felt guilty about the time he spent in the real world. When the world was red, time was stopped, and then, if bad things were happening to Bonny Lee, they stopped too. He could keep time at a standstill by walking the entire way, but he had to measure his own energies on the scale also. The sun was almost down. He could not afford to let the day end, because he could not be certain he would be able to see well enough in the combination of darkness and faint red light.

In his haste, he made a miscalculation. The woman ahead of him spurted ahead as though to make a red light before it changed, then changed her mind and jammed her brakes on. He piled the rental into the back of her plum-gray Continental, in a scream of rubber and expensive metallic clangor. As he sat dazed, she came yawping out of her car, her face red and ugly with anger. His door had sprung open. Off to the right he saw a cop striding toward the scene.

He grabbed the watch and stopped all the noise and motion. It took an effort of will to remember that, when the world was red, there was no need for haste. The rear end collision had happened in the center lane of three lanes of southbound traffic. Other cars had stopped all around them. He got out and checked the other cars. The first car in the left lane was a convertible. A conveniently small man sat behind the wheel. He had his fingertips on the wheel, and he was staring over at the accident, at the tall woman, stopped in the middle of a yelp. Kirby climbed in and levered the small man up and out from under the wheel. He shoved him out beyond the car, climbed down, took his ankles and towed him back to the rental and, with the increasing ease of experience in such matters, worked him into proper position, his fingertips on the steering wheel, his head still looking back over his right shoulder. He knew that maximum confusion would serve his purposes. He put his baseball cap on the small man, and wedged the man's tweed hat on his own head. As a final touch, he removed the policeman's service revolver, worked it snugly into the hand of the irate woman, pointed it up into the air, and gave a final solid pressure to the trigger finger. He clambered into the convertible, slid under the wheel, and turned the city back on, looking toward the little group as he did so. The woman fired into the air, hauled her hand down and stared at it. The cop started at the sound of the shot and began pawing his empty holster. The little man snapped his head around, stared with utter disbelief at the crumpled car, the cop, the woman with the gun, leaped out and began to run. The light changed and Kirby drove on, reasonably confident it was a matter that would never be completely straightened out.

As soon as he realized he was within reasonable walking distance of the Marina, he pulled over to the curb and stopped and then stopped the final slant of sunlight. He shoved his shoes inside his shirt, took the dark glasses off, and headed toward the Marina. Walking among the pink silent people was like walking through a stone orchard. Sometimes, in his haste, he brushed against them. They were rigid, unreal. A man stood lighting a pipe. The flame looked fashioned of pinkish brass. A woman huffed cigarette smoke from her mouth and it was unmoving in the air, like some strange semi-transparent plastic plume.

He went through the Marina gates and out onto the large central dock. The bay ripples were stilled, molten lead that had set and been oiled and polished and was touched with the red reflections of sunset.

The *Glorianna* was there, at the end of the T, not quite as large as he had expected her to be. Eighty feet, perhaps. A bald, mustachioed man stood forward, looking toward the city, stopped in the act of coiling a heavy line. The *Glorianna* had so much cabin space in ratio to deck space, she looked slightly ungainly, but she seemed to have enough beam and freeboard to be a good sea boat. He went up the gangway and onto the deck. She was pale and trim, spotless, luxurious, comfortable. He could find no one else topsides. All hatches were closed, so he assumed she was air-conditioned. He tried to get in, but in the red world he was insubstantial in relation to the objects in stasis. He was like a mouse trying to open a refrigerator.

When he had determined which was the most plausible entrance to the stateroom, he spent just long enough out of the red world to work the latch and pull the door halfway open.

He went in, leaving it open behind him. He went down the several steps of the short ladderway to the narrow passageway between the port and starboard staterooms. The master stateroom seemed to be forward, dead ahead. The door was ajar. By putting his shoulder against it he was able to slowly force it far enough open to be able to sidle in. Charla stood in the burgundy murk, in quarter profile, a glass in her left hand, gesticulating at Joseph with her right. She wore a short loose robe and her hair hung glossy to her shoulders. Joseph leaned against the paneled wall near the bed, his arms folded, his expression skeptical. He wore a dark business suit, white shirt, figured tie.

Kirby walked over and stared at Charla from close range. It startled him that he could have forgotten how perfect in texture, how remarkable and how sensuous her face was. It shook him slightly. He had thought he had gained enough sweet insulation from Bonny Lee to be immune to this older woman. But being this close to her made his knees feel loose and uncertain. He felt compelled to proclaim his newfound freedom from the obsession she had so quickly established, and so he leered at her and said, "Hi, sweetheart," and reached a hand toward her and fondled her. It was an unsuccessful performance. The leer didn't fit his mouth. The words were dead, as though he had spoken them directly into a wad of insulation. And the remarkable breasts felt like plastic bowls behind chain mesh.

He was about to turn and go in search of Bonny Lee and Betsy when he realized that something might be gained by listening to them. If they were here alone, it was unlikely either of the girls were being harmed. He searched the luxurious cabin for a suitable hiding place. On a less roomy craft, the area under the bed would have been used for stowage. But it was empty under there, and there was room enough. With the watch in hand, he could halt the scene if suddenly there was any hint of danger. He wiggled into the constricted area and, once he was concealed, bent the edge of the hanging spread back the way it had been.

The instant he depressed the stem of the watch he heard a great staccato torrent of a language he could not understand. The sound stopped abruptly. She said something in the rising inflection of a question, and walked over and slammed the door. She said something in the firm voice of command.

He answered casually, indifferently.

"If I say we speak English, Joseph, we shall speak English. Why did the door swing open? Rene is the only one with fluent English and he's ashore. I didn't get where I am by trusting anyone."

"Even yourself," Joseph said.

"We can't be too careful in this matter. Please don't make bad jokes. We tried the utmost care with Krepps, and failed miserably, several times. I must have whatever it is which gave him such strength, Joseph."

The bed creaked as Joseph sat on it. With his cheek against the rug, Kirby could look out and see Charla's bare feet. They moved over to stand in front of Joseph, as Joseph said in an ironic tone, "What do you expect? A device to read minds? A cloak of invisibility?"

"He read our minds, Joseph. He guessed our plans. He was a devil! Winter has whatever it is. But he is less of a man than the old one was. Now we can get it before he learns to use it well."

"Whatever it is. And if he knows what it is."

"I'm convinced he does. I told you the things he said."

"He could have been bluffing."

"But it will be nice to be certain, one way or the other."

Joseph sighed audibly. "It is still a most delicate matter. I would feel much better if that damned girl hadn't been so quick and so clever. What if she informs the police? That will complicate matters."

Charla laughed and sat beside Joseph. Kirby could have reached and touched her bare heel. "That one is not interested in the police. The way it was done, I was reminded of myself, long ago. Naturally those idiots you hired were not expert, but even if they had been competent she might still have—"

"Just how did she manage it?"

"One of them had a place he thought would be safe, to keep her there until we could bring her here, or at least prepare her to be brought here so she would be quiet and humble and answer properly if she were asked questions. He told me about the place. It seemed adequate. I should have been warned by the way she eluded Rene and Raoul, but I was concerned for her. She seemed totally unconscious. When I held a cigarette near her hand, there was no movement. I was planning how best to handle it if she were seriously hurt. The apartment we would use was over on the beach. It is on a canal. We could park behind it, out of sight, so no questions would be asked. I had them use care lifting her out of the car. Suddenly there was a veritable explosion, and I sat down rather painfully, and one of your idiots was rolling around groaning and hugging himself and the other was blinded by blood from his clawed forehead running into his eyes. The girl was running. She ran forty feet and dived over a low wall into the canal. By the time I reached the wall she was almost around a bend, swimming very strongly, leaving me with her cheap purse and a bruised seat. No, Joseph, that one will not go to the police. She knows who Winter is. She has the smell of money in her nostrils now, and when she has composed herself, she will think of some way to make the money come true. The police won't assist her in that. I do not know if Winter has known her long, but I would say she has possibilities, that one, hah? We could find her useful, I think. More than poor Betsy ever was. With Winter as a lure, possibly we can trap her. I found her address in the purse, so I sent your idiots to watch it and intercept her should she return to her place."

"And bring her here?"

"Of course not! Take her to that beach apartment and phone us here that they have her."

"But what if she goes back to the house?"

"Rene has been instructed. They will hold her there."

"This is a tiresome country, Charla," Joseph said. "In any reasonably well-managed country all of this would be restricted to a few officials, and you would know the price of the officials in matters of this sort. Here they scream delicate matters over the air and spread them all over their vulgar newspapers, and every moron on the street becomes a potential problem. We should never attempt any sort of business matter here. It was always better elsewhere, particularly in Spain, when Juan March would help with the arrangements."

"Don't whine, darling. We had no choice. Now Winter and the Farnham woman are in our custody. And Betsy will be given no further chance to become a problem. And even if we fail to pick up that Beaumont girl, who will believe her? And even if they should, we'll be well out of reach. We'll have all the time in the world to find out everything, and plan how to make use of it. Believe me, it will work just as smoothly as it would have the way we first planned it, before all this dreadful hue and cry began. Kirby Winter was troublesome for a time, but that is ended."

"I do not care for this business of the packing cases," Joseph said.

"Then how else can we bring them aboard so easily? Daniel will drive the truck out there at eleven, and we'll have them stowed aboard a little after midnight, sleeping sweetly. If that police search completely overlooked that hull compartment, darling, why do you think the customs people will find it tomorrow? And we can show them the packing cases, filled with completely innocent supplies, to prove what came aboard in the night. Darling Joseph, when those two innocents awaken, they'll be in cozy beds, far at sea, without any idea how it was done or where they are being taken. And after all business details have been attended to, I think Miss Farnham might find the crew's quarters educational. Unless you have any amusing ideas."

"Her picture didn't enchant me, Charla dear."

"She's a bloodless, stilted, self-important little wretch, dear, with a quick temper and a natural talent for virginity, but she did appear slender and seemed to move well. I rather doubt that even with your talents you could debauch her."

"Is that a challenge, my dear?"

"I could, of course, but it would be a different sort of venture entirely."

"I'll decide after I have had a look at her."

"You're losing your sense of adventure, Joseph."

There was a low laugh, a rustle of moment, and Charla's heels were swung up and out of sight. "It is much more likely, my dear," he said, his voice slightly muffled, "that as I grow older I find it increasingly difficult to settle for anything less than the best the world can provide."

"Yet you continue to make comparisons."

"To reassure us both. Just as you do."

"How sweet! How very sweet!"

Kirby, with sweaty fingers, put a halt to whatever was going on, as well as to the rest of all concurrent cultural phenomena. He wormed his way out from under the bed. Charla had emerged from the robe. She had her head thrown back, her eyes closed, her lips smiling and parted. Her attitude made the business suit look particularly incongruous. He went over to the door and turned and looked at them again. He decided he could risk a fraction of a second to get the door open, without being noticed. He managed it and then, in the redness, pushed the door open far enough to slide out. Once he was in the corridor he braced himself and pushed it shut again. He could not latch it, but he could shut it almost all the way. He used other seconds of real time to test the doors of the other four staterooms. Three were empty. One was locked.

He considered the problem, and then spent five nervous moments in real time, ready to turn it off if he heard anyone approaching. When five minutes were up, he turned back to red. The master stateroom door had not been latched. He pulled it open. The business suit was not on the floor. It was arranged on a chair with a meticulous neatness. After one electrified glance at the bed, he decided he was cured of all lingering fragments of the Charla obsession. He had been uneasily apprehensive of making his invisible intrusion upon some scene of an evil so unspeakable it would fry his brain like grease on a skillet. But of all possible visions the one he had not expected had been that look of low comedy, like clowns belaboring each other with inflated bladders, like Harpo honking his cane, like a massive pratfall in a still shot from a Keystone Komedy. And what made it even more intensely ludicrous was the obvious air of deadly seriousness of the participants.

As he manipulated the soft lead sheathing that was Joseph Locordolos' sedate business suit, he realized that all reports to the contrary, as a spectator sport this activity was not even likely to replace tournament chess. As he pried pockets open, groping for keys, his tendency toward a howl of helpless laughter was smothered by a shocking thought. Suppose when he and Bonny Lee—would it have appeared as—

And, with a certain wry despair he realized it might seem the same. Thus he took another step toward joining the human race, the sweaty, ridiculous, pretentious, self-deluding, aspiring, flesh-trapped march of man.

The keys, six of them, were on a gold ring. He hung them in midair while he kneaded the suit back into orderliness, flattening it by leaning on it with open palms. He took the keys and swung the dead weight of the door open and shut again, without looking directly toward the sportive Charla and fun-loving Joseph.

It had to be a small key, and the second one he tried worked. He swung the door open. Betsy stared at him in complete astonishment. She had evidently been standing, looking out through the heavy glass of the sealed porthole. Her tan hair was rumpled, her face pale and without make-up. She wore a pale orange corduroy coverall arrangement, with short sleeves, a zipper down the front and a big silver buckle. It was a bad color for her and did not fit her properly.

"What in the world—"

He touched his fingers to his lips, closed the door and started to lock it with the key and then saw the oblong bolt and slid it into its socket. When he looked at her again she was trying to smile at him, and the tears were streaming out of her eyes. She came to him and he held her in his arms. She trembled and held him tightly, but made no sound of crying. She had a faintly sour smell and he wondered if it was the odor of pain and fear.

Finally she turned away and took a lurching step toward the deep bunk, turned and sat heavily, bent over and put her head between her knees. In a few moments she straightened up, smiling almost shyly. "Sorry. I almost fainted. I never faint." Her face twisted. "I guess it took a lot out of me. She—hurt me so."

He sat with her on the bunk, half facing her. "It was my fault."

"No," she said flatly. "Mine. I had to get cute. I had to try all the angles. I thought I could con her. I couldn't believe she'd ever really—do anything to me. And when I realized she was, I was going to be terribly brave. Joan at the stake. But in such a shamefully short time I was begging and babbling and betraying everybody. I'm so sorry, Kirby. I'm so ashamed. I told them where to find you and Wilma. Please forgive me."

"You should have told before she hurt you."

"And I would, the next time. It's such a simple way she does it, too. Just one of those damned electric reducing machines. She just ties those pad things on where you want them least, and revs the current up until you feel your own muscles beginning to tear you up. And not a mark, afterward. She's monstrous, Kirby. How did you get here? Where are they?"

"Keep your voice down, Betsy. They're just down the corridor, in the big stateroom. I think everything is going to be all right."

"Wilma didn't have a clue. My God, Kirby, she's a dreadful little prig. Terribly loyal. But she doesn't believe there really is any special thing they're after, unless she has it and doesn't know it. Where is she?"

"In a safe place for now, for a while, anyway. They had her for a time. Two of the men from the crew. Rene and Raoul."

"I remember Rene. Raoul is a new one, I guess. Rene is tough and quick and powerful and completely loyal to Charla. I never liked the way he'd look at me."

"They had both of us, in that house where Wilma was, but we—got away from them."

She looked startled. "Got away from them and—you got aboard and got into this cabin? That's very good indeed, Kirby. Maybe I made a low estimate."

"Joseph and Charla don't know I got away from them yet. They were going to bring me and Wilma aboard tonight in packing cases."

"Are you sure you didn't save them half the trouble?"

"I don't think so. I think it's going to be all right. You see —I found out what they're after."

"You did?"

"And I haven't any good ideas about how I can solve a lot of these damn legal problems, but I think I can get you off this boat."

"What is it? A handy dandy thought control machine? Or does it just melt big holes in the sides of boats?"

"You're sounding more like yourself."

"So I'm a little skeptical. Show me."

"It has—certain limitations, and I don't know how it works, and maybe I don't know how to get maximum use out of it yet. But I'll demonstrate it. It—it may frighten you, Betsy. It may frighten you quite badly because it—offends all reason. You'll try not to get hysterical if—it frightens you?"

"That's a luxury I don't think I can afford, Kirby Winter."

"All you need to know is the objective results."

"You mean it has something to do with that old—"

He stopped the flow of rational time, wondered whether he should get her used to it by degrees, then decided she was mentally strong enough to cope. He slowly pulled her rigid body out of the bunk, forced her over to a chair, leaned his weight on her thighs and pushed her down into it. Then he went over and stood by the door and picked time up where he had left it.

"—watch?" she said. She gave a leap of violent surprise, turned deathly pale, shut her eyes tightly and opened them again and stared at him. "My word," she whispered. "I didn't know what to expect, but this is—" She frowned. "Did I black out somehow?"

"No time passed at all. It was instantaneous."

"You moved me to here, and you to over there. What is the range?"

"Let's say it's about as far as I can carry a kitchen stove."

"You carried me somehow?"

"With difficulty."

"While time took time out?"

"Exactly."

"You could carry me past someone and they wouldn't notice?"

"No more than you would."

She nodded her head, quite slowly. "Your revered uncle, my friend, had quite an edge. An edge, in fact, so filled with interesting possibilities, it makes that twenty-seven million you gave away look like candy for the children. Why didn't he use it to—make himself king of the world? He could have managed it. Like a man with a rifle in the dawn of history."

"Maybe being king would have bored him. Being Santa Claus was more his style. Or maybe he had to keep what he had from being too obvious, or other men would have started looking in the same direction."

She nodded again. "Charla was convinced there was something to look for." She lost her thoughtful expression and stared across the room at him with a look of fearful intensity. "One thing we do know, Kirby Winter. A thing like that must never belong to my aunt. Never. She's bought every kind of immunity they sell, and she uses it all without mercy."

Suddenly there was a hurried sound in the corridor, a mutter of voices, and then a sound of heavy hammering.

Above the bunk there was a hiss and click of electronic circuits, and then Charla's voice came into the room, the low purring tones vastly amplified.

"My darlings!" she said. "How terribly fortunate I left that circuit open! And how glad I am we had the patience to listen. Dear Joseph even had the presence of mind to begin taping it after the first few words. We can play it back for clues, you know, but possibly we have enough. How did you put it, dear? A way to make time take time out. I have suddenly lost my respect for Omar Krepps. With that ability, he did very little with it, comparatively. While I'm talking I can't hear you, of course. That sound you must have heard was a timber being wedged between your door and the opposite side of the corridor. Apparently your miracle will not melt prison walls. I hope not. So at least we have created an impasse, have we not? And it will give us all time to think."

Kirby shuddered and looked at Betsy. Her eyes were closed and she was biting down on a bloodless lip. "I didn't know," she whispered. "I didn't know. But, knowing her, I should have guessed."

He went over to her and put his lips close to her ear. "All we have to do is get them to open that door."

"It is really quite amusing," Charla said, "that what I should have been looking for is actually that old gold watch you showed me, Kirby dear. The little telescope is a rather nice disarming touch. Really, I expected some sort of procedural thing, notes and formulae, something like that. But this really seems far more practical, a portable, useful, innocent-appearing device. What did you say, Joseph? Excuse me a moment, darlings."

"Damned witch," Betsy said distinctly.

Charla spoke through the concealed speaker again. "Joseph has had a fruitful idea. We shall have a hole burnt in your steel door, darlings, just large enough for the watch, and then you can pass it out through the hole. Otherwise I think you might find things becoming highly unpleasant."

When the hiss of the circuit stopped, Kirby said, "Before I'll do that, Charla, I'll take the end of the chain and I'll slam it against the inside of this steel door until I'm damned well certain it's unusable, unidentifiable junk."

"Dog in the manger?" Charla asked.

"Precisely."

"You bluff well, Kirby."

"No bluff, Charla. I'm infected by a chronic disease called a sense of responsibility. I'm a very noble fellow. I'd rather destroy it than have you have it to use."

"Nobility confuses me," Charla said. "Isn't it the traditional disease of adolescence? Aren't you rather old for it, Kirby?"

"I'm having a delayed adolescence, Mrs. O'Rourke. But you can check it out, if you don't believe me. Cut the hole in the door. The minute the chunk falls out, I start battering this gizmo to bits."

There was no answer, no faint hiss that preceded each speech.

"You've got her worried," Betsy whispered.

"She should be worried," Kirby said in a normal tone. "I mean every damn word of it. I can't get out of here. Okay. So nobody gets to use it."

Charla spoke again. "It would make me terribly angry, Kirby," she said with a tone of gentle regret. "I think both of you would have to die in the most unimaginable agony. You see, Betsy would have to share your heroics. And Miss Farnham. And Miss Beaumont. It's quite a heavy responsibility upon you, dear Kirby. I know it will trouble you."

When the hiss stopped Betsy asked in a thin and shaking voice, "What if he gives it to you, Charla?"

"Freedom, my dear. And a generous gift of money. I shan't be small about it."

He whispered to Betsy. "She won't want anybody around to tell what she has." Betsy sat quite still, then gave a nod of dreadful comprehension.

Charla laughed softly. "Or, if that seems to be too good to be true, I can at least promise something so quick and so painless you'll never know what happened. We have a lot of time for you to think it over, dears. No one will come aboard until we ask for clearance. So do talk it over for a bit."

"Charla?" Betsy called. "Charla!"

The speaker remained silent.

Chapter Twelve

Betsy Alden lay in the bunk on her back, her eyes wide open, her face expressionless, while Kirby Winter prowled the stateroom. It was fifteen feet long by eleven feet wide. There was an alcove with a sliding door containing a head, a small stainless steel lavatory, and a medicine cabinet. He inspected the two sealed portholes, too small for escape even if he could find something to shatter the heavy glass. He located the air-conditioning inlet and the exhaust vent. Twice he put himself into the red world of stasis.

One idea began to seem more and more feasible. He sat on the bunk and said, "I think I've got something."

"Nothing will work," she said listlessly.

"Listen to it, at least."

"We're whipped, Kirby."

He yanked her up and slapped her face sharply. "Damn you, Betsy. At least listen!"

She listened. She thought the plan was madness. But she could think of nothing better. Once she had accepted it, her help was efficient. They soaked blankets in water, getting them as saturated as possible. They spread them in one corner. She helped him heap all the other bedding and combustibles near the door. The fire started slowly at first, but when they were certain it had caught, they crawled under the sodden blankets, and had wet towels ready to wrap around their faces. Smoke became thick in the cabin.

Suddenly Charla spoke, with anger in her tone. "Very clever, dears, but it won't work, you know. Are you holding rags by the outlet?"

When the hiss stopped, Kirby began to cough, trying to sound as if he were choking to death. The furniture was beginning to crackle, and he hoped she could hear that. He felt heat on his face. He prodded Betsy. She was ready for her cue. She gave a scream of such convincing agony he wondered for a moment if the fire had somehow reached her. "Help!" she screamed. "Help me! Let me out!" She screamed again, and faded it off into a grisly bubbling sound.

He heard the commotion in the corridor. He knew what would happen next. They would feel the steel door, and feel the heat coming through it. The blankets were beginning to steam. There were shouts and a sound of hammering and then the door which he had unlatched was burst open, and just as he worked the watch to stop it all, he saw something aimed toward him in the murk, heard a sharp cracking sound. The flame stopped. The steam was motionless. The heat was gone. The blankets felt like slabs of molded oak. He worked his way out. Joseph stood just inside the door, almost in the static flames, aiming a long-barreled pistol with a rigid little tongue of flame protruding from the muzzle. Staying below the layer of smoke, Kirby searched the air between himself and the muzzle, and found the small slug suspended at the midway point. Assuming, he thought with a hollow feeling in his belly, a velocity of a thousand feet per second, and it had another seven feet to go before catching me squarely in the face, had I been seven one thousandths of a second slower—

Suddenly, to his astonishment, he saw that the bullet had a perceptible movement. He glanced at the gold watch and saw he had given himself a little over a half hour. It was the first thing he had seen move in the red world. He went close to it and timed its velocity, and it seemed to him that as he counted off ten seconds, it moved almost one full inch. It was a clue to the ratio between the two worlds. Two minutes per foot. Or a ratio of two minutes to one one thousandth of a second. Thus, one full hour of red time equalled three hundredths of a second of objective time. Suddenly he stirred out of his speculative trance. When he moved his face into smoke it felt like thick rubbery cobwebs. He pulled the girl up to a convenient height and, crouched below the smoke, pulled her past Joseph and into the corridor. Charla stood beyond the door, her expression anxious. The emotion he felt toward her was not fear or hate or anger, but merely a vast impatience, an irritability. He left Betsy suspended and went back in and plucked the lead snail out of the air and took it out into the corridor, aimed it at Charla's bland honeyed forehead and pushed it as forcefully as he could, releasing it an inch from the center of her forehead. He went back toward the flames, slowly bent Joseph's golden arm until the muzzle was directly under Joseph's chin, aimed upward, the silent tongue of blue flame a half inch from the jowl. He gave the trigger finger a forceful tug. He towed the girl along the corridor to the steps up to the cockpit hatch. It was ajar. He pushed it open and went back and got her and forced her out into the night. The sun had set over the land and the sky was like a banked fire but it was not as difficult to see as he had anticipated.

As he towed her along the dock he staggered with his weariness. He did not know how long he could continue. He had to find a safe place. He moved off the dock and into deep shadows and set her upright and leaned her against a tree. He peered at the dial of the gold watch and found there were a few minutes left. He put his thumb on the watch stem and he knew it was a trigger. They deserved to die. Yet he had the curious feeling that he would also be destroyed if he pressed it. Why should he pass ultimate judgment?

Suddenly, in all his weariness, he had a feeling of antic pleasure, of a wild exhilaration. Bonny Lee was free. Wilma was safe. Betsy was safe. The world was new again, and there was nothing able to stop him. He turned and ran through the bloody twilight as fast as he could. He went back into the yacht. The lead slug was touching her smooth forehead. He pulled it away, pushed it toward the flames. He pulled the muzzle away from Joseph's chin. He stepped back just as the red time ended. The pistol cracked, the flames crackled, Charla's face was changed by a look of vast alarm. He spun the world red again, stilling the flames. He looked at them as he now knew his uncle must have looked at them in times past. Ridiculous people. Fair game. A mildly interesting irritant in a greedy world. Death had too much stature, too much dignity, to be awarded them now. The watch could provide more suitable punishments. But at the moment he was too exhausted to follow through. He found a cabin and stretched out, set the watch to a full hour, suspended a heavy ashtray a few inches over his chest and went peacefully to sleep.

He awoke much refreshed, stopped objective time again and went to see what he could do about Charla and Joseph. He took Charla off the yacht. When he was near where he had left Betsy, he took a breathing space and walked over and looked at her. She had taken three steps away from the tree, and she looked terribly confused.

He tugged the stubborn burden of Charla all the way to the nearest intersection, stopping frequently to look around for something suitable. He found it at the intersection, waiting for the light to change. It was a big gray truck with Navy markings. He peered in over the tailgate. About thirty men sat on the benches that ran along either side of the truck. They were not recruits. They had that bronzed competent look of career men, who, when faced with any unusual situation, would not be at a loss.

Sadly, slowly, he bent the short robe off the suspended figure of Charla. After the fevered dreams of performing this very act, it seemed wasteful that it had to be done with so little emotion. Regretfully he admired the exquisite structure and texture of her. He pushed her into a handy position, clambered over the tailgate and hauled her inside. He stretched her out across five military laps, pressed her down solidly, and climbed back out of the truck. It would give her, he thought, some unforgettable moments. He looked into the truck at the tableau in red marble, the bored male faces unaware of the rich burden. If he had gauged their reactions properly, the very first response would be the firm clasp of a bronzed hairy hand, right over her startled mouth.

It had taken twenty minutes to dispose of Charla. He went back after Joseph. He was not only a more difficult burden, but it was troublesome to think of some situation which would be as memorable to him as Charla's awakening would be to her. He pushed and tugged and floated Joseph all the way to the intersection, then left him suspended in air while he scouted a nearby cocktail lounge. It was doing an excellent business. He walked through to the back beyond the rest rooms and found a storeroom. The door was ajar. The key was in the lock. He went back among the throng and selected three women. He picked three mature ones without wedding rings, three who looked glossy and competent and somewhat virulent. They had style, prominent jaw lines and a few well-concealed traces of erosion. He trudged them back to the hallway outside the storeroom, one at a time. As he undressed them, one at a time, in midair, and levered them into the small dark room, it occurred to him that he was becoming so adept at it he could apply for a position fixing department store windows. The third one gave him pause. She had a truly astonishing tattoo.

By the time he plodded in with Joseph, time was growing short. He stripped him hastily, shouldered him in with his new acquaintances and slowly pulled the door shut. Clothing was suspended in the air all around him. He tried to turn the key, but he could not. Time had almost run out anyway. He switched the watch to normal time, turned the key and took it out of the lock and immediately switched back to enough red time to leave and get back to Betsy. The second touch on the watch stem cut short the very beginning of a scream. The clothing had fallen to the hallway floor.

He walked back to Betsy. He stood beyond her line of vision and turned the world on. She turned and saw him and gasped. "This—this is something nobody could ever get used to! But the damned thing works!"

He looked toward the intersection. The light changed. The Navy truck started up and moved slowly away through the dusk. He looked over and saw the billowing of smoke against the dark sky. He heard a distant sound of sirens approaching.

"It worked," he said.

"We came within an inch of getting murdered or fried and you stand there grinning like a moron! What's the matter with you?"

"Murdered, fried or shot."

"Shot?"

"You missed that part of it, Betsy dear."

She looked at him with a haggard, accusing face. "And you carried me right past them?"

"Yes indeed."

"And they just—stood there?"

"Like statues."

She moved closer to him. "Could you have killed them?"

"Yes."

"And you didn't?"

He thought her mouth had an exceptionally ugly look. They were in a small park area sheltered from the flow of headlights and the blue glare of the mercury vapor lights on the avenue. Her damp stained orange coveralls smelled of smoke. Her hair was tangled and her face was smudged.

"I had that idea, to tell you the truth."

"You fool! You do it again, you hear? Make everything stop. Go back aboard and kill them. Who could ever prove anything? Go kill both of them. They'll never give up. They'll never give up until they're dead."

He studied her. And he remembered how close he had come to doing just what she now suggested. Nothing would have ever been the same again. The watch, Bonny Lee, all would have been changed. And he would have lost one of the most precious attributes of this unique ability to make time stand still—the additive of wry mischief, of ironic joy. Bonny Lee had understood that instinctively. Murder would have turned the watch into a perpetual solemnity and a perpetual guilt—because, regardless of provocation, the owner of the watch was beyond the need to kill.

"Betsy dear, Charla and Joseph are too busy right now."

"Busy!"

"Aunt Charla is sort of riding around enjoying the evening. And Joseph is making some new friends."

"You act as if this is all some kind of a joke!" she said furiously.

He heard men shouting on the dock. The fire trucks arrived. He took Betsy by the arm and walked her away from there, staying in the shadows and on the darker sides of the streets. When they came to a shopping area where a cut-rate department store was open late, he left her in a shadowy place and went into the frozen silence and stillness of the store and found fresh clothing for himself, taking care to select the lightest weight sandals he could find. He changed, selected clothing for her, packed it into a lightweight suitcase and towed it on out. He realized he had been careful not to take anything that anyone was looking directly at. He was acquiring the habit of a basic ethic of using the time-stop. Do not frighten the innocent unnecessarily. With Charla and Joseph he had violated this concept. The sailors were the innocents, and he did not imagine they would seriously question the origin of the gift. And there was enough subjective phenomena in cocktail lounges to make objective magic almost unnoticeable.

When he returned to Betsy he did not bother to reappear

in the same place and position. She started violently. They walked further into a small park. He opened the suitcase on a bench. She went behind bushes and changed to the cotton dress and Orlon cardigan he had brought her, and stuffed Charla's sodden playsuit under a bush. At a drinking fountain under a street lamp he held the mirror he had brought her while she wiped the smudges from her face and used the hair brush he had brought her, and used the stolen lipstick.

He risked a cruising cab and had the driver stop a block away from the Hotel Birdline. She went in with the money he gave her and rented a room, using a name they had agreed upon. He loafed in the shadows for ten minutes, and then halted time and went into the hotel. He looked at the register and saw they had given her room 303. He went up the stairs. She had left the door ajar as agreed. When he materialized instantaneously in front of her, her leap of surprise was smaller than before. He closed the door and said, "You're doing better, Miss Betsy."

"I think I'm just too tired to react. What is the world like when you're—doing that?"

"Absolutely silent. Red light. No motion anywhere. It's like being in a strange kind of a dream."

"Does it seem evil? Or is that a silly question."

"It could be evil. I don't think it's a silly question. I guess it would depend on the person using it. I guess it would sort of—multiply whatever you are by ten. Because it's absolute freedom. You can make your fantasies come true. And if your fantasies are—sick, then that's the way you'll use it. Maybe it's just like any other kind of power. I haven't really had time to think about the implications. And not much time now. You'll be safe here and I have a girl to find."

"Just any girl?"

"Not exactly."

"Your face is dirty."

"I'll use guest rights on the shower."

"Of course. Go ahead."

He showered and put the stolen clothing back on. He reached into his pocket and found the watch gone. He ran out of the bathroom. She was sitting huddled on the edge of the bed. She held the watch out to him at arm's length. Her eyes looked haunted. "I didn't have the guts," she whispered.

"What did you have in mind?"

"Please don't be angry. I just wanted to try. But I couldn't. Maybe—I was afraid of my own fantasies. They aren't—particularly nice." She lifted her chin with a kind of tired defiance. "I would have killed them."

"I know."

"For many many reasons. But you didn't. So maybe you have the right to use that magic, and I don't."

"You had the sense not to try. That's something."

She stood up and sighed and moved into his arms. She turned her mouth up to him and he kissed her without passion.

"Will you come back here?" she asked.

"I don't know. I'll leave money in case I can't. I'll phone at least."

When she looked up at him her eyes seemed softer, more gray than green. There was a faint smell of smoke caught in that palomino hair. Her back was hard and slender, under his hands. "I owe you lots," she said. "And I think you are quite a guy. If you can make any use at all of a sort of neurotic but very grateful girl, and you want to come back here, feel free." She pushed herself away. "Have I said something so terribly amusing?"

"I'm sorry. It isn't you. It's me. I was thinking of all the other nights I spent in this pleasure palace. It was just sort of ironic for the moment. Betsy, you are very tired and very sweet and very desirable."

"Desirable in general. Nothing specific."

"I'm sorry. Nothing specific."

"Then I'm sorry, too, because I do feel sort of specific." She sighed and smiled and touched his cheek. "Go find your girl."

Two blocks from the hotel he suddenly came upon a disguise which would render him completely invisible in nighttime Miami. It was a little past nine o'clock. He removed the disguise from a man who was in no condition to realize he was being robbed. Kirby donned the disguise and looked at his reflection in a store window. A comedy derby, a bright red plastic cane and a big round beribboned badge on which was printed "Eddie Beeler—Lubbock, Texas." He lurched slightly, faked a soft hiccup and nodded at himself with satisfaction.

He hailed a cab and asked to be taken to Rio's in North Miami.

The driver said, "You wanta go where the action is, you don't wanta go there, sport."

"Going to meet some buddies there."

"Okay, so what you do, you go in and bring them out and I'll take you where the action is."

The driver started up. He had the news on. Kirby asked him to turn up the volume. ". . . were involved in the search for Kirby Winter and Wilma Farnham when police traced a shipment of Winter's personal possessions to the yacht. Prompt action by area firefighting units prevented serious damage to the luxury vessel. The scene of the fire looked like attempted arson, but the three crew members aboard at the time can shed no light on the matter. The stateroom was occupied by Betsy Alden, actress niece of Mrs. O'Rourke, and as yet the police have been unable to locate either Miss Alden or Mrs. O'Rourke. While the fire was being brought under control, Joseph Locordolos, owner of the *Glorianna*, was being apprehended in a nearby cocktail lounge. Locordolos, severely battered and lacerated by the women upon whom he was forcing his attentions, and in a semi-hysterical condition, was booked for assault, exposure and lewd behavior, and is reported as not yet being in condition to be questioned regarding the two women who were aboard or the origin of the fire.

"A further element of mystery concerns the other two members of the crew of the *Glorianna*, Rene Bichat and Raoul Feron who were apprehended earlier today in the Hallandale home of Professor Wellerly of Florida Eastern. When Metro police went to the house in response to an anonymous phone tip, they found considerable damage to the house and found the two seamen in the shuttered living room, bound hand and foot. The two men have refused to explain their presence there and are being held.

"Evidence collected on the scene indicates Wilma Farnham may have been hiding out in the Wellerly home. Professor Wellerly and his family are in Europe, and he is a friend of Roger Farnham, Miss Farnham's brother, who denies any knowledge of his sister's whereabouts.

"Another factor, as yet unexplained, was the presence of a sports car behind the Wellerly residence, registered in the name of Bonny Lee Beaumont, a night club entertainer now working in the Greater Miami area. As yet police have been unable to contact Miss Beaumont.

"It is now believed that there was a closer connection between the people aboard the *Glorianna* and Kirby Winter and the Farnham woman than was first presumed. But an aura of mystery thickens around the millions embezzled from the estate of the late Omar Krepps."

The news ended. The driver turned the radio down and said, "Why the hell do they have to make it sound so hard? This Winter had it all set up for his buddies to bring that Glory Annie here and take him off with his broad and the money. But it's so much money and so much heat, everybody wants a bigger cut, so they start fighting among themselves and they screw up the whole deal for everybody. Why is that so hard to figure?"

"So where are they now?"

"Who knows, sport? This town has a million transient rooms, and there's so many ways to get out of it, you can't seal it off. Right? And there's enough confusion going on, how can anybody find anybody? It's like the whole town is going nuts. Beach riots, crazy traffic jams, people all over claiming they're seeing spooks. What it is, it's the humidity. It gets just to the right place and this town always starts to unravel. I seen it before."

When they reached Rio's, Kirby told the driver there would be no point in his waiting. The structure looked as though a pagoda had been mated with Mount Vernon, then boarded up and used as a proving ground for neon tubes. It sat in the middle of an asphalt field half full of cars. At intervals, a little worm of blue neon would appear way over on the left, out of total blackness. It would start to move across, picking up speed, picking up more width, additional colors until, when it reached the far right it occupied the whole height of the building. Then it turned into a huge white waterfall. Then it said RIO'S—in red—big enough to drive a truck through the O. And, as it was shouting RIO'S, three banks of floodlights flicked on, one after the other, illuminating three plywood girls, thirty feet tall. The first one was a brunette labeled Perry Meson. The middle one was Bonny Lee. The third was a redhead disastrously named Pooty-Tat O'Shaugnessy. They were all smiling. They were bare, except for the strategic placement of their name signs. They were all of a height, standing elbow to elbow, reproduced by some color photomural process, and the six breasts aligned, big as bushel baskets, had a fearsome implausibility which induced, rather than lust, a feeling of inadequacy. This peculiar vision of his love gave Kirby a feeling of petulance and indignation, like a small boy discovering he is expected to share his candied apple with the entire first grade. It was but a minor compensation to note that the incredible Pooty-Tat made the other two look immature. RIO'S flickered off and the lighted cutouts lingered another two seconds. The building was in total darkness for a moment and then the little blue worm reappeared.

When he hauled the heavy door open, he was assailed by a blast of noise so tangible he wondered that it did not push him back out. He went through the hat check foyer without relinquishing funny hat or cane, and moved into the smoky gloom. Waiters pounced, scurried, slid through tiny spaces between the shadowy tables. Everyone seemed to be yelling to be heard over the brass din of a small and exceptionally noisy group of musicians on a cantilevered shelf playing an accelerated version of "Smoke Gets in Your Eyes," with the compulsive, crashing beat of a twist number. A lot of people seemed to be yelling "Go!" in time to the beat. At the far end of the large room, on a small platform stage, bathed in a hot pink spotlight stood Miss Pooty-Tat O'Shaugnessy wearing nought but a drowsy smile, a sequined G-string and two little silk tassels. She had her fingers laced at the nape of her neck and seemed totally relaxed, except that one little red tassel was revolving clockwise, the other counterclockwise, each completing one revolution exactly on the smashing beat.

"Parm me!" a waiter snarled and shoved Kirby out of his trance. He went to the crowded bar and found a four-inch space between two beefy men. The service was fast, the drink small, weak and expensive. When the harried bartender brought his change, Kirby tried to ask when Bonny Lee would be on, but the barman was gone before he could get the words out. At the final thump of the last bar, Pooty-Tat added a bump to the other activities, and the pink spot went off.

"She ain't on tonight," one of the beefy men said.

"Cop trouble, somebody said," the other man said.

"How come?" the first man said.

"Her car got used on a B and E that went sour and they made her through the plates, but she should have showed and said it was borrowed. You fade and they nail you every time, like accessory."

When the bartender started to snatch Kirby's empty glass, Kirby grabbed him by the wrist and said, "How can I get in touch with Bonny Lee?"

The man yanked himself free and said, "Try a classified ad, doll."

Five minutes later, as Kirby was wondering what to try next, there was a tap on his shoulder. He turned and saw an old waiter with a face like a tired bulldog. The waiter moved away, giving a little jerk of his head for Kirby to follow him. Ten feet from the bar the waiter stopped.

"I play a little game, okay? Like I say a front name and you give me the rest of it, okay? Bernie?"

Kirby stared at him blankly. As the waiter shrugged and started to turn away, Kirby said, "Sabbith?"

"Slow thinker, huh. Come on with me."

Kirby followed him along the side of the big room, through a door, down a corridor and past a noisy kitchen to other doors. He knocked on one of them. "Yes?" a high clear voice called.

"It's Raymond. I got with me maybe the guy you wannit."

"Let him in, love. And thank you so much."

Raymond opened the door and let him in. It was a small, incredibly cluttered room, harshly and unpleasantly lighted. Pooty-Tat sat on a ratty couch eating a steak sandwich, sharing the couch with a precarious pile of clothes, cartons, magazines, empty Coke bottles, paper editions, phonograph records and other debris. She wore a blue denim smock.

"Do sit down," she said. The dressing table bench was the only place available. She had a high voice, a rather chilly and precise English accent, with that special clarity of tone English girls often have.

"Actually, love, I hardly expected such a festive look. But the little scar is just where she said it would be, so you must be the one. Do take off that insane hat, Mr. Winter."

"Is she all right?"

"You do ask that rather nicely. Concern, anxiety. As far as I know, she is perfectly all right."

"Where is she?"

"In due time, Mr. Winter. I have been wondering about you. We are all terribly fond of Bonny Lee. A limited background of course, but marvelous instincts. Sometimes her instincts fail her, though, and she does become involved with some horrid sod. Then we do what we can, you see."

"I would like to know where—"

"Are you quite certain you are good for her, Mr. Winter? You do seem to have involved her in some sort of stickiness. And you're even more of a fugitive than she at the moment. I can't pretend to know much about it, but haven't you made off with rather a lot of money? Don't look so alarmed, love. I trust her completely, and she trusts me. I wouldn't turn you in."

"I didn't mean to get her into any trouble or danger."

"You certainly *seem* harmless enough. You have quite an earnest look. You see, I was just getting up when she rang me up, and I had to scurry over to the Beach and pick her up. She'd cadged a dime to phone me, and she was in a drugstore, absolutely sopping wet, terribly busy fending off a randy little clerk. But she would not take time to change. She was frantic with worry about you. I couldn't even drive fast enough to suit her. We went to the health school and picked up three of my friends. I have this ridiculous letch for horribly muscular men. They're invariably dumb as oxen and sexually not very enterprising, but sometimes they are useful if one anticipates a brawl. So then we went scooting to Hallandale, with Bonny Lee on the edge of the seat using rather bad language, but the place was crawling with police officers. We parked a block away and I sent my brightest oaf to go find out what was up. No sign of you, he said, or of some girl Bonny Lee was asking about. Just two rather bitter and surly fellows, low types apparently, being led into a police vehicle. So then we took my fellows back to their muscle flexing. Bonny Lee was wondering what she should do about her poor little abandoned car. She had stopped fretting about you. In fact she seemed awfully amused about something, but wouldn't give me a clue. I took her to that horrid nest amongst those squadrons of tireless old ladies, but quite suddenly she scrooched down and hissed at me to go right on by. It seems two unsavory types were parked on her street, the two she had apparently eluded by plunging into a canal. She was all for our gathering up my friends once more and returning to give them a bashing about, but I must say I had begun to have quite enough of this darting about, and I became a bit cross, so I took her back to my place where at last she had a chance to get out of that dank clothing and rinse the salt out of her hair."

"Is she there now?"

"You are an impatient fellow. She was going to come to work until we heard over the radio that the police wanted a chat with her. She had a perfectly reasonable impulse to turn herself in and explain, but the more she thought about how she would explain things, the less she wanted to try. And she thought that if they did happen to hold her for questioning, you might hear about it and do some utterly idiotic thing like dashing to her rescue. She seemed to assume you would be searching for her, and when I expressed small reasonable doubt, she became quite ugly about it. She was afraid you might go to her place, and there was no way to warn you. We made arrangements about how I might contact you and identify you should you come here."

There was a muffled roar, a concerted shout. Miss O'Shaugnessy tilted her head. "Dear Perry. She always gets that same response to that part of her act. The child is incredibly flexible."

"I'm anxious to see Bonny Lee."

"Of *course* you are, and I would have sent you dashing to my place if you'd arrived earlier. But it is after eleven, you know. And I had a dear friend arriving at my place at eleven to nap and wait for me, an absolute bronzed giant of an airlines pilot, with the most astonishing external voluntary muscle structure I've ever seen. The deltoideus, triceps brachia, latissimus dorsi and trapezius are like great marvelous wads of brown weathered stone. The poor lamb has just enough awareness to push all his little buttons and levers to get his aircraft from here to there and back, and he crinkles charmingly when he smiles, but it would be too confusing to him to find Bonny Lee at my place. He wouldn't know how to react, and it would upset him. So it was arranged that she would leave before eleven. She has my little car and she is wearing some of my clothing, and she will be at Bernie Sabbith's apartment at midnight. She hopes you will meet her there, but in the event you don't, she'd planned to enlist the help of Bernie and his friends in whatever gruesome difficulties you two seem to have gotten into. Actually, I think all Bernie can contribute to any situation is additional confusion, but perhaps some use can be made of that. So, you see, you have time to spare. And you've been watching every morsel of this sandwich, you know."

She went to the kitchen. A few minutes after she returned, a sandwich and coffee was brought to her little dressing room.

"Does—uh—Bonny Lee do the same sort of act you do, Miss O'Shaugnessy?"

"My name is Lizbeth, love. Lizbeth Perkins, actually. You are a rather stuffy fellow, aren't you? What if she did exactly the same routines? Would it make her unworthy of you?"

"I just wondered," he said, miserably.

"Have no fear, love. The degree one is required to strip is in inverse ratio to one's other talents. Your darling has a lovely voice, and she's getting better all the time with those bongos. And she moves about well. I suspect the pictures outside upset you? Bonny Lee was upset too, and if you look closely, you'll see that though Perry and I are as nature made us, some clever wretch with an airbrush removed Bonny Lee's little frivolous bandeau. But she wasn't agitated about the exposure, love. She was jealous of her category—entertainer rather than stripper. You men are such dismal creatures, really, beset with Edwardian scruples. I can't sing a note, and as a child I trained for ballet, but whoever heard of a prima ballerina measuring forty-one, twenty-five, thirty-seven? What those slack-jawed idiots out there fail to realize is how many hundreds and hundreds of sweaty hours of brute labor it has taken for me to develop the skill to flex all the muscles of my body, singly or in any desired sequence. It's not what one could call a skill of any historic significance, Mr. Winter, but it pleases the fools, supports me well, and keeps me in a condition of astonishing health. Is it somehow more reprehensible than being able to bash a small ball a long distance with a club? Dear me, I do hope Bonny Lee hasn't become emotionally involved with a dingy little moralist."

"I didn't mean to—"

"Hush, love. I'm merely educating you to a proper level to appreciate Bonny Lee. She is a dear child, loving and honest and gay. And you must enjoy her for exactly what she is, the way one enjoys sunshine and gardens. If you try to confine her or restrict her or change her into what you think is a more suitable image, she will very probably break your heart. She's terribly young, you know. Old in some ways, young in others. In time she might well become very famous, if clods like you can keep from making her feel coarse and insecure."

"I think I see what you mean."

"I hope you do, love. If I didn't suspect you have possibilities, I wouldn't have wasted the time and the words."

"I'm not very—deft about girls, Lizbeth."

"So much the better. Deft men fall into dim patterns. And the dreadful clue to all of them is that they seem to feel they are doing the girl some enormous favor. I like a man to feel grateful, and bloody few of them do. And the worldly ones seem to feel obligated to prove their skill by showing off a whole arsenal of nasty little tricks which they seem to feel should induce an absolute frenzy. My word, I've had it up to here with being compared to a cello or a sports car. I'm a rather direct woman, Mr. Winter, and I like love to be direct and pleasant and on the cozy side, and as comfortable as one can make it. So don't fret about being unaccustomed to girls. I suspect Bonny Lee finds it all rather sweet. And don't you dare brood about her other affairs. You'll merely poison your own mind and spoil it for both of you. She will be totally, absolutely faithful to you for as long as the game will last, and that is all you can expect or should hope for."

He finished the last of the coffee and put the cup aside. "This is all very interesting, and I suppose you are an unusual woman, and maybe you can't help being so damned defensive, but I am getting Goddamned well tired of listening to a lot of little lectures from women. I am tired of having my head patted, and I am sick of a lot of over-simplified little bite-sized pieces of philosophy about life and love. I just happen to think the world is a little more complex than that. And with your kind indulgence, Lizbeth, I shall go right on making my own stuffy and sentimental and unreasonable mistakes in my own way. I have had a very long day, Lizbeth. The mind of man cannot comprehend the kind of a day I have had. Mentally and emotionally, I am right at the frayed end of the last bit of string there is. I do not defend or attack your right to flex muscles I never heard of. I make no attempt to typecast you, so please do me the same favor. I appreciate your assistance to Bonny Lee, and your concern for her. But my attitudes and responses, are, I am afraid, my personal business. If I have annoyed you, I'm sorry. But I do have to be leaving."

She looked at him very thoughtfully. She nodded. "Now didn't she just come up with something! Possibly the hat and the cane and the badge warped my judgment, love. You might come back one day, Mr. Winter. If you're free. But spend some time on the weights and bars first. No more lectures. Not a word of advice. You do seem quite able to cope. All I can do is wish you luck."

She put out her hand. It was a small hand, rather plump, but implicit in the quick squeeze she gave him was the warning that with an effortless twist she could probably sail him over her shoulder like a quoit.

Chapter Thirteen

Some very freehand parking had occurred in the alley by Bernie Sabbith's apartment. As Kirby climbed the outside staircase he heard guffaws and breaking glass. The door was open a few inches. He knocked, but after he realized no one could hear him, he pushed the door open and went in.

All the tricky lights were on, and the big music system was throwing a mighty wattage into all the built-in speakers. A table bar had been set up and a man in a white jacket was mixing drinks as fast as he could. At first glance there seemed to be fifty people in the apartment, but he soon realized the mirrors had doubled the apparent number.

There seemed to be a group of curiously identical young men, all dark, all spankingly clean, all wearing dark narrow suits, knit ties, white button down shirts, all smiling with a certain ironic tilt to one eyebrow, all holding chunky glasses containing ice and dark whisky. The rest of the young men seemed as young, but they looked as if they cut each other's hair, got their clothes out of mission barrels and bathed on bank holidays.

The girls seemed divided into two groups, too—a pack of languid starved ones in high fashion clothes, and a bouncy, racy, noisy batch in odds and ends of this and that. A fat little girl in a ratty red leotard came bounding toward him with yelps of delight lost in the general confusion.

"Let me guess!" she yelled. "You are a conventioneer! Your name is—uh—Eddie Beeler! You heard the sounds of action, O Conventioneer, and you have traced it with incredible instinct to the very fount of *all* action! I, Gretchen Firethorn myself, shall be your guide and mentor, O Eddie."

"Which one is Bernie Sabbith, please?"

"Oh shoot!" she said. "You spoil everything. Couldn't you

have just wandered in, for God's sake? That's Bernie, over there in the khakis and the white jacket, not the little one making drinks. Further. The one plastering the blonde against that mirror."

As Kirby hesitated, the fat girl took the funny hat, the cane and the badge, in what seemed to be one swift motion and bounded off, whooping. He worked his way between the twisters to where Sabbith was mumbling to the semi-smothered blonde. Bernie was a tall and angular man, seemingly constructed entirely of elbows and knuckles.

When Kirby finally got the man's attention, he swung around and stuck his hand out and said, "Glad you could make it, pal. The bar's right over there. Glad you could show." He turned back to the blonde.

"Have you seen Bonny Lee Beaumont?"

Bernie turned around again. "Bonny Lee! Where is she? You bring her, pal?"

"No. I'm looking for her."

"She isn't here tonight, pal. There's the bar. Get yourself a—"

"She's supposed to arrive at midnight."

The blonde started to slide sideways. Bernie grabbed her and straightened her up again. "Pal, some day I'd like to have a nice long chat, but right now you're a drag. Noonan!" One of the dark-suited ones presented himself. "Noonan, get this conversationalist out of my hair, like a pal."

Noonan gently led Kirby away. "Mr. Sabbith seems to be busy at the moment. What is the angle of impact, sir? Chamber of Commerce? Press, radio, television, talent?"

"I'm supposed to meet a girl here."

"Sir, if that was the guarantee, that you shall have. With a few spoken-for exceptions, I can offer you your choice of any member of our happy crew, our tight little ship. I would suggest one of the ragamuffin types, one of our off-camera laborers in the vineyard. If, on the other hand, you want the model type, I suggest you take two. Their energy level is so low, sir, they save their tiny sparkle for the deathless moment when they hold up the product."

"I'm supposed to meet a specific girl here!" Kirby shouted over the music. "I know her." As he made a helpless gesture, somebody put a drink in his hand.

"Can't you remember her name?"

"I *know* her name!"

"But you don't know what she looks like?"

"She's going to *arrive!* I want to *wait* for her!"

"Sir, you seem too solemn about all this. This is an epocal night in the short brilliant history of Parmalon."

"Of what?"

Noonan staggered and clutched his heart. "Don't do that to me, fellow. Parmalon! Seven shades, seven lotions, seven secret ingredients, the seven lovely lives of a beautiful woman. And we are down here, sir, bankrolled to do ten tropical commercials which will tear the living hearts right out of all the frump housewives in America." He tapped Kirby solidly on the chest. "Do you know who Bernie Sabbith is?"

"I think so."

"He is Guts. He is shining Brass. We are surrounded by the Loyal Ones, on and off camera. Shrewd agency minds. Fantastic technicians. Talent, beauty, dignity and greed." He thumped Kirby again. "Sabbith went in there as the writer. Do you know what he is now? He is the writer, *and* the director, *and* the producer, with twenty-eight grand apiece in hand for each and every message. That is what we celebrate, fellow. And we tolerate no solemnity, no groaning of the bored. Gather a damsel, grasp the wine, howl and prance, fellow. Let us see a little forthright debauchery. What is your trade, fellow?"

Kirby looked him squarely in the eye. "Philanthropy."

"Good God, another agency man?"

More glasses broke. A spindly girl did a comedy trampoline act on the giant bed, to mild applause. The next record was Cuban, from the time when Cubans were cheerful, flexible folk.

A vision floated over to Noonan and Kirby. She was the young Ingrid, a younger Greta, a juvenile Marlena, drifting, pensive, faintly confused as though she had just been awakened, or had just been given a good one behind the ear. She had great sad tilted dreamy gray-blue eyes, oval shadowed hollows in her cheeks, a golden drift of cobweb hair, a white length of throat. She seemed to be on the edge of tears, and in her dusky voice was a throb of heartbreak.

"Noony," she said, "this one come down with the scurds?"

Noonan was most gentle with her, as though she were the

only survivor of some inconceivable disaster. "No, dear. I'm sorry."

"Diddly bring the scurds?"

Noonan patted her thin shoulder gently. "Some one else is bringing them, dear. Don't you fret. What did you say your name is, sir?"

"Eddie. Eddie Beeler."

"Eddie, may I present Minta Burleigh. Minta, dear. Show Eddie what you do. Minta?"

She looked at Noonan, at the floor and at her empty hands and said mournfully, "Whaddle I use?" Noonan gave her his cigarette case. She turned slowly and focused on Kirby. She held the cigarette case up. She tilted her head. She smiled at Kirby, and suddenly she was specific, obvious, glowing, direct —like something that emerges from the fog and bears down upon you. "For that seventh loveliness," she said in a throbbing, dramatic contralto, "Parmalon! In the jeweled decorator case, for the woman who cares so much." Her lights went out like an unplugged Christmas tree and she listlessly handed the case back to Noonan.

"She's worried about some skirts," Noonan explained. "There's a color matching problem in a medium shot where she walks toward camera."

"Fugging scurds," Minta murmured.

"Be nice to Eddie, dear," Noonan said. "I got to go calm Harry down again."

Minta tottered slightly and looked at Kirby. The vast eyes seemed to cross slightly for a moment. She turned her hand out, held her wrist up where Kirby could read what someone had printed with a ball-point pen on the tender, transparent, blue-veined skin. "Worm I sacked?" she asked.

"Sultana. Seven-twenty," he read.

She swayed toward him, hooked her weight on his belt and laid her gentle cheek against his chest. "Sokay," she sighed. "Juss no messing the hair, no bruise the mouth."

Bonny Lee appeared just beyond Minta, looking at Kirby with an odd expression. "Having fun?"

Kirby made gentle efforts to disentangle Minta. He was afraid of fracturing or dislocating something. "I've been waiting for you," he explained.

"Sorta killin' time, sweetie? Where'd you get the disaster case?"

Minta swayed around and looked at Bonny Lee. "Where are all the peasants coming from?"

Bonny Lee slowly drew back a clenched right fist. Kirby spotted one of the dark-suited ones standing a little to one side, his eyes closed, swaying in time to the Latin beat. He put his hands on Minta's narrow waist, picked her up and set her down against the man with the closed eyes. She had been as easy to lift as a child. She immediately hooked her weight onto the man's belt and laid her gentle cheek against his chest. The man didn't open his eyes. In a few seconds they began to dance, moving slightly to every fourth bar of the music.

"It was just like that, Bonny Lee," Kirby said.

She gave him a narrow look. "Sure. Just in case I never showed, huh?"

"Bonny Lee, we've got too much to talk about to get started off this way. I've been terribly worried about you. I've got to tell you what happened. We've got to figure out what to do next."

"Look like you already knew." She looked around at the party. "Man, we're going to get no help out of this outfit. They gone past the point. Let me say hi to Bernie and we'll take off."

"I see no reason why you have to say anything to him."

"Oh, you don't!"

"No, I don't!"

"So you rove free as a bird and I can't even say hello! Is that it?"

"You got the wrong idea about that girl, Bonny Lee. But I don't have any wrong ideas about Bernie Sabbith."

She moved closer and glowered at him. "The only idea you got about Bernie is he's a friend, and right now no more than a friend, and I say hello to friends."

"Never more than a friend. Get that clear!"

Suddenly she looked amused. "Just listen to us, hey? Sure, Kirby. Never more than a friend. And that's all you have, too. Friends."

He saw her wend her way through the confusions to Bernie's side. When he hugged her, Kirby glowered at them. He turned and went off in pursuit of the fat girl. She was forlorn at giving up the hat, the cane and the badge. Bonny Lee came back to Kirby, near the door, and she seemed to stumble against him, put her arm around him. He felt her hand in the side pocket of the cord jacket. Suddenly she appeared in a new place two feet to the right of where she had been. She handed him the watch, and she was smiling cheerfully.

In the middle of the big room, Minta Burleigh went mad. All eyes were on her as she leaped, yelped, spun, flailed in a frenzy of the dance. Her Slav eyes were crazed, and the cords in her pale throat stood out. Her partner got in the way and got a crack across the chops which staggered him. As the dance began to diminish, Bonny Lee urged Kirby toward the door. The door closed behind them, cutting the major part of the din, and Kirby could hear Bonny Lee chuckling as they went down the stairs to the alley.

"What did you do?" he demanded.

"Packed her pants with shaved ice, lover. Guess there's life left in her. But, gawddamn, she's built scrawny."

Lizbeth's car, an English Ford sedan, was parked at the mouth of the alley. They got in and as soon as they'd closed the doors, Bonny Lee made a small furry sound in her throat and came into his arms, filled with a ready warmth and kisses and strength of round arms, and at long last said, "How come I could get to miss you so dang much? And you a city type fella."

"What has that got to—"

"Trouble is, you think too much. By the time you through walking around something, thinking at it, it like to take off. I just couldn't figure how you'd try to find me, but I guess you finally decided trying Rio's. How'd you like Lizbeth? You catch her act?"

"Yes, I—"

"And I went round and round with that Charla friend of yours. There's a woman mean as a snake, Kirby. And she had those two hoodlum boys to quieten me, but they weren't enough, not for a girl who one time when she was thirteen got run into the piney woods from a tent meeting by seven old boys full of shine, twicet as tough, each one, as those boys Charla had trying to keep holt of me. In those moony woods, I chunked two of them with rocks, tipped one into a crick, kicked one ontill he screamed like a girl and plain outrun the other three. They picked them the wrong gal, just like that Charla did. No man has ever forced me, nor ever will."

"I want to tell you—"

"So things can get ordered out for you, a little at a time, if you go at it direct, and I took something else off you tonight, that waiter you slugged."

"What?"

"By now he's told the police he's taking back the complaint on you, and even if he hasn't, you got this paper I brang you, sweetheart."

He looked at the paper in the flame of a match. On it was written, "The man hitting me taking my cloths, he was short fat bald maybe sixty year. I say it Mr. Winter so my name is on newspaper, for important." It was signed by the waiter and by two witnesses.

"How did you get this?"

"I was at Lizbeth's place and getting restless, so when I heard about the fire I thought maybe those two boys wouldn't be waiting at my place any more, so I went to see and they were gone. And I wanted my own clothes on account of in the top half of Lizbeth's there's room enough for me and a set of drums. I got into some of my own clothes and took money from under the mattress and went to the Elise. That waiter and I had a little talk. Somewhere while I was talking he got the idea he better settle small and get out, or somebody might float him away on the tide. So he took five hundred, and his signature is a little bit wiggly, but it's good enough I think. It was just a little favor, lover. If I could get to talk personal to them two hungry cops, I bet you I could fix that up too."

"I'm beginning to think you could."

"Anyhow, when we got back to that little pink house with those muscly fellas of Lizbeth's, I knew you'd got hold of that golden watch and used it good, and taken that Wilma girl away with you, so I stopped being so fretful about you, but I sure wish you'd taken my car so we'd have one less trouble. Sugar, you better tell me all of what happened, every dang bit of it, and you better be real complete, because I have it in my mind you went off with Wilma and here it is after midnight. There's time in there to burn a boat and do too much else too."

They were turned, facing each other in the small car. He held her hands and told her all that had happened. When he came to the situation with Joseph and Charla, the way he had left them when he had carried Betsy off the boat, her fingers dug into his hands. When he told her about how he had changed his mind and gotten back to them barely in time, her grip softened.

"Hold me some," she said in a low voice. He held her.

"How much difference would it have made if I didn't get back?"

"Maybe none, to us," she whispered. "We could make us up some reasons why it was a thing to do. But it would have been a dirty thing."

"I sense that. But why?"

"Why a dirty thing? Because they'd be bugs with you stomping them. And people aren't bugs. Not even those people. Anyways, if you'd used it to kill folks, I couldn't ever use it again to do something happy, like packing ice in around that ol' scrawny girl up there."

She bounced back away from him and said, "Sweetie, you got a tendency to treat that watch too solemn. Afore you know it, we'll be bowing down to that darn thing, and then it will be the watch in charge instead of us. I say if there isn't fun in something, the hell with it."

"You think I should use it more—frivolously?"

"It would be good for you."

"What should I have done to Charla then? What would you have done?"

"Hmmm. I'd want to scare that mean ol' gal and unfancy her a little."

"Like, for example, stripping her and stuffing her into a truck full of sailors?"

She kissed him quickly. "If you can even think up something like that, honey, it means you're coming along just fine. Just fine."

"That's what I did."

"What!"

"And the truck drove slowly away."

She whooped, yelped, bounced, pounded his chest with her fist and laughed until she cried. And he got almost as much reaction from Joseph's untidy fate.

Suddenly she sobered, and her eyes narrowed. She leaned toward him in the faint glow of street light. "Speaking of you a-takin' the clothes off that fat little blonde woman, just how good did you get along with that Wilma girl and that Betsy?"

"I told you Wilma is in that motel in Hallandale. And I left Betsy at the Birdline."

"Gals stashed all over town, huh?"

"It's either feast or famine."

"I'm all the feast you need, Yankee. I'm a banquet all day long, so when we go check on those gals, we *both* go. Wilma first, I guess. We have to make sure they stay put before they go wandering around messing things up."

"And then what?"

"I was thinking about that," she said quietly.

"We can run. You and me. A long, long way."

"And leave a mess like this? The law would never give up."

"What else is there to do?"

"That old uncle of yours left you in a real good mess. And I keep thinking maybe he had a reason. And maybe the reason is in that letter he left."

"But I can't get that for a year."

"Maybe he left you a way to get it a lot sooner."

Suddenly he realized what she meant. "Of course!"

"And he could have meant for you to get hold of it sooner than a year, Kirby."

He pulled her close and said, "You're a very bright girl, Bonny Lee Beaumont."

Unreckoned minutes later she began to make languid efforts to untangle herself. "First," she said regretfully, "let's go check on all your other women."

Chapter Fourteen

On Wednesday morning, young Mr. Vitts, of Wintermore, Stabile, Schamway and Mertz received the anonymous, puzzling phone call. It preyed on his mind as the morning wore on. He knew it had to be nonsense, yet he knew he would not feel easy until he had assured himself that the packet entrusted to him was exactly where he had placed it, exactly where it belonged. At eleven, canceling his other appointments, he went to the bank. He signed the vault card, went with the attendant and operated his half of the double lock and took the japanned metal box to a private cubicle.

He opened the lid and saw the labeled packet Mr. Wintermore had entrusted to him, and felt like a fool at having wasted time coming to the bank to stare at it, just because some crackpot had told him it was gone.

And suddenly it was gone.

He shut his eyes tightly and opened them again and looked into the box. The packet was gone. He put a trembling hand into the box and fingered the emptiness. He slumped onto the small bench and closed his eyes. He knew he was overworked. A man who could not trust the evidence of his own senses had no business accepting fiduciary responsibilities. He knew he would have to go at once to Mr. Wintermore and confess that the Krepps packet had disappeared, and he had no idea where it had gone. He would ask for some leave, and consider himself fortunate if he was not forced to resign.

When he stood up, he moved like a very old man. The packet was back in the lock box. Had it been a cobra, he could not have recoiled more swiftly. It took him a few moments to acquire the courage to touch it, then lift it out of the lock box. At first it seemed to him to be of slightly different weight and dimension than he remembered, and it looked as if it had been resealed, but then logic came to his rescue. No one could possibly have touched it. He'd had a mild hallucination based on nervous tension and overwork. There was no need to tell Mr. Wintermore about it. Everything was entirely in order. He would try to get a little more rest in the future, a little more exercise and sunshine. He returned the box to the vault and walked back to his office, consciously breathing more deeply than was his custom.

Most of the documentation within the packet consisted of a detailed, witnessed, notarized certification of where the twenty-seven million had gone, affirming that O.K. Devices was primarily an eleemosynary operation, and because taxes had been paid on monies diverted to O.K.D., no claims for deductions had been in order.

Bonny Lee knelt on the bed behind Kirby and read over his shoulder as he read Uncle Omar's personal letter to her.

"My dear Nephew: It is entirely possible that you will never be able to comprehend this letter. You will think it evidence of senility, unless you have discovered *It*, and made use of *It* to gain access to this letter—a matter you should find rather simple—well in advance of schedule.

"I have taken elaborate safeguards. One, of course, was my attempt to shape your mind and character so you would be capable of properly using It, but at no time did I feel that you had reached the point of development where I could merely hand It over to you, as though giving you the world and all that is in it. I decided to make it all so difficult for you, the very act of discovering the capacities and making use of them would be sufficient trial by fire to solidify those aspects of your personality which I felt too indefinite to make you worthy of such a strange trust.

"The other safeguards are technical, and I fear so complete that the odds are against It ever being used by anyone after my death. The first device was extremely cumbersome, created nausea in the user, and was operative for but three minutes at a time. Over the years I simplified and perfected it. All technical notes regarding it have been destroyed. All you need know, if you have discovered Its capacities, is that it is permanently sealed, and uses cosmic radiation as a power source, accumulating it and storing it with such rapidity, no use is so excessive as to weaken It. Yet should any fifty-day period pass without its being used, the accumulation will overburden the storage capacity and fuse the basically simple device beyond all possibility of constructive analysis. This is one safeguard. In addition, should any attempt be made to open the sealed mechanism, the same result will be obtained. Lastly, due to a microscopic diminution of the essential element of the device, through use, I estimate that it will last no less than twenty and no more than twenty-five years from the date of this letter.

"I might add here that I took into account one psychological safeguard. I have directed Wintermore to hand it to you personally, and he is the least likely man I know to either let it out of his hands prematurely, or to fiddle with it and thus accidentally learn its properties.

"If you have waited a full year to read this letter, my boy, you will have no idea what I am talking about.

"If, on the other hand, you have learned the properties of the object, and have used it to solve certain problems I set up for you, then you will realize why I have surrounded it with these safeguards. Morally, perhaps I should have destroyed it when I knew I had not long to live. But possibly it was vanity which kept me from doing so. If you know what it will do, you can perceive the horrid burden of responsibility in having discovered the phenomenon, in having made selfish use of it, in having, I hope, partially atoned for such use, and having faced the dreadful image of a world where such a thing would be available to unscrupulous men.

"I even face the fact that some other person may be reading this letter, and you will never see it. In that event, it is possible I have indeed loosed a demon on the world.

"But if you have it, know what it is, and understand this letter, my boy, I need not charge you with any special duties and responsibilities. What you are will determine how you use it, and I have tried to shape you to that end. If the burden seems too great, all you need do is set it aside for fifty days.

"In these, my last words to you, I caution you about one thing, and one thing only. Keep it to yourself. Do not share its use with anyone. The man who owns it and can use it is the most powerful man the world has ever seen. It is not a power which can be safely shared."

Wilma Farnham, with sufficient advance notice to attract the widest possible coverage by the news media, and the maximum attendance by the executive personnel of Krepps Enterprises, governmental authorities and assorted attorneys of all parties at interest, made the first public appearance, with hair, make-up and clothing selected by Bonny Lee Beaumont.

Wilma, carefully coached by Kirby and Bonny Lee, made an intricate deal with the opposition. Once it was agreed that, if she could present satisfactory documentation as to the disposition of the twenty-seven millions, all criminal charges against Kirby Winter would be dropped, and all civil charges would be limited to those which could be established on the basis of the documentation she would present, she calmly produced the detailed statements.

KREPPS GAVE IT ALL AWAY, the headlines said.

The incident of Bonny Lee's little car was readily solved. Wilma swore she had borrowed it.

Betsy Alden was the next one to turn herself in. She had walked off the *Glorianna* an hour before the fire and had been for a time at the apartment of one Bernard Sabbith (verified by Mr. Sabbith) and had then gone to a downtown hotel and registered under a pseudonym (there was no law against it) and had remained there until she had discovered, at this late date, that the police wanted to talk to her.

ACTRESS CLEARED, smaller headlines said.

By the time Kirby Winter made his public appearance, the public imagination had gone bounding on ahead to new phenomena, as always—in this particular instance eleven young men in Coral Gables, insurance agents, store managers, stock salesmen and the like, whose discreet little wife-swapping club had worked like a charm for over two years until it had been discovered that one of them had been rigging the basis of selection by using a marked deck. They became suspicious of him when they noted that he was the only one who never ended up with his own wife. After having been disciplined with more enthusiasm than good judgment, he made full confession from his hospital bed.

The only residue of public opinion regarding Kirby Winter was a feeling of dull indignation that he had not, after all, stolen millions. He did not help matters by projecting a public image of a mild and rather wordy and tiresome man who wanted to talk of nothing but the Good Works of the late Omar Krepps. And the public has a minimum interest in Good Works. KREPPS HEIR TELLS OF GIVEAWAY, the very small headlines said.

Betsy Alden disappeared without further publicity. Sabbith took her back to New York with him. She has since been seen on major networks, telling why her clothes are fluffier, her drains are spotless and her nasal passages are open.

Wilma Farnham, after a few lessons from Bonny Lee, became a demure little ivoried odalisque with a weighty hairdo, bright blue contact lenses, a whispery voice and dresses which looked too tight to sit down in. Walton Grumby kept asking her to come to the K.E. offices and explain over and over what her duties had been with O.K. Devices. When he decided to go to Paris, Cairo and Rangoon to spot check the reported disbursement of cash, he took her along, just in case he happened to think of any additional questions.

After a partial recovery from a wide spectrum of traumatic nervous disorders, Joseph Locordolos was permitted to return to the *Glorianna*. Criminal charges were dropped and he settled civil actions out of court at considerable expense. His visa was cancelled, as were the visas of the five crew members. They were ordered to remain aboard the *Glorianna* until repairs had been completed. Joseph did all in his power to delay the repairs, hoping that Charla would reappear before he would be forced to leave port. He was very worried about her. He kept wondering what horrid thing Winter could have done to her, if perhaps he had killed her and hidden the body. When he thought of Charla dead, it made tears come to his eyes.

On the eighth day after the fire, Charla came calmly aboard. It was mid-morning. She walked into the main lounge and said, "Hello, Joseph." She sat down. He had jumped to his feet. He looked at her with consternation. She was perhaps fifteen pounds lighter. Her cheeks were hollow. Her eyes looked enormous. Her lovely flaxen hair had been cropped quite short. She wore a cheap little blouse and a cheap little skirt and she carried a big vulgar red purse.

He ran to her, knelt beside her chair and flung his arms

around her and sobbed into her neck. "Oh, my poor darling, what has happened to you!"

"How are you, Joseph?" she asked. Her voice had a formless, faraway quality.

"How am I?" he cried. "I am *terrible!*" He sprang to his feet, and, pacing back and forth, he described the outrage that had been perpetrated upon him. "They were like tigers! Veritable tigers!" he declared. "And he did it with that devil's device, the same thing his uncle used upon all of us, but never so—exuberantly. My God, the expense it has been! I still can't sleep. I keep waking up. In my sleep I see that tattoo." He knelt beside her again. "We must have that device, Charla. We must have it. That soft fool should have killed us when he had the chance. Listen, my dearest. I have purchased information. He went from here to New York. He is with Bonny Lee Beaumont, the girl who escaped from you. An entertainer. They plan to go to Paris." He stopped and looked at her closely. She seemed dazed. "Darling, you are not listening!"

She was staring at the paneled wall of the lounge. "Do you know what AWOL means, dear?" she asked.

"How should I know what that means?"

"Absent without official leave. Oh, they were very disturbed, you know. To have thirty-three of them go AWOL all at once, with an official vehicle." She turned her head and looked mildly at him. "The vehicle was the truck, you see. They were on their way from Port Everglades to Key West. That's where their destroyer is. Key West."

Joseph struck himself in the head with his fist. "What are you talking about? Where have you been?"

"Suddenly I was in a truck, with a lot of sailors."

"How hideous!"

"A destroyer is the smallest seagoing combat ship. It is generally from three hundred to four hundred feet long and displaces from two thousand to three thousand tons. Destroyers are used mainly to screen other ships, to picket certain areas and to escort ships."

"Charla!"

"Destroyers are long-range, high-speed, hard-hitting ships. For protection they rely on watertight compartments and speed. Sailors call destroyers 'tin cans' because of their thin metal hulls."

He grabbed her and shook her until her teeth chattered, but the moment he released her, the sing-song recital was resumed.

"The most common type of destroyer in the U.S. Navy is known as the 692 Class or 'long hull', developed during World War II. They have two main engine groups of high-pressure steam turbines that total over sixty thousand horsepower. Engines, boilers and other machinery for propulsion occupy nearly three-fourths of their length below the main deck."

He bent over in front of her and looked into her eyes. He saw for the first time a horrid benignity there, a calmness, a curious smugness—as though all searches were ended, all fires quenched.

"Listen to me, my dear. We shall leave tomorrow. We shall go to Nassau, Charla, and from there we shall fly to Paris. And there we will find this Kirby Winter and we—"

"No, dear," she said calmly, sweetly.

"What?"

She stood up and yawned and stretched. He noticed that in spite of the way she had leaned down, her color was excellent. She started toward the hatch. "I just came aboard to get some clothes and some money."

He followed her. "But where are you going?" he pleaded.

She turned and gave him a blank stare. In a tone of voice which indicated she thought it an incomparably stupid question, she said, "Back to Key West, of course."

"But Charla!"

"They're waiting for me, dear. Destroyers are armed with torpedoes in tubes on deck, multipurpose five-inch guns, and depth charges."

She went into the stateroom. He heard her in there, humming. He could not remember the name of the song. It had something to do with anchors. He stood in the doorway. She started to change her clothes. But as soon as she was undressed, Joseph had to turn abruptly away and go to his stateroom, and lie down. When he heard her leaving, he called, "I'll wait for you in Nassau!"

After she left, he wondered how long it would be before she turned up. He hoped it would be a reasonable length of time—long enough for him to adjust to her brand-new tattoo.

And at the moment Charla was clambering expertly into

the waiting gray jeep, Kirby Winter, thirty-five thousand feet over the Atlantic, was lifting a glass of champagne to the angel lips of his white-headed wench and drowning quite happily in her rogue eyes.